Compass of Health

Using the Art of
SASANG MEDICINE
to Maximize Your Health

JOSEPH K. KIM, PH.D., O.M.D.

NEW PAGE BOOKS
A division of The Career Press, Inc.
Franklin Lakes, NJ

COMPASS OF HEALTH
Edited by Karen Prager
Typeset by Robert Brink and Kristen Mohn
Cover design by The Visual Group
Printed in the U.S.A. by Book-mart Press

To order this title, please call toll-free 1-800-CAREER-1 (NJ and Canada: 201-848-0310) to order using VISA or MasterCard, or for further information on books from Career Press.

The Career Press, Inc., 3 Tice Road, PO Box 687,
Franklin Lakes, NJ 07417
www.careerpress.com
www.newpagebooks.com

Library of Congress Cataloging-in-Publication Data

Kim, Joseph, K.
    Compass of health : using the art of sasang medicine to maximize your health/ by Joseph K. Kim.
        p. cm.
    Includes index.
    ISBN 1-56414-559-X (pbk.)
    1. Medicine, Korean. 2. Health. I. Title.

R628 .K54 2001
615.5'3'09519—dc21

00-054889

Dedication

To my parents, for their loving support
and encouragement.

To the memory of Dr. Jae Ma Lee, the founder of
Sasang Medicine, whose remarkable and profound insight has
inspired every word written in this book.

For Mirela

A woman who guests!

Wishing you Good Health,

Harmony & Happiness

With Light & Love

Eric

Acknowledgments

My sincere gratitude goes to all of the following people whose contributions in time, energy, guidance, and support have made this book possible:

Dr. Jae Yong Shin, for his inspiration, wisdom, and unwavering support.

Dr. Jae Do Hahm, for his continual advice and encouragement.

My senior colleague, Dr. David Sunghwan Lee, for his countless invaluable insights that were indispensable to me.

My friends and colleagues, Dr. Jung Min Kim, Dr. Sun Ho Hong and Dr. In Ho Cho, for the innumerable enlightening hours spent discussing theories of Sasang Medicine.

Dr. Suk Jun Park and Dr. Chang Nam Ko of the Oriental Science Research Society in Korea, for providing me with much needed information.

Dr. Kyu Suk Ahn of Kyung Hee University of Korea, for his indispensable assistance and ideas in Chapter 4.

Dr. Dal Rae Kim, Dr. Kyung Yo Kim, Dr. Yong Tae Cho, and Dr. Suk Chul Hong, for their friendship, teachings, and scholarship.

Dr. Henry Yu (founder of Yuin University), Dr. Bong Dal Kim (founder of Emperor's College), and Dr. David Park (founder and president of South Baylo University), for their constant encouragement and support.

Ms. Cecilia Moddelmog, freelance editor, for her editorial assistance in Chapter 12.

Mr. Soo An Kim, freelance artist, for creating all of the drawings that accompany the text.

Ms. Paige Wheeler, my agent, for her unstinting support.

Ms. Karen Prager, my editor at New Page Books, for her excellent editorial work.

Mr. Victor Kim, my dear friend and senior, for his ever-present guidance and wisdom.

Finally, during the long and arduous process of writing and rewriting this book, several of my students at Emperor's College of Traditional Oriental Medicine provided invaluable insight and assistance. I would like to especially thank Rita Yoon and Randy Otaka for their careful editorial work on the entire manuscript. I could not have finished the book without their help.

Contents

Part III: Love and Work

Part IV: Application

Author's Note

Words that have no direct equivalents in English, such as Tai Chi, Qi, Yin, and Yang have been capitalized. The physiological actions of organs, as interpreted in Sasang Medicine, are different from that of Western physiology. Thus, organs have been capitalized to differentiate them from Western anatomical organs.

The advice given in this book regarding diet, tea, and exercises does not replace proper medical care. Before following the recommendations in this book, please consult a physician if you have any medical condition.

The names and identifying information of patients in the clinical examples have been changed to protect patient confidentiality.

Introduction

A young fish once asked the wisest fish in the sea, "Where is the Great Ocean?" The wise fish merely rolled his eyes about, laughed, and answered, "Where is the Great Ocean? Where is the Great Ocean?"
—Zen fable

The modern world is complex and grows more so with each passing day. Although many of us struggle to make sense of it and find our place within it, it continually distracts us with new choices and alternatives. Confronted by the overwhelming possibilities offered by this information age, we often feel as though we are standing at an intersection in our lives, paralyzed by a thousand arrows pointing to a thousand different destinations. Where are we to go? The irony of our situation lies in the fact that we are imprisoned by our own freedom. Our world has expanded from a puddle to a great ocean, and instead of rejoicing, we find ourselves confused and uncertain.

The answer to our dilemma does not lie outside of us. It does not lie in indulging in the endless promises dangling before us. Rather, the answer lies within ourselves. If we are clear about who we are, then we will be clear about where we should go and what we should do.

Like many people, I was both inspired and challenged by the question, "Who am I?" With this question in mind, I studied and practiced Eastern philosophy, medicine, meditation, martial arts, and Qi Gong for many years. But the question remained an unresolved enigma.

Equally enigmatic questions arose when I observed other people. Why did people act the way they did, and why did people look the way they did? These questions related to apparently idiosyncratic details: Why could some people drink ice cold drinks by the gallon without a hint of discomfort, and others preferred drinks without ice? Why were some people endowed with broad shoulders, while others had an inescapable potbelly? Why were some people always easygoing and relaxed, while others always seemed to be in a rush? I was also fascinated by famous people, the cultural icons who left their marks on history and influenced the world. I wondered what made them the way that they are, what about them separated them from ordinary people.

It was only after I came into contact with Sasang (pronounced Sah-Sahng) medicine, first through my father, a practitioner of Eastern medicine and medical doctor in Korea, and then through my own studies under several masters, that I experienced a turning point in answering these questions. Sasang Medicine is a form of Korean constitutional medicine that relates an individual's physical, emotional, and pathological characteristics to one of four different energetic foundations: Taiyang (greater Yang), Shaoyang (lesser Yang), Taiyin (greater Yin), and Shaoyin (lesser Yin). Knowing their constitutions allows people to understand themselves on a fundamental level and is the best way to attain health and well-being. Knowing the constitution of others, meanwhile, allows us to understand their characteristics and how best to relate to them.

Sasang Medicine gave me a gauge with which to examine, reflect upon, and comprehend myself and others. Through it, I gained a deeper understanding of myself and of the people around me. Sasang Medicine provided me with the compass and the map for my journey through life.

As I have discovered understanding and health through Sasang Medicine, I feel it my duty to spread this knowledge to the West. In doing so, I am only carrying on the efforts of the founder of Sasang Medicine, Dr. Jae Ma Lee. A deeply insightful and compassionate individual, he strove to create a medical system that would be useful not only in times of illness, but that would also help individuals realize their highest potential in physical, mental, and spiritual health. Dr. Lee hoped that, through the process of self-cultivation outlined by Sasang Medicine, common people could experience the truth of the words of Mencius, the great Confucian philosopher:

"All things are complete within us.

There is no greater delight than to realize this through self-cultivation...One who knows completely his own nature, knows Heaven."

It is my sincere wish that this book, like a compass, helps you on your journey toward your Great Ocean, the highest potential of your particular embodiment.

How This Book Is Organized

The quest for health is like a journey, and *Compass of Health* reflects this. The journey begins in Part I. In the six chapters of this section, you will be introduced to the philosophical underpinnings of Sasang Medicine and to the physical, psychological, and pathological aspects of the four constitutions. Part II discusses five aspects of life, which you can modify to help you on your journey. These five aspects are: 1. diet, 2. teas, 3. exercise, meditation, and Qi Gong, 4. centering the mind, and 5. acupuncture.

The third part of the book concerns itself with the application of Sasang Medicine in everyday life. The section is titled "Love and Work," referring to the two dimensions of life that many psychologists consider to be most important in determining the health of an individual. The first chapter of this section concerns itself with the way in which the different constitutions relate with one another. With this understanding as a foundation, you will know what type of person is right for you, as well as the best ways to get along with those who aren't. The second chapter of this section discusses work. Our careers should agree with our body types, and this chapter tells us how we can make it so.

Part IV is an entertaining and educational section that applies the ideas of Sasang Medicine to famous historical figures and fictional characters. By studying these figures, you will gain a deeper understanding of not only the four body types, but also yourself.

Part I

The Middle
of Nowhere

Chapter 1

The Path to Health

The farther one goes, the less one knows.
—Lao Tzu

The path to health differs for each of us. We each possess inherent strengths and weaknesses, setting in motion our different natures and different needs. Yet we drift in a sea of uniform health advice, making us feel as though we were in the middle of nowhere. Although the surface of this sea may appear flat and calm, it conceals wayward currents that may carry us far from our intended destinations. Take aspirin for example. Aspirin is considered to be an all-purpose pain reliever. Yet for those who have weak stomach linings or for those with thin blood, aspirin can cause serious complications, far more serious than the headache or cramp for which it was indicated.

How do we know what is right for us? How do we find our paths to health?

The answer lies within ourselves. Our bodies and minds have built-in navigation mechanisms. When something goes awry, our bodies and minds emit signals. These signals may take a variety of forms—pain, such as headaches and stomachaches, or emotional discomforts, such as anxiety and depression. These symptoms let us know that we are misusing our bodies and minds in some manner and veering off the course of health. If we are attentive to these signals and adjust our paths accordingly, then we will improve.

In a more metaphysical sense, it is said that the universe may be found in a single grain of sand. Similarly, our bodies and minds may be seen as microcosms reflecting the entire world. If we wish to understand or navigate through our external world, we need only look at the internal world within ourselves for the map.

I invite you to embark on a journey to discover this world within yourself. Trace your body. Traverse your mind. And chart your own course to health.

Sasang—Nature's Four Symbols

As with any expedition, you'll need a compass. Without this fundamental navigational tool, how will you know what is North, South, East, or West? How will you identify your starting point or your destination? How will you determine the path linking the two?

This book introduces a revolutionary new way to navigate through the terrain of your body and mind. It is called Sasang Medicine. Heretofore unknown to the West, Sasang Medicine is a unique system of Eastern medicine and natural health care developed in Korea. Sasang is derived from the Korean words "sa," meaning four, and "sang," translated as "symbols of natural phenomena." Therefore, "Sasang" means "nature's four symbols."

Nature has bestowed upon us four symbols with which to guide all phenomena. To navigate within the world, we need a minimum of four cardinal directions—North, South, East, West. This is because these four directions reflect our body's four sides: front, back, right, and left. Whether we are in the middle of a flat plane, on the summit of a mountain peak, or sailing the seas, we orient ourselves by comparing the four sides of our bodies (front, back, right, left) with the four directions of the universe (North, South, East, West).

All maps are based upon this four-directional configuration. The four directions are reproduced on a map whenever a vertical line and a horizontal line intersect at a single point. This intersection simultaneously creates a center and organizes the space around it into a grid. Whenever we need to locate something on a map, all we need to know are the horizontal and vertical coordinates, or the longitude and latitude, of the place in question. The simplicity, efficiency, and ubiquity of this system demonstrate the power of the number four with regard to space.

The four symbols not only effectively divide space, they also divide time. Although the weather varies from day to day, there are only four fundamentally different seasons—winter, spring, summer, and fall. Winter months are characterized by cold and hibernation. In the spring, nature awakens; animals begin to emerge, plants begin to sprout. In the heat of summer, activity is in full force; flowers bloom, bees buzz. As autumn approaches, leaves fall and birds depart. Nature takes on new colors in preparation for another winter.

What is true for the macrocosm is also true for the microcosm. The fundamental character of life also obeys the guiding principle of the four symbols. Genetics, the science of inherited traits, is based on four basic building blocks—adenine, thymine, cytosine, and guanine. These four base pairs serve as the "letters" of the genetic code that spell out the "words" and "sentences" of the DNA molecule, your genes, and ultimately, your biological inheritance. Blood also revolves around four principles. Despite our infinite biological differences, only four blood types exist within humans—O, A, B, and AB.

As you can see, nature's four symbols reverberate all around you. You need only tune yourself into them to see nature's pattern and your place in it.

The Four Body Types

Sasang Medicine explains your body and mind according to nature's four principles. The Eastern philosophical concept of Yin and Yang serves as the background, or the first division, of the four symbols. Variations in the degree of Yin and Yang serve as the second division. The four resultant symbols resonate within our bodies and minds to create four different constitutions or body types.

What exactly is a body type? Sasang Medicine defines a body type as the physical, psychological, and spiritual manifestation of Yin and Yang energies within the body. The four body types of Sasang Medicine are:

1. Taiyang (greater Yang).
2. Shaoyang (lesser Yang).
3. Taiyin (greater Yin).
4. Shaoyin (lesser Yin).

According to the flux and flow of Yin and Yang, different body types possess tendencies toward particular physical shapes, external appearances, and personalities. For instance, Taiyangs tend to be resolute, dogmatic individuals with relatively large heads.

The different body types are also predisposed to certain diseases. Disease results when your mind and body become unbalanced and can no longer maintain harmony. Therefore, knowing your constitutional makeup, the areas in which you are strong and weak, plays a significant role in finding the proper approach to healing yourself.

Sasang Medicine

In contrast to Western medicine, Sasang Medicine operates from a holistic perspective, taking an individual's body, mind, emotions, spirit, and environment (physical as well as social). Only then does it come up with a health plan. Treatment is diffuse, addressing the whole person, not just specific symptoms. In addition, it is ideal in Sasang Medicine for patients to involve themselves in their treatment. Patients become more aware of their imbalances and learn to control their emotions and behaviors to restore health.

Each body type maintains its own particular harmony and health given its particular Yin-Yang dynamics. Thus, Sasang Medicine tailors health regimens of acupuncture, diet, herbal supplements, and exercises to fit each individual's particular needs. Health in Sasang Medicine is not a single, uniform concept, but a living process that manifests differently according to an individual's body type.

Dr. Lee—founder of Sasang Medicine

Sasang Medicine was founded by Dr. Jae Ma Lee, a Korean doctor and philosopher (1836-1900). Throughout his life, Dr. Lee suffered from chronic ailments that could not be healed through the medical traditions of his time. As a child, he began to suffer from Fan Wei Ye Ge syndrome, a combination of vomiting and inability to swallow, and Jie Yi syndrome, a form of lower body weakness that caused difficulty in walking, with no signs of pain, swelling, or paralysis.

As his condition grew worse, Dr. Lee traveled throughout Korea in search of a cure. He sought out famous doctors in the cities, Buddhist monks in the temples, and shamans in the forests, but no one could help him. Despite his constant disappointments, Dr. Lee continued to seek out different healers.

After repeated failures, however, Dr. Lee came to the realization that health could only come from within and not without. Armed with this understanding, he studied medicine on his own. He tested a variety of treatment methods from the medical classics in order to find his own cure.

By observing his own positive and negative reactions to various treatments, Dr. Lee discovered that he had a special constitution called Taiyang. His body type only responded to a select group of herbs. Although this in itself was an amazing discovery, Dr. Lee extended the findings from his own experiences to conclude that everyone was born with one of four unique body types, each possessing particular qualities in terms of health, disease manifestation, and treatment methods. Dr. Lee spent the remainder of his life devoted to the development of this medicine, which he called Sasang Medicine.

Originally a Confucian scholar, Dr. Lee had studied the teachings of Mencius, who propagated the theory of Sadan (Four Beginnings), a moral code emphasizing benevolence, righteousness, propriety, and wisdom. He had also studied neo-Confucian ideas concerning the emotions of anger, joy, sadness, and pleasure.

In creating Sasang Medicine, Dr. Lee included elements from both of these traditions and infused them with Taoist philosophy. Dr. Lee spent the majority of his life refining his philosophical ideals and looking for ways to practically apply the core tenet of Confucianism: "To cultivate oneself and to benefit or give service to others." He believed that through the cultivation body and mind, people can elevate themselves to the higher states of consciousness. This could only be accomplished through a deep understanding of one's own constitution and the constitutions of others.

Look Within to Find Your Place

If we look at Dr. Lee's life as a model of the path to health, we discover that true progress only comes when we look within and clearly perceive where we are. If we search for something outside of ourselves to make us feel better, then we are doomed to fail in our quest for true well-being. We will remain lost in the middle of nowhere, in terms of both our health and self-knowledge.

The key, then, lies in looking within. It lies in perceiving the path to health not as a road leading somewhere else, but as a road always bringing us back to ourselves. By aligning ourselves with our ideal center, we can find our place in the world. In other words, we transform ourselves from being lost in the middle of nowhere to being found through the middle of nowhere.

What precisely is this middle of nowhere, and how do we align ourselves with it? Sasang Medicine addresses this question. This unique Eastern medical system views the whole of humanity and identifies our locus in the cosmos via four fundamental poles. Like a compass, Sasang Medicine acts as the central axis that creates order out of the chaos.

Chapter 2

Yin-Yang: The Energetic Axis

The Yang energy of Heaven and the Yin energy of
Earth interact, giving birth to all things in creation.
—*Yellow Emperor's Inner Classic*

A compass is able to serve as a navigational tool because it is sensitive to the magnetic field of the Earth. Without this magnetic field, a compass would be useless. Its needle would be unable to align with the North and South Poles, and would point instead to any large concentration of metal, electricity, or magnetic force.

Like a compass, we need to be sensitive to an energetic axis. Without such sensitivity, we follow whatever is shiny, stimulating, or otherwise attractive, thus losing our way. What is this energetic axis? Although there are no words to adequately describe it, in the East, it is referred to as Yin-Yang.

What Are Yin and Yang?

Yin and Yang have actually been bandied about enough in the West for them to become common, albeit misunderstood, terms. They are often considered mere opposites: Yin is negative, Yang is positive; Yin is evil, Yang is good. Moreover, there is a tendency in the West to think that one is better than the other. For example, when people say that Yang is good, the implication is that it should be emphasized to the exclusion of its opposite, the evil Yin.

Although Yin and Yang oppose each other, they also depend on each other. Take the North Pole (Yin) and the South Pole (Yang) as an example. Without the North Pole, it would be impossible to talk about the South Pole because North is defined by its opposite, South. If we were to choose a point on the globe to serve as the North Pole, then we would simultaneously determine the point opposite it on the globe as the South Pole. By determining one, we invariably determine the other. Like all Yin-Yang pairs, the North Pole and South Pole are created together.

A magnetic field exists between the North and South Poles. This further demonstrates the interdependency of Yin and Yang. It also demonstrates the fact that Yin and Yang pairs establish a field of interaction between themselves. This field exerts an influence upon everything else. The North and South Poles maintain an ongoing communication with each other through the magnetic field. Everything in between and around cannot help but eavesdrop on their conversation.

Just as the North and South Poles act as the magnetic axis of the Earth, Yin and Yang act as the energetic axis of the universe. If we can understand Yin and Yang, then, like a compass, we can orient ourselves to the ways of the universe and attain our goal of optimal health.

Origins of Yin and Yang

In order to truly understand what Yin and Yang are, it is necessary to delve into the soil of Eastern culture. The *I Ching (Book of Change)* introduced the Yin-Yang theory of Eastern philosophy to the world in written form some 3,000 years ago. This classic text is one of the most revered books in the East, but in the West, it is primarily regarded as a book of divination. According to this book, Tai Chi, translated as the Supreme Ultimate, gave birth to two fundamental forces, Yin and Yang.

The following diagram (Fig. 2.1) represents the concepts of Tai Chi and Yin-Yang.

Figure 2.1: A Tai Chi symbol

The whole circle represents Tai Chi and the two sides (dark and light) represent Yin and Yang. When Tai Chi divides, it produces Yin and Yang. When Yin and Yang unite, they form Tai Chi.

Tai Chi implies a whole and undivided state. It encompasses all phenomena, but is not yet differentiated. One way we can look at Tai Chi and the formation of Yin and Yang is to examine our own creation as human beings. Imagine a zygote, a fertilized egg. At first, it is whole and undivided. This is similar to Tai Chi, the undifferentiated matrix of the universe. When the zygote undergoes the process of cell division, it becomes two cells. These two cells may represent Yin and Yang, the first and most fundamental division of the universe. These two cells divide again, forming four cells, then eight, and so on, until a complete embryo develops. Now imagine a single seed. Seeds, though simple and small, can eventually grow up to be trees 100 feet tall through the same process of cell division. Zygotes or seeds are like Tai Chi in that they contain the potential for all creation.

When Tai Chi divides, two formless, intangible modes called Yin and Yang are created. These two modes are the relative principle underlying all creation. Simply stated, Yin and Yang reflect the fundamental orientation of the universe. They are its most basic polar energies.

One simple yet profound way in which the polar nature of Yin and Yang is symbolically represented is through the use of lines. A broken line represents Yin, and a straight, unbroken line represents Yang (Fig. 2.2). The break in the Yin line represents rest, an interval, or a pause between activities. It can also represent an opening or a space that can accept things (expressing the receptive nature of Yin). On the other hand, the straight Yang line represents constant, ceaseless activity, without rest. It is unable to accept anything because it has no opening or space.

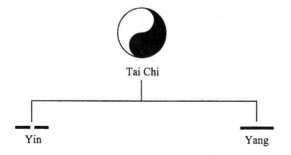

Figure 2.2: Tai Chi and Yin-Yang

Common Yin-Yang Pairings

Remember that Yin and Yang always exist relative to each other and to some context. Thus, strictly speaking, it makes little sense to say, "That person is Yang," unless you specified something or someone that was Yin, providing a basis of comparison. Nevertheless, by convention, Yin has come to be associated with certain qualities, and Yang has come to be associated with others. Here is a list of the common associations.

YIN	YANG
Cold	Hot
Descending	Ascending
Passive	Active
Slow	Quick
Stillness	Movement
Potential energy	Kinetic Energy
Conservation	Transformation
Contraction	Expansion
Centripetal	Centrifugal

Yin-Yang in Daily Life and Nature

YIN	YANG
Moon	Sun
Night	Day
Cloudy day	Clear day
Autumn/Winter	Spring/Summer
Water	Fire
Earth	Heaven
Plants	Animals

We see Yin and Yang at play in daily life. The sun rises at dawn, giving birth to day (Yang). The sun gradually descends, giving way to the moon as night falls (Yin). This simple observation of the daily cycle clearly shows that Yin and Yang are neither good nor bad, but equally essential elements of nature's flux and flow.

Yin can be likened to the autumn and the winter seasons, the months when sunlight is in decline. Like water, the nature of Yin energy is inactivity, coldness, and downward or inward motion. Yin causes energy to settle into substance or matter.

Yang seasons are the spring and summer, the seasons when sunlight is most plentiful. Like fire, the nature of Yang energy is activity, heat, and upward or outward motion. Yang energizes matter into more rarefied, intangible states, as opposed to the more solidified states of Yin.

When you are out in nature, you notice the tranquil stillness created by the trees, flowers, and grass (Yin). You also notice the sounds and movements created by various animals (Yang). Plants are Yin and animals are Yang because plants remain in a fixed location (Yin), whereas animals are constantly moving (Yang).

Yin-Yang: A Description of Change

Thus far, we have tended to emphasize the static qualities of Yin and Yang. For example, we associated Yin and Yang with the North Pole and the South Pole, two landmarks that are so unchanging that all navigation is based upon them. Although they definitely have an orienting tendency, ultimately, Yin and Yang are used to describe the process of change. Here are four general principles of change in the Yin-Yang theory:

- **Yin and Yang are interchangeable.** In other words, Yin can change into Yang, and Yang can change into Yin. This idea was demonstrated powerfully when Albert Einstein discovered the equation $e=mc^2$. Before $e=mc^2$, energy (Yang) and matter (Yin) were held to be two distinct qualities. After Einstein's discovery, it was revealed that energy and matter were merely two extremes of a spectrum, and that each was constantly changing into the other.

- **Yin and Yang are cyclical in nature.** In other words, extending the idea of the previous principle, Yin becomes Yang becomes Yin becomes Yang ad infinitum. There is no endpoint to the process of change. Time, in fact, is told through the rhythm of different Yin-Yang cycles. A day is a single cycle through day and night; a month is a single cycle of the moon; a year is a cycle through the four seasons. Paradoxically, it is precisely because Yin and Yang keep changing into each other that the basic rhythms of our lives remain constant. If the cycles of Yin and Yang stop, then our sense of rhythm and time would be lost.

☯ **Everything contains the seed of its opposite.** There is no such thing as pure Yin or pure Yang. Whenever something approaches purity, it gives birth to its own opposite and its own destruction. For example, when the sun is at high noon directly overhead, it automatically gives birth to the darkness that grows through the afternoon and blackens the sky at night.

One way of expressing this somewhat elusive principle is the saying, "What goes up must come down." Of course, in Yin-Yang theory, it is equally important to emphasize the opposite: "What goes down must come up."

☯ **Yin and Yang are infinitely divisible.** In other words, it is impossible to isolate Yin from Yang. The attempt to do so only recreates other Yin-Yang pairs. For example, all magnets have a north pole and a south pole. If you break a magnet in an attempt to isolate the north pole from the south pole, you will only succeed in creating two magnets, each with a north pole and a south pole. Repeated attempts will only recreate more bipolar (two-poled) magnets. Similarly, the tie between Yin and Yang can never be severed.

All changes have their foundation in the interplay between Yin and Yang. This interplay is a poetic dance. Like the ebb and flow of the tide, Yin unfailingly becomes Yang, and Yang inevitably becomes Yin. Through this endless transformation, opposites are balanced, and differences are unified into a whole. In this unification (which never actually happens because it is always in the process of happening), Yin and Yang simultaneously remember and forget that which they truly are: complementary aspects of one source—the Tai Chi.

Yin and Yang in Sasang Medicine

As stated previously, Yin and Yang serve as the first division in Sasang Medicine. This division makes some of us more Yang and some of us more Yin. Physically, Yang manifests as greater upper body development and a faster metabolism, while Yin manifests as greater lower body develop-ment and a slower metabolism. Psychologically, Yang manifests as a more extroverted, aggressive personality, while Yin manifests as a more intro-verted, conservative personality.

The goal of Sasang Medicine is to harmonize our fundamental Yin-Yang imbalances. For example, for a Yang type person, treatment would primarily focus upon strengthening the Yin aspect, so as to bring about a relative balance. Whatever our type, our goal should not be the emphasis of one aspect over the other, but rather alignment with the Yin and Yang of the universe.

Aligning Ourselves With Yin and Yang

It is necessary that we capture the essence of, and align ourselves with, Yin and Yang if we are to attain anything in this world. Failing to do so will inevitably lead to imbalance. Furthermore, the exclusive emphasis of one aspect over the other is unhealthy and unnatural. Nothing in the universe is or can be pure Yin or pure Yang. Thus, forceful methods used to attain pure Yin or pure Yang are doomed to fail. It is impossible to sever Yang from Yin.

In the East, it is held that nothing can be accomplished without re-specting the balance of Yin and Yang. This is true of all things, but par-ticularly so for health cultivation. Yin and Yang reflect the basic orienta-tion of the universe, and our bodies and minds are parts of that universe. Respecting our bodies and minds, then, means respecting Yin and Yang.

How do we align ourselves with Yin and Yang? First of all, we must change our attitude from one focused upon external accomplishment ("Where am I going?") to one centered upon balance ("Where am I?"). Second, we must appreciate and obey the natural patterns and cycles of the universe, both within and outside of ourselves. During the day, we should be active; during the night, we should rest. When we are hungry, we should eat; when we are thirsty, we should drink. Although this seems like common sense, modern life has so divorced us from our natural ways that we must work to rediscover them within ourselves. Yin and Yang are alive within us. If we listen, we will hear the common harmony weaving through our hearts and the universe around us.

Chapter 3

Sasang: The Compass

*The Sages created symbols and images in order to
thoroughly express their ideas.*
—Confucius, *I Ching*

A compass serves as a navigational tool. Although the most important piece of this tool is the magnetized needle, the designation of the four directions beneath it is also important. Without this designation, the needle lacks context. And without a context, the needle loses meaning and significance for us. What good is the fact that a magnetized needle points North if we cannot relate it to the four directions that we know and understand?

Similarly, Yin-Yang, the energetic axis, is not enough. We need a means to relate to Yin-Yang so that it has meaning for us. This is the purpose behind Sasang, Nature's Four Symbols.

The Importance of Symbols

Before we can adequately discuss what Sasang means, we must understand what a symbol does. A symbol gives something inexpressible an expressible form. Yin-Yang, the energetic axis of the universe, is inexpressible because it is too pure, too perfect, and too simple. Living in an impure, imperfect, complex world, it is very difficult for us to feel it, and almost impossible for us to align with it. Therefore, the Yin-Yang axis expresses itself in the universe through Sasang, the Four Symbolic Forms (Fig. 3.1). Through Sasang, we are able to feel Yin-Yang and to transform our world from a confusing maze into a paradise.

(Note: The following diagram represents how the Tai Chi differentiates first into Yin-Yang, and then into Sasang. Whenever anything divides, it must divide into a Yin-Yang pair. Thus, although one might think that Yin would divide into two Yins [Taiyin and Shaoyin], it actually must differentiate into a Yin-Yang pair, meaning that Shaoyang would be more appropriate than Shaoyin. The same is true for the division of Yang.

For the sake of convenience, however, and to make the distinction between Yin and Yang clearer, throughout most of this book Taiyin and Shaoyin are grouped under Yin; Taiyang and Shaoyang are grouped under Yang.)

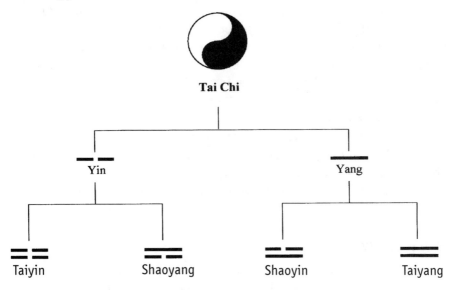

Figure 3.1: Sasang Division

The Tilt of Imperfection

Yin-Yang embodies perfect balance. Yet, we live in an imperfect world. To be a true symbol, Sasang must bridge the perfection of Yin-Yang with the imperfection of our world. Only as a hybrid can it express Yin-Yang in a tangible manner.

The introduction of imperfection, or tilt, to the perfect balance of Yin and Yang naturally creates four qualities. Instead of equal amounts of Yin and Yang, an imbalance introduces a Greater Yang, a Lesser Yang, a Greater Yin, and a Lesser Yin. In order to see how this is so, let us take a look at the Earth.

What if the Earth had a strict vertical axis? If it did, then the upper hemisphere and the lower hemisphere would both be heated and cooled equally. The relative equalization of temperature around the world would lead to a great reduction in the weather we experience, for weather is nothing more than a reflection of temperature imbalances. Not only would weather be stabilized on a day-to-day basis, it would also grow monotonous on a seasonal level, so that summer would be indistinguishable from winter. Life as we know it probably could not exist.

Fortunately, the Earth does not rotate on a strict vertical axis. It is tilted approximately 25 degrees. This tilt creates an imbalance. On the sunlit half of the Earth, one hemisphere has more area, so it receives more light than the other hemisphere. On the shadowed half of the Earth, one hemisphere has more area, so it is more in the dark than the other hemisphere. As a result, there is a significant difference in temperature between the two hemispheres. This manifests as daily weather, and on a larger scale, as the four seasons.

Yin-Yang resembles a perfect, hypothetical Earth with a strict vertical axis. The real Earth is tilted, and it is this tilt that creates four distinctly different regions and four distinctly different seasons. Similarly, the "tilt of imperfection" forces Yin-Yang to express itself through the filter of Sasang.

Why four?

Why four? What is so special about this number? There is some logic to the number four. It is the closest multiple of two. The fact that four is a multiple of two is significant, because Sasang, as a symbol of Yin-Yang, must reflect the binary nature of Yin-Yang. The fact that it is the *closest* multiple is also significant, as Sasang allows us to approach Yin-Yang.

There is another way to explain the significance of four through the Yin-Yang theory. Because four is an even number, it is Yin in nature.

Even numbers are fixed and come in pairs. They represent dependence, stillness, and balance. Odd numbers "stick out," thus representing independence and movement. As such, Sasang provides the certain foundation (Yin) from which all movements (Yang) can take place.

We may also argue for the significance of four through its universality in human culture. The Greeks conceived that Four Elements—Wind, Fire, Earth, and Water—composed the universe and governed all processes within it. India and other cultures of the East had similar philosophies. In China, for example, four mystical animals were thought to govern the four directions: the Turtle was the guardian of the North, the Phoenix the guardian of the South, the Tiger the guardian of the West, and the Dragon the guardian of the East. Thus, we may say that four is implicitly understood as a special number in the global language.

But the number four has significance beyond human culture. In fact, its significance in human culture is only a reflection of its significance in nature. If we merely look at our own bodies, we see a myriad of examples of the number four. We have four limbs, for example. On our face, there are four sense organs—eyes, ears, nose, and mouth—corresponding to four important abilities—hearing, sight, smell, and taste. Sasang also manifests through our genetic code and blood types, as previously mentioned.

We have already discussed how the tilt in the Earth's axis creates four different regions. This spatial division of four can be described in an even more basic sense. Consider the four-sided shape, the square or rectangle. The square is significant in that it is the most repeatable and stackable shape in existence. Thus:

- Grids and maps use the square to divide area.
- Paper is most commonly fashioned into a rectangular shape, perhaps to facilitate such division, or perhaps because the human mind naturally frames things in a square.
- Bricks are the basic building blocks of most architecture.
- Buildings themselves, more often than not, have a square or rectangular shape. Even the pyramid, which has triangular walls, has a square base. Like the four cornerstones that set the foundation of most buildings, Sasang sets the foundation for the form or shape of everything in the universe. It is what provides stability to all things in creation.

Another spatial form based upon the number four is the + sign. The + sign is commonly used to designate the center of a graph. The point of intersection between the vertical line and the horizontal line is conventionally designated as the origin. The lines point away from the origin, heading away from it in four directions. The + sign is used for the face of compasses, with each line symbolizing one of the four cardinal directions, and the center serving as the axis for the spinning magnetic needle.

The + sign is often used to explain the creation of the four body types. The origin represents perfect balance, or the Yin-Yang axis. The vertical line represents the continuum between Yang on top and Yin on the bottom. The horizontal line represents the continuum between Tai (greater) to the left, and Shao (lesser) to the right. As mankind cannot exist in a perfectly balanced state, everybody adopts a tilt upon birth, manifesting in one of the four quadrants of the graph. If, for example, an individual is tilted such that he or she has a greater amount of Yang, then that person is born with a Taiyang body type (the upper left quadrant).

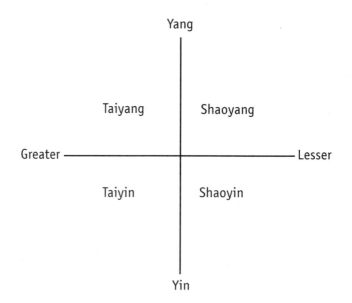

Sasang can also be described in terms of time. We experience time in stages. We do not experience 12 hours of uniformly intense sunlight, followed by 12 hours of darkness. If we did, we would likely fry during the first half of the day and freeze during the second half. Many of the most significant cycles of time are experienced in four stages:

- The daily cycle: dawn, noon, dusk, midnight.
- The yearly cycle: spring, summer, autumn, winter.
- The life cycle: childhood, adolescence, adulthood, old age.

To explain the first two cycles, we may invoke the aid of the + sign again. This time, however, the elements of the + sign take on a different meaning. With regards to the daily cycle, for example, the Earth beneath our feet occupies the position of the origin. The vertical and horizontal lines, meanwhile, designate significant positions of the sun. Although the sun does not orbit the Earth, it is subjectively experienced as though it did. Thus:

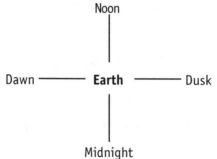

The four seasons may be illustrated in a similar manner, with the sun occupying the position of the origin, and the vertical and horizontal lines representing significant positions of the Earth in its yearly orbit.

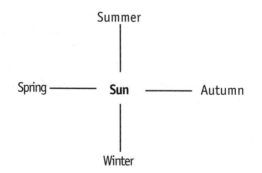

The four positions of the orbiting body, whether it is the sun or the Earth, correspond to four different qualities. Therefore, although both dawn and noon are considered to be part of the day, they are very different from each other. Dawn has a quiet, fresh feeling to it. Noon, on the

other hand, is in the "heat of things." The qualitative difference caused by
the four positions is even more evident in the four seasons. Spring has a
feeling of birth and renewal; summer, a spirit of play and excessiveness;
autumn, a sense of responsibility; winter, a quiet, meditative air. The seasons correspond to the four stages of life.

The Four Body Types

In our physical universe, perfection (Tai Chi) does not exist. Only
God, or whatever your particular interpretation of a Divine Being happens to be, is perfect. We tilt away from the perfect balance of Yin-Yang
(Tai Chi) in varying degrees when we are born. As a result, we manifest as
one of four body types.

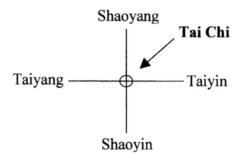

The circle in the center represents the perfect balance of Yin and
Yang, called Tai Chi. Again, this is the state where Yin and Yang energies
have united in perfect harmony. The closer we are to the center, the more
balanced we are in body, mind, and spirit. Our goal is to come as close as
we can to the centered state. In order to do this, we need to know what our
particular tilt or body type is. Understanding this will enable us to approach Tai Chi, as we learn to offset our imbalances.

Greater and lesser

If you recall, the tilt in the Earth's axis creates four distinct regions
on the surface of the globe. These four regions differ in the amount of
light or shadow they receive. Similarly, the four body types result from an
imbalance in Yin and Yang. With regards to Yang, there are Taiyang
(greater), and Shaoyang (lesser); with regards to Yin, there are Taiyin and
Shaoyin.

Although we make a distinction between these four body types, it is important to remember that they all possess both Yin and Yang. What makes them differ from each other is the degree of Yin and Yang that they possess. The differences in Yin and Yang in each type can be expressed in the following way:

- Taiyang (greater Yang): Yang within Yang.
- Shaoyang (lesser Yang): Yin within Yang.
- Taiyin (greater Yin): Yin within Yin.
- Shaoyin (lesser Yin): Yang within Yin.

As you can see, the main difference between the greater, or Tai, constitutions and the lesser, or Shao, constitutions lies in the amount and strength of Yin or Yang energy. Therefore, even though Taiyang and Shaoyang are Yang body types, Taiyang has a greater amount of and stronger Yang energy, whereas Shaoyang has a lesser amount of and weaker Yang energy. The same is true for the Yin types; Taiyin has a greater amount of and stronger Yin energy and Shaoyin has a lesser amount of and weaker Yin.

I Ching symbols and body types

The difference between the four body types is not just a quantitative one. It is also qualitative. Just as the four seasons have distinctly different qualities, so do the four body types. We can begin to see these qualitative differences by looking at Sasang as expressed through the following four bigrams of the I Ching (see also figure 3.1 from the beginning of this chapter).

Taiyin   **Taiyang**

Taiyin has a double Yin line, and thus is the most Yin among all the constitutions. These two broken lines create spaces that allow things to gather and accumulate inside. Thus, they express the fact that Taiyins are able to hold the greatest amount of physical mass and are the most prone to obesity. The lines also express the fact that Taiyins can accept a lot psychologically; of the four constitutions, they are the most tolerant, forgiving, persistent and patient. As the breaks in the lines represent pauses, rests, or interrupted motion, it is no surprise that Taiyins are the slowest constitution, both in regards to internal metabolism and external behavior. There are more Taiyins than any other body type in the human population. Remember that Yin corresponds to more physical mass and structure, so Taiyins can materialize or embody more easily.

The Taiyang constitution, on the other hand, is pure Yang as the Yang lines double up. Taiyangs are like a tornado with 400 mph winds, or a hydrogen bomb on the verge of exploding. Both of these phenomena are capable of destructive power on an astronomical scale. The top line in their bigram represents their exterior appearance, and the bottom line represents their internal character. The fact that both are Yang (hard, unyielding) gives you a sense of Taiyangs' unbreakable strength. Indeed, Taiyangs are the most resolute, revolutionary, and fearless of the four body types. Their surplus Yang also makes them extremely urgent, arrogant, uncooperative, and rude. Oftentimes, there is not enough Yin energy to hold this great amount of Yang energy; thus, it is difficult for Taiyang energy to manifest in human form. As a result, we see fewer Taiyang persons in nature than any other constitution.

Shaoyin   **Shaoyang**

Shaoyins have a Yin line on the outside (on top) and a Yang line inside (below). Thus, externally they appear fragile, weak, soft, and introverted. Inside, however, they are tough, resilient, calculating, methodical, and immovable once they make up their minds.

Shaoyangs have a Yang line on the outside and a Yin line on the inside. They are strong outwardly, but weak inside. Externally, they are robust, quick, and tough, but inside, they are gentle and tender. They are extroverted, sentimental, compassionate, and tolerant of others.

At last, the compass is complete. We not only have a magnetized needle, that is, Yin-Yang, but four directions with which to interpret and orient it, that is, Sasang. Now, we may begin our journey. On the following pages, you will find a questionnaire that will help you determine your body type and allow you to take the first step on the path to self-understanding.

Identifying your constitution

The following questionnaire is designed to help you identify your constitution. The questionnaire is divided into four sections: The first deals with your general mental and behavioral characteristics; the second, your personal, business, and social lives; the third, your physical characteristics; and the last, some general questions on your health. Read through the whole questionnaire, placing a check mark next to each answer with which you identify. There are certain overlaps in the answers, because some answers apply to more than one constitution. Nevertheless, still check all of the answers that apply to you. Relax and take your time. Try to be reflective, honest, and unbiased in your answers.

After you have completed the questions, count the number of checks you have made in each column to find your totals. Write your totals at the end of each of the four parts of the questionnaire in the space provided. At the end of the questionnaire, there is a table for you to fill in your scores. Add up your scores from the four parts to find your overall totals. The overall totals that you obtain from this chart will provide you with a good estimation of your body type. For example, if you come up with 20 check marks for Taiyang, 40 for Shaoyang, 10 for Taiyin, and 15 for Shaoyin, then you are most likely of the Shaoyang body type. As it is possible for you to take on traits of other constitutions, you may come up with a tie score. Nevertheless, remember that you are born of only one dominant constitution, even if it may not be strongly evident in your score. To break the tie, use only the score on Section III (physical characteristics). If you still have a tie in Section III, or are still uncertain about your body type, consider a consultation with a practitioner of Sasang Medicine for a professional evaluation of your body type.

This questionnaire is a tool. Use it to steer you toward a better understanding of your constitution and a deeper insight into your relationships.

Part I: General Mental and Behavioral Characteristics

Taiyang	Shaoyang	Taiyin	Shaoyin

Most prominent characteristics

Taiyang	Shaoyang	Taiyin	Shaoyin

☐ resolute
☐ dogmatic
☐ arrogant/
  self-righteous
☐ creative/
  ingenious
☐ revolutionary
☐ charismatic
☐ heroic
	☐ cheerful
	☐ mischievous
	☐ decisive
	☐ extroverted
	☐ quick to act
	☐ brave/chivalrous
	☐ righteous
		☐ magnanimous
		☐ prudent
		☐ taciturn
		☐ stubborn
		☐ ambitious
		☐ decorous
		☐ persistent/
		  tenacious
			☐ crafty
			☐ indecisive
			☐ introverted/timid
			☐ decorous
			☐ stubborn
			☐ meticulous
			☐ deeply reflective/
			  meditative

Appearance/General impression

Taiyang	Shaoyang	Taiyin	Shaoyin

☐ fearless/arrogant
☐ neat/elegant
	☐ sharp/intelligent
	☐ riotous
		☐ benevolent
		☐ dignified &
		  reserved
			☐ soft, gentle & calm
			☐ detail-oriented &
			  tidy

You at your best

Taiyang	Shaoyang	Taiyin	Shaoyin

☐ benevolent/
  compassionate
☐ strong leader
☐ pioneering/
  original
☐ courageous
☐ optimistic
☐ reformer
	☐ life of the party
	☐ quick reasoning/
	  decision-making
	☐ outspoken
	☐ altruistic & quick
	  to help others
	☐ optimistic
	☐ passionate worker
		☐ responsible
		☐ humorous
		☐ patient
		☐ even-tempered
		☐ optimistic
		☐ stoic
			☐ precise &
			  methodical
			☐ frank & candid
			☐ prudent
			☐ considerate of
			  others
			☐ non-contentious
			☐ patient &
			  persevering

You at your worst

Taiyang	Shaoyang	Taiyin	Shaoyin

☐ dictator/despot
☐ rebellious/
  uncooperative
☐ easily angered
☐ rude/impertinent
☐ debauching
☐ urgent
☐ antisocial/outcast
	☐ fickle
	☐ rash/impulsive
	☐ not patient or
	  persistent in
	  study or work
	☐ angry/belligerent
	☐ vain/show-off
	☐ prodigal
	☐ neglectful of family/
	  domestic/
	  internal life
		☐ greedy/selfish
		☐ lazy
		☐ wicked
		☐ cowardly/overly
		  cautious
		☐ closed-minded
		☐ pleasure-seeking
		☐ procrastinating
			☐ selfish
			☐ pessimistic
			☐ jealous/envious
			☐ procrastinating
			☐ moody/silent
			☐ nervous/
			  apprehensive
			☐ stingy

Part I: Total ( )   Total ( )   Total ( )   Total ( )

Part II: Personal, Business, and Social Life

Taiyang	Shaoyang	Taiyin	Shaoyin

1. How do you handle your personal and business work?

Taiyang	Shaoyang	Taiyin	Shaoyin
☐ I am always resolute and firm in starting and finishing projects, no matter what.	☐ I am quick in starting new projects, but seldom finish anything.	☐ I am a slow starter, but once the ball gets rolling, I carry things through to the end.	☐ I wait until I am certain of success before starting anything, but I usually finish what I start.
☐ I do things on a grand scale quickly, and without planning.	☐ I like to get things done quickly because I get bored easily.	☐ Slow, steady, and easy-does-it is my approach to work.	☐ I am precise and meticulous in my work.
☐ I cannot sit still or work on one thing for an extended period of time.	☐ I cannot sit still or work on one thing for an extended period of time.	☐ I can sit and work patiently in one location for a long time.	☐ I can sit and work patiently in one location for a long time.

2. Your response to a new situation is:

Taiyang	Shaoyang	Taiyin	Shaoyin
☐ "Ready or not, here I come!" I create new situations.	☐ I am optimistic and enthusiastic in new and unfamiliar situations.	☐ Though I don't enjoy them, I am steady and reliable in unfamiliar situations.	☐ I am self-protective in any situation, especially new and unfamiliar ones.

3. How do you respond to an opportunity?

Taiyang	Shaoyang	Taiyin	Shaoyin
☐ I make my own opportunities!	☐ When I see an opportunity, I quickly go after it.	☐ I wait patiently for opportunities to arise. When they are within my reach, I grasp them tightly, and never let go.	☐ I wait and wait, and lose my chance.

4. How do you generally make decisions?

Taiyang	Shaoyang	Taiyin	Shaoyin
☐ I resolutely make my decisions and they are always correct!	☐ I quickly make decisions without weighing the pros and cons.	☐ I ponder over all decisions slowly, cautiously, and thoroughly.	☐ I am indecisive by nature, and prefer to defer decision-making to others.

Taiyang	Shaoyang	Taiyin	Shaoyin
5. Appearing or speaking before a crowd or relating to strangers:			
☐ I make my presence known to everyone (even strangers) in the same manner.	☐ I feel comfortable appearing or speaking before an audience.	☐ I experience difficulty appearing or speaking before an audience.	☐ I experience difficulty appearing or speaking before an audience.
☐ I say whatever comes to mind whenever I want to.	☐ I say whatever comes to mind whenever I want to.	☐ I do not speak until I feel certain that my ideas are correct.	☐ I do not speak until I feel certain that my ideas are correct.
☐ I enjoy being the center of attention.	☐ I enjoy attention, and actively seek it.	☐ I don't try to stand out (but I wish people noticed me).	☐ I shy away from the attention of others.
6. How do you generally respond to stress?			
☐ anger/rage	☐ irritability	☐ fear	☐ procrastination
☐ aggression	☐ anger	☐ procrastination	☐ insecurity
☐ stoically "take it"	☐ anxiety	☐ lethargy	☐ anxiety/worry
☐ take action	☐ take action	☐ conservatism	☐ indecisiveness
7. Your personal and social relationships:			
☐ I can meet and talk to anyone, anytime.	☐ I enjoy going out and meeting new people; I love parties and crowds.	☐ I like meeting new people, but I'd rather spend time with family and friends.	☐ I have difficulty meeting new people, whether for business or social reasons.
☐ Although I know many people, I really do not have any close friends. My friends must share my ideals.	☐ I'm not picky about making new friends, and do so with ease and enjoyment. Thus, I have many friends.	☐ I can easily make friends with anyone, and have good relationships with everyone.	☐ I am picky in forming friendships, and socialize only with those with whom I share a close affinity.

Taiyang	Shaoyang	Taiyin	Shaoyin
8. On making mistakes:			
☐ I never make mistakes. Mistakes are due to others, and I criticize them for it. (Even if I do make a mistake, I never regret it.)	☐ I often make mistakes, but I quickly forget about it. I can easily forgive others when they make mistakes.	☐ I work slowly, and rarely make mistakes. When there is a mistake, I can easily forgive myself or others for it.	☐ I hate making mistakes, so I approach work carefully. I have a hard time forgiving mistakes in either myself or others.
9. When I fail:			
☐ It is never my fault. It is always someone else's fault.	☐ I quickly forget about it and plan my next move.	☐ I get down on myself but come back no matter what it takes.	☐ I worry and stay depressed for a long time. It's hard for me to start fresh again.
10. When someone mistreats you:			
☐ I explode on the spot, no matter who the person is.	☐ I let my anger show, and shout and retort right back at the person.	☐ I dismiss it, or talk things out. Although I may be hurt, I pretend I'm fine.	☐ I get angry and annoyed, but I usually just back away.
Part II: Total ( )	Total ( )	Total ( )	Total ( )

Part III: Physical Characteristics				
	Taiyang	**Shaoyang**	**Taiyin**	**Shaoyin**
Overall body structure	☐ thin body with large head ☐ body resembles inverted triangle with narrow waist	☐ average-sized body with me-dium-sized bones ☐ body resembles inverted triangle, with wide, athletic shoulders and narrow hips/ buttocks	☐ large-sized body with thick bones and stocky build ☐ greater waist and lower body development; either obese with pot-belly, or overall strong and heavy appearance	☐ small-sized body with thin bones ☐ body resembles ladder; well-developed hips, buttocks, and lower body with narrow shoulders and chest; but overall well-balanced
Head size/shape	☐ large head, bulging at the crown/thick stiff neck	☐ protruding forehead and back of head	☐ large and round or large and square head	☐ round or thin, oval head
Overall facial feature	☐ strong, intimidating look; or elegant, neat appearance ☐ wide forehead and protruding cheeks	☐ sensitive, but bright and animated ☐ small thin lips; sharp chin	☐ serene and dignified ☐ fleshy, large face; round, large nose; thick lips	☐ gentle and quiet or nervous and timid ☐ overall face small; small features, but well-balanced
Eyes	☐ crystal-like, fierce, piercing, intimidating	☐ clear and sparkling or sharp and intense	☐ large, cow-like, or large and bright	☐ pleasant, gentle, without focus (sleepy eyes)
Skin	☐ soft	☐ dry, thin, and smooth	☐ solid and thick; fairly rough; large skin pores	☐ soft and tender; slightly moist and swollen; small skin pores

Part III: Physical Characteristics (cont'd)				
	Taiyang	**Shaoyang**	**Taiyin**	**Shaoyin**
Voice	☐harsh, metallic; or sonorous, overflowing with vigor	☐clear and crisp	☐thick, impure (muffled) and heavy	☐somewhat calm, quiet, and gentle
Walk/ Gait	☐light and weak; straight stiff posture, resembling a robot	☐straight posture; light and fast tempo; whole body shakes (looks unstable)	☐ slow and stable with measured gait (heavy regal steps)	☐ natural and gentle; careful and stable; may walk with upper body leaning forward
Part III:	Total ( )	Total ( )	Total ( )	Total ( )

Part IV: General and Health Questions

Taiyang	Shaoyang	Taiyin	Shaoyin

1. How is your general bowel movement?

Taiyang	Shaoyang	Taiyin	Shaoyin
☐ I usually pass a great amount of large, well-formed stools.	☐ I tend to get constipated easily.	☐ I tend to get constipated and it makes me feel somewhat uncomfortable.	☐ I tend to get diarrhea easily, and it really makes me tired.
☐ I can sometimes be constipated up to 6 or 7 days without problems, but if it goes over a week, then it bothers me.	☐ I have a hard time dealing with constipation; it can make my chest feel hot and congested.	☐ I tend to have alternating diarrhea and constipation, but it doesn't bother me.	☐ I am usually constipated for 2 to 3 days, but it doesn't bother me.

2. How much do you generally sweat and how do you feel after sweating profusely?

Taiyang	Shaoyang	Taiyin	Shaoyin
☐ I don't sweat much and I feel okay after sweating.	☐ I don't sweat much and I feel okay after sweating.	☐ I tend to sweat a lot and feel energized when I do. I love sitting in saunas for long periods of time.	☐ I generally do not sweat much and feel very tired when I do. I do not generally like sitting in saunas.

3. What type of foods and drinks do you like?

Taiyang	Shaoyang	Taiyin	Shaoyin
☐ vegetables and fruits, raw and undercooked foods ☐ cool or cold drinks	☐ all types of foods, but especially cool and cold foods (salads, vegetables, fruits) ☐ cool or cold drinks	☐ everything ☐ room temperature or cold drinks	☐ hot, spicy, warm, and well-cooked foods ☐ room temperature or warm drinks

4. What season(s) do you like?

Taiyang	Shaoyang	Taiyin	Shaoyin
☐ cool/cold seasons	☐ cool/cold seasons	☐ any season except hot and damp	☐ warm/hot seasons

Part IV: General and Health Questions (contd)

Taiyang	Shaoyang	Taiyin	Shaoyin

5. Your manner of speech:

Taiyang	Shaoyang	Taiyin	Shaoyin
□ urgent	□ fast, garrulous	□ usually taciturn, but once I start, I talk in a cheerful manner	□ usually quiet, but I talk a lot with people who are close

6. From which of the following ailments or conditions do you frequently suffer?

Taiyang	Shaoyang	Taiyin	Shaoyin
□ vomiting	□ urination or sexual problems	□ palpitations	□ indigestion
□ weakness in waist and legs	□ forgetfulness	□ weak lungs	□ sighing
□ difficulty swallowing	□ constipation	□ hypertension	□ low energy
□ hiccups	□ lower back pain	□ weight gain	□ abdominal pain

Part IV: Total ( )   Total ( )   Total ( )   Total ( )

Overall Test Scores

Categories	Taiyang	Shaoyang	Taiyin	Shaoyin
Part I				
Part II				
Part III				
Part IV				
Overall score				

Now that you have identified your body type, it is time to explore its various aspects and delve deeper into your own self-understanding. The next three chapters will help to paint a clearer picture of the four constitutions through detailed explanations of the physical, mental-emotional, and pathological predispositions of the four body types. With this information, you will get a sense of what your fundamental tendencies are. This knowledge will help you get grounded, so you know where you stand on the journey to health.

In Part Two, you will learn what steps you can take on this journey to approach balance and harmony. You will be empowered with the basic information you need to develop your own personalized regimen for self-cultivation and make your own way to realizing your true potential.

Chapter 4

The Physical Landscape

The human body is the universe in miniature. That which cannot be found in the body is not to be found in the universe. Hence the philosopher's formula, that the universe within reflects the universe without. It follows, therefore, that if our knowledge of our own body could be perfect, we would know the universe.
—Mahatma Gandhi

Human beings receive their life from the Yin Qi and Yang Qi of Heaven and Earth, and derive their form according to the principle of the four seasons.
—Yellow Emperor's Inner Classic

Your body is not a happenstance phenomenon. You look the way you do for a reason. Your contours, curves, and facial impressions are vital elements of nature's panorama. In fact, you might say that your body is your personal landscape. It holds landmarks telling you who you are. Perceive its subtleties and you'll find your own meaning.

Any practitioner of Feng Shui (literally, Wind-Water), or the art of geomancy, will tell you how important the lay of the land is. Landscape determines the manner in which vital energy (Qi) flows through a place. A box-valley, for example, will tend to pool or stagnate the Qi, whereas an open plain will tend to disperse it, like flowing water without riverbanks. The nature of this flow will in turn determine such subtle factors as good or bad weather, or even auspicious or inauspicious fortune.

Our physical bodies are similar to landscapes. Based upon the shape we are born with, the energy in our bodies flows in certain ways. This flow in turn determines our mental and emotional temperament, and even our "luck." This is the reason why the physical body is so important in Sasang Medicine; as in Feng Shui, shape or form determines destiny.

The idea that the body reflects the spirit is neither new nor unique. In the Bible, for example, the body is called "the temple of the soul." What makes Sasang Medicine special is that it correlates the shape of the vessel (the physical body) with the nature of its contents (the spirit or soul). It accomplishes this by looking at the flow of Qi. Thus, before we can talk about the four body types, we must answer the question, "What is Qi?"

What Is Qi?

Qi is the subtle, fundamental force that creates and permeates all phenomena. Nothing exists without Qi. Qi can be roughly translated as dynamic force, cosmic force, fundamental life force, life energy, and bio-energy. Some people have tried to define Qi as electromagnetic force. It seems more appropriate to consider electromagnetic energy as but one form of the manifestation of Qi. Other forces in nature, like strong and weak nuclear forces or gravity, may also be considered manifestations of Qi. In India, Qi is called prana. Whatever it is called, or however it is seen, Qi is the ultimate matrix of the universe, spreading out in both physical and metaphysical dimensions. It is Qi that concerns practitioners of Eastern medicine as well as those who practice other forms of energetic medicine.

Physically, Qi is the dynamic energy for all phenomena in the universe; psychologically, it is the mood or vibe of humans; physiologically, it is the bio-energy that keeps organisms alive; socially, it is one's social position, trend, or situation.

Yin-Yang, Qi, and Physical Development

Everything in the universe is created out of Qi energy. In order for any form to manifest in the physical plane, Qi must condense into solid matter. This is true of our bodies as well. The actual manner in which Qi manifests in our bodies depends upon Yin and Yang.

We are born as one of four constitutions, as illustrated in the last chapter. Each constitution correlates to a different ratio of Yin and Yang. A Shaoyin person, for example, has excessive Yin and deficient Yang. In

Chapter 2, we saw that Yin and Yang are associated with directions (among other things); Yin is associated with downward and inward directions, whereas Yang is associated with upward and outward directions. A person's Yin-Yang ratio determines the predominant direction that the Qi will move in his body. Thus, for a Shaoyin person, the excessive Yin will cause the Qi to move in a downward direction.

As the Qi moves to certain areas of the body according to the forces of Yin and Yang, those areas become saturated with Qi energy. Wherever the Qi goes, blood and other nutrients follow. Hence, those regions experience greater physical and/or mental development. On the other hand, if less Qi goes to a certain area, that area will not receive as much blood and nutrition, and therefore will be relatively less developed.

Recall that Yin and Yang are also associated with temperature and speed. Yin is associated with coldness and slowness, while Yang is associated with warmth and speed. If we take all of these factors into consideration, we can make general characterizations of the influence of Yin and Yang on our physical formation:

YIN	YANG
Greater lower body development:	Greater upper body development:
❂ Waist	❂ Head
❂ Neck	❂ Hips
❂ Buttocks	❂ Chest
❂ Legs	❂ Shoulders
❂ Colder bodies and extremeties	❂ Warmer bodies and extremeties
Slower metabolism	Faster metabolism

This chart demonstrates the general influence of Yin and Yang upon our body types, but does not address the finer distinctions of Sasang (between Taiyin and Shaoyin, and Taiyang and Shaoyang). For example, although both Yang constitutions have greater upper body development, and both Yin constitutions have greater lower body development, the specific area of greatest development differs among the four constitutions. Taiyang is most developed in the head and neck, Shaoyang in the chest and shoulders, Taiyin in the abdomen and waist, and Shaoyin in the hips and buttocks.

The Tai Chi symbol and body types

We may obtain an interesting view of the body types by dividing the Tai Chi symbol in half and turning those halves in different directions. The resulting shapes give us rough profiles of the different body types, illustrating where the Qi energy goes and where development is greatest.

Taiyang

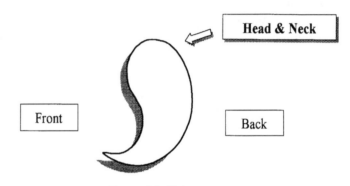

Figure 4.1: Taiyang

Figure 4.1 represents the Taiyangs. The region corresponding to the head (top and rear) protrudes the most, representing the concentration of energy in the head and neck in this constitution. This shape conjures up images of an alien (ET), Godzilla, a dragon, or a male lion.

Shaoyang

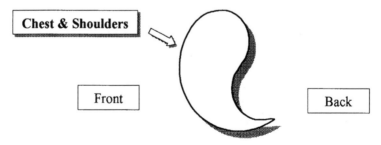

Figure 4.2: Shaoyang

Figure 4.2 represents the Shaoyangs. In the diagram above, you can see that the energy is focused on the front upper region of the figure (the area of the chest and shoulders), revealing that Shaoyangs have the greatest development there. You can visualize a soldier or a body builder standing, keeping his shoulders back and sticking his chest out.

Taiyin

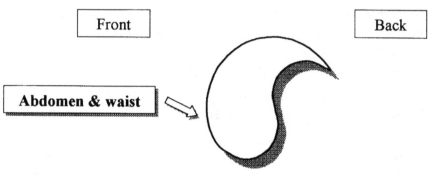

Figure 4.3: Taiyin

Figure 4.3 represents the Taiyins. The diagram reveals that Taiyin energy is focused on the front and lower part of the body (especially the abdomen area). Imagine the stereotypical potbelly of a businessman or of Santa Claus when viewed from the side.

Shaoyin

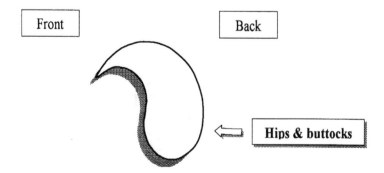

Figure 4.4: Shaoyin

Figure 4.4 represents the Shaoyins. It is bottom heavy and the energy is primarily concentrated in the rear lower portion. Similarly, Shaoyins are bottom heavy people, with energy concentrated mainly in their hips and buttocks. Try to visualize a kangaroo, a squirrel, or a rat viewed from the side.

Four Energetic Directions and Body Structure

We have seen through the Tai Chi symbol that Qi concentrates in different areas of the body. Now let us examine the direction that the Qi takes from the front. Think of four directions: up, down, obliquely up, and obliquely down. These directions correspond to the four body types:

- ❧ Taiyang: Energy rises straight upward.
- ❧ Shaoyang: Energy rises obliquely upward.
- ❧ Taiyin: Energy descends obliquely downward.
- ❧ Shaoyin: Energy descends straight down.

The center from which the Qi energy moves is the acupuncture point REN-12, situated halfway between the solar plexus and the navel. If we picture this point as the center of the body, with vectors extending out in the four directions indicated above, we can easily see how the body types come to be (Fig. 4.5). (Note: The idea of REN-12 as the center from which energy radiates to create the four body types, as well as the diagrams used to illustrate this idea, were originated by Professors Kyu Yong Chi and Kyu Suk Ahn of the Department of Pathology, Oriental Medical College, Kyung Hee University, Seoul.)

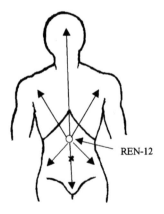

Figure 4.5: Four Energetic Directions

The next four diagrams depicting each constitution are exemplary of each body type. However, every body type varies somewhat in size and configuration. Thus, the following are but a set of general guidelines exemplifying the four energetic directions as mentioned above.

Taiyang

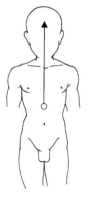

Figure 4.6: Taiyang

The above diagram shows that the Qi in Taiyangs ascends straight up. It rises through the neck, focusing in the head region. Because blood and nutrition follow the Qi, these areas experience the greatest amount of development. For this reason, the head of a Taiyang person resembles a bud or a flower sprouting forth from a plant or a tree. On the other hand, because the Qi ascends, it is lacking in the lower portion of the body, resulting in a weak waist and legs. Thus Taiyangs are, on the whole, quite top-heavy.

Shaoyang

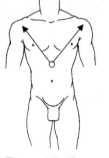

Figure 4.7: Shaoyang

The Qi of the Shaoyang ascends obliquely, exploding up and out, like a billowing cloud of smoke. This pattern of energy movement widens the ribcage, making the chest and shoulder regions larger and stronger. It also makes the waist and hips narrower and weaker, giving Shaoyangs an upside down triangle figure. This body structure, the ideal build of a gymnast, can be compared to the spreading branches of a tree. In the animal kingdom, Shaoyangs are analogous to birds. The wingspan of birds taper down to small buttocks and legs, just as with Shaoyangs. Monkeys and chimpanzees also exemplify the Shaoyang body type, with their wide shoulders and long arms.

Taiyin

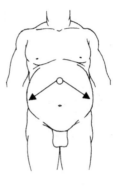

Figure 4.8: Taiyin

The Qi of Taiyins descends obliquely, traveling to the abdomen and waist region. This gives Taiyins a thick trunk (much like a tree's) and a wide, stable appearance. Although Taiyins are large overall, the trunk or waist is the region of greatest accumulation. Visualize big, heavyweight wrestlers, Olympic power lifters, and sumo wrestlers. Taiyins in the animal kingdom include hippopotami, elephants, dinosaurs, and rhinoceroses.

Shaoyin

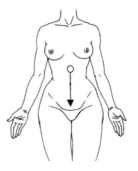

Figure 4.9: Shaoyin

In Shaoyins, the Qi drops straight down like an icy waterfall, pooling in the pelvic cavity and the buttocks region. This gives Shaoyins well-developed hips, as well as strong legs (like the roots of a tree). Although Shaoyins tend to be small in size, we may see large, heavyset Shaoyins in everyday life. Whether small or large, however, the basic body type remains the same: Shaoyins always have the greatest physical development in their hips, buttocks, and legs. Thus, their appearance for the most part resembles a ladder, narrow at the top and wide at the bottom. Although this description sounds awkward, they often are anything but. Many Shaoyins have well-balanced, proportional figures. The hip and leg development of the Shaoyin body type allows them to sprint swiftly and make powerful, graceful leaps; some of the best ballet dancers, figure skaters, high jumpers, and short distance runners are Shaoyins. Animals resembling the Shaoyin body type include kangaroos, ducks, squirrels, and rats.

The 4 Body Types in Detail

Now that we have talked about the general differences in development among the four body types, we are ready to look at our physical landscape in greater detail. Your landscape can be described in terms of 1. external physique and 2. internal physiology. The external physique consists of the physical frame, including the development of bone and muscle, and the overall body shape. The internal physiology concerns the strength or weakness of organs in the body, and the excess or deficiency of Yin and Yang.

Taiyang

Taiyangs are the rarest of all body types. According to Dr. Jae Ma Lee, only one out of 1,000 people is Taiyang. This is because Taiyangs have the most Yang energy of all the body types, and Yang energy is difficult to embody in physical form (a Yin process).

External Physical Appearance

Taiyangs have the greatest amount of development in the most Yang (highest) part of the body, namely the head and neck. The Taiyang head is generally large and round, and the front, the back, and the top of the head are well developed. In many Taiyangs, the head juts forward, like a gargoyle waiting to attack. Often, Taiyangs appear to have thick, stiff, strong necks, as though in a cast. Combined, the head and neck can lend an aggressive, combative appearance to Taiyangs. If you look at the head and neck development of such famous Taiyangs as Napoleon, Lenin, and Beethoven, you can see this quite clearly.

Taiyangs have distinctive facial features. Their facial characteristics are clearly defined, with small, sharp eyes. They are notably piercing and crystal-like, such that Taiyangs may appear scary, cold-blooded, and intimidating. The cheeks look as though they were pushed forward from the ears to the eyes. Many Taiyangs have fairly wide foreheads, but their chins are somewhat small and pointed, giving their faces an upside-down triangular shape. Some Taiyangs, however, have a rounder face. In any case, their overall expressions tend to make them look sharp, sensitive, and troublesome, or progressive and intelligent. Their skin color is paler than the other types of constitutions, and their skin texture tends to be soft, with small pores.

The Taiyang body shape resembles an inverted triangle. The upper body shows great development, making the low back, waist, buttocks, and legs appear weak in comparison. As a result, the Taiyang standing position looks weak and unstable. The Taiyang person is generally on the thin side with weak or undeveloped musculature (you will rarely find an obese Taiyang body type). There are, however, a few Taiyangs with larger bodies. Still, even these large Taiyangs are usually of smaller stature.

The external appearance of Taiyang body types can be likened to a stereotypical alien. Aliens are commonly depicted with inordinately large heads housing big brains, perched atop thin, small bodies with wiry limbs.

Internal Physiology

Taiyangs have a surplus of Yang and a slight weakness of Yin. Their Yang energy is extremely powerful and explosive, and manifests in strong, outward, dispersing tendencies that manifest in rapid physiological processes. Everything moves quickly, easily, and smoothly within the Taiyang person. This results in a thin body, because the rapid, dispersing energy dissipates the Yin and fluids inside of them, while burning up foods before they can be stored as fat.

Taiyangs have strong Lungs and weak Livers (please bear in mind that these organ systems refer to energetic patterns as described in Eastern medicine, and not to the physical organs of Western medicine). The strong Lungs manifest in the strong outward and dispersing energy described above. The Liver, meanwhile, is responsible for much of the gathering and accumulating energy in the body, and plays a major role in the development and growth of the uterus and reproductive system. In Taiyangs, the weak Liver often manifests in a weak reproductive system. An otherwise healthy Taiyang woman has a weaker uterus than women of other constitutions, and she has a greater chance of infertility or miscarriage. If she does manage to get pregnant, a Taiyang woman will likely experience a difficult pregnancy. This is another reason why people of the Taiyang constitution are difficult to find in everyday life.

Shaoyang

Shaoyangs are also Yang, but are the lesser of the two Yang constitutions. Unlike Taiyangs, their energy has already dispersed somewhat, like a waning sun. Physically, their shoulders and chest are well developed (Yang), but their waists and lower bodies (Yin) seem frail in comparison. Shaoyangs generally tend to have warm bodies (Yang) and possess fast metabolisms (Yang).

External Appearance

Shaoyangs' eyes are their most prominent facial features. Although not necessarily large, they have a sharp, intense look to them, much like those of a boxer sizing up his opponent. Shaoyangs are always on the lookout, scanning their surroundings or gazing into the distance. Their deeply penetrating gaze is inescapable. The eyes of many famous Shaoyangs have an aggressive quality to them. Some notable examples include the glares of Bruce Lee, Muhammad Ali, Robert DeNiro, and Arnold Schwarzenneger. Other Shaoyangs, meanwhile, tend to have clear, sparkling eyes, like Elizabeth Taylor, Jacqueline Kennedy Onassis, Julie Andrews, and Elvis Presley.

The Shaoyang head is generally small and narrow, often with a protruding forehead and occiput. Their noses are usually high or sharp-tipped. Their mouths are generally small, and their lips are generally thin. The Shaoyang chin is usually pointy and thin. Protruding, turned-up chins are frequently associated with this constitution. The overall shape of the head and face is somewhat elongated and oval. Although they may look sensitive upon an initial meeting, their overall expressions are bright, animated and joyful. Some Shaoyangs have a dark complexion, stemming from an inherent weakness in their Kidneys. This is especially true if they have engaged in excessive sexual activity, which further weakens the Kidneys.

Like Taiyangs, Shaoyangs have more Yang energy, so they have greater upper body development. Unlike Taiyangs, however, Shaoyangs are more developed in the shoulder and chest regions. Imagine Taiyang energy as being perched on the top tier of a totem pole with Shaoyang energy resting just below it. In Shaoyangs, the shoulders appear raised and the chest is wide and open, as in the stereotypical athlete or body-builder. The ribcage is well developed with a wide sterno-costal angle.

Shaoyangs' waists and hips look meager in comparison to their upper bodies. Although Shaoyang women have a full and well-developed upper body, the lower body is especially narrow, making them lose the elegant, hourglass feminine figure. Some Shaoyang women have wide hips, but they are still narrower than the hips of Taiyins and Shaoyins. On the whole, Shaoyangs resemble an upside down triangle in their physical appearance. This body shape, together with their Kidney weakness, makes it more difficult for Shaoyang women to conceive (though not as difficult as for Taiyang women) than Yin body types.

Despite the athletic appearance of their bodies, many Shaoyangs have weak bone framework, which can give them the appearance of being sickly and debilitated. This is also due to the weakness in their Kidneys and their relationship to the bones. Shaoyangs' skin tends to be thin, without much moisture, and is smooth. In general, Shaoyangs do not sweat much. Their hands and feet are generally warm.

Some Shaoyangs are small in stature with a neat and tidy appearance, similar to Shaoyins. For this reason, you must exercise care in differentiating these two types.

Internal Physiology

Shaoyangs are generally on the thin side, as they have a difficult time gaining weight. This is due to the excess Yang energy and weak Yin energy that rules this constitution. This Yang energy drives a rapid metabolism that leaves no time for assimilated nutrients to accumulate in the body. In fact, one would be hard pressed to find an obese Shaoyang person (most people who constantly eat yet do not gain weight belong to this constitution). As they grow older, however, Shaoyang people may gain some weight due to a slowing of their metabolisms. This is especially true of Shaoyang women after childbirth. Occasionally, you can see Shaoyangs who are somewhat obese; their abdomen protrudes in a round fashion rather than drooping straight down.

The Shaoyang constitution possesses a strong Spleen and weak Kidneys. The Spleen is responsible for digestion. As we have just discussed, Shaoyangs have no problems in this regard; in fact, the strong Spleen tends to make their digestion and metabolism too efficient. The Kidneys, meanwhile, are closely related to reproductive energy. The weak Kidneys of Shaoyangs result in weak reproductive energy, with difficulty in conception. The Kidneys are also responsible for bone growth and development, which is why some Shaoyangs tend to experience problems related to weak bone structure.

Taiyin

Taiyin and Shaoyin types generally have greater lower body development, due to the descending of Yin energy. As Taiyins are the greater Yin, they hold more mass and embody more easily, as previously mentioned. They are physically heavier, thick boned, and slower. Internally, they possess the slowest metabolism of all four constitutions.

External Physical Appearance

The shape of the Taiyin face is generally round or square (although it may be oval). Whatever shape the face is, it is fleshy like the rest of the body. This fleshy countenance, combined with Taiyins' magnanimous personalities, gives them an appearance of benevolence, serenity, and peacefulness.

Unbalanced Taiyins may have a fearful look in their eyes, resembling that of a frightened doe or cow. Their eyes can also be large and somewhat dull. Normally, though, Taiyins have large, bright eyes. This feature, combined with their large bodies, gives Taiyin women a graceful and dignified appearance. The ends of the eyes of some Taiyin men are raised, however, giving them a somewhat scary or angry countenance.

Taiyins may possess particularly large and round noses that stands out prominently from their faces (as with W.C. Fields or Babe Ruth). Their mouths are generally large, with thicker lips. The chin region is often more developed than the rest of the face. As a matter of fact, many Taiyins develop double chins. Taiyins have a weakness in their circulatory system, so many have an overall reddish complexion, or a face that turns red easily. In fact, compared to other body types, Taiyins generally tend to have darker complexions.

Although Taiyins have large heads compared to the rest of their bodies, their overall appearance is weak and isolated, due to the lack of Yang energy in the upper part of the body. The back of the neck is generally short and weak looking when compared to the rest of the body.

The inherent physiological ability of Taiyins to accumulate plenty of energy and Blood in the body produces many Taiyins with strong physiques and great strength. Due to their Yin nature, the lower part of their bodies is especially well developed, mainly in the waist and lower back regions. Whereas some Taiyins may look clumsy and slow, others have a sturdy, stable, and well-grounded look, like an autumn tree that has borne many fruits. In this specific type, the whole body looks strong, with plenty of flesh. The bone structure is large and sturdy, with large hands and feet. Sometimes, Taiyins of this ilk appear arrogant or conceited because of their protruding belly and thick waist. Examples of strongly built Taiyins are the heavyweights in all sports—boxing, wrestling, weight lifting, or even Sumo wrestling.

In general, the Taiyin body type possesses thick and rough skin with large pores. Again, they tend to have darker skin than other types. They tend to either sweat easily with little or no exertion, or profusely with heavy exertion. Though the hands and feet are large, the fingers and toes look relatively short in comparison. Furthermore, their limbs appear short in relation to their trunks. Taiyin hands are thick and warm and tend to chap easily in the winter.

Although Taiyins in general are of a stocky build, thin persons can exist within this constitution. It is easy to mix up Taiyins and Shaoyins, so careful observation should be made in distinguishing these two types.

Internal Physiology

Taiyins have surplus Yin with a slight weakness of Yang. This Yin energy manifests as an inward, gathering tendency. This tendency causes an excessive accumulation of Yin substances in the body. These Yin substances include retained fluids, fatty tissues, mucus, and other unmetabolized pathological substances. Their accumulation results in a body that is more often than not on the obese side. It also results in a general slowing of physiological processes (metabolism).

The Liver in Sasang Medicine is responsible for accumulating energy and Blood within the body. In Taiyins, the Liver is strong, so they tend to accumulate mass very easily. Their Lungs, on the other hand, are very weak, so Taiyins have a difficult time dispersing and metabolizing the accumulated mass and energy upwards and outwards. This enhances the accumulative tendency of the Taiyins. The weakness of the Lungs also causes Taiyins to generally have weak circulatory and respiratory systems.

Shaoyin

Shaoyins are also Yin, but are the lesser of the two Yin constitutions. Unlike Taiyins', Shaoyins' Yin is weaker, causing them to hold less mass and thus have smaller bodies. Similar to Taiyins, they have greater development in their lower bodies, especially in their hips and buttocks. Nevertheless, their overall appearance is well proportioned.

External Physical Appearance

Many Shaoyins have either a round or a thin, oval shaped face. Their facial features are well proportioned, but closely woven together. Their eyes, ears, nose, and mouth tend to be on the smaller side, especially when compared to Taiyins'.

Shaoyin eyes seem to lack luster and some Shaoyins have so-called "sleepy eyes," drooping eyelids. They have bright and clear complexions, but they can get a sickly yellow color when their constitutionally weak digestive systems become even weaker. A gentle, quiet, and modest visage characterizes Shaoyins, but many show a lack of vitality in their face. Nonetheless, you can find an abundance of attractive and charming people in this body type—particularly Shaoyin women. Marilyn Monroe and Meg Ryan, for example, are of the Shaoyin constitution.

Like the Taiyin constitution, the Shaoyin has more Yin characteristics than Yang. The lower body, especially the hips and buttocks, is large, firm, and well developed. The energy of the Shaoyin is concentrated in the lower rear part of the body, giving Shaoyins a strong and stable sitting position, unlike the Shaoyang type. The shoulders and chest, meanwhile, are narrow, weak, frail, and bent slightly forward. Thus the Shaoyin body resembles a ladder—wide at the bottom and narrow at the top.

Whether Shaoyins are short or tall, their upper and lower bodies are usually well proportioned. Although they are usually on the thin side, overweight Shaoyins can be found, especially as they get older. Nevertheless, at the initial encounter, Shaoyins give a tidy and neat impression due to their countenance and physique.

In general, Shaoyins tend to sweat very little and have rather soft and tender skin, with small pores that are closely knitted together. Their muscles are soft and delicate, and look somewhat swollen. This is due to a weakness in the Qi energy, which controls water metabolism. In other words, there is not enough energy to properly circulate the water, resulting in a puffy appearance. Shaoyin hands are generally cold, but unlike Taiyins', they do not chap easily during winter.

Shaoyin women are the most fertile and are best suited to carry their babies to full term because of their well-developed hip and buttocks regions. Strong Kidneys, which are related to the reproductive system, are another dominant contributing factor. Shaoyin women have an easy delivery of multiple births. This is in contrast to both the Taiyang and Shaoyang constitutions.

Internal Physiology

Shaoyins are lesser Yin. This means that they have a surplus of Yin, but a deficient amount of Yang. As Yang energy is warming, this makes Shaoyins the coldest of the four constitutions. As Yang energy is active, its deficiency makes Shaoyins somewhat lacking in vitality.

Shaoyins have weak Spleens and strong Kidneys. The weak Spleen manifests as weak digestive energy. Shaoyins have difficulty digesting food, and will easily become fatigued if they overtax their Spleens with a large meal, or with cold, raw foods. In addition, they frequently suffer from loose stools and diarrhea. The strong Kidneys, meanwhile, manifest in strong reproductive energy and strong bones.

Chapter 5

The Mental Climate

It is a thorny undertaking, and more so than it seems, to follow a movement so wandering as that of our mind, to penetrate the opaque depths of its innermost folds, to pick out and immobilize the innumerable flutterings that agitate it.
—Michel Eyquem de Montaigne, *Essays*

Perceiving the body is straightforward. You need only your eyes to canvass your physique. But the state of your mind changes from day to day and from moment to moment. According to time, place, circumstance, and situation, your mind takes on different forms.

The amorphous and unpredictable nature of the mind is like the weather, which is affected by temperature, pressure, and innumerable other factors. Weather is at once conditioned by the physical environment and transcendent over it. In the same way, your mind may be heavily determined by your body, yet it may at the same time retain patterns of its own. But if our mental states are constantly changing and conditional, how do we determine the fixed, mental natures of our body types?

The 4 Seasons of the Mind

It is nearly impossible to predict the weather on a day-to-day basis. However, it is possible to predict the general trend of the weather in a given season. Similarly, although it is not possible to perceive all of the peculiarities and idiosyncrasies of an individual's mind, it is possible to perceive a general pattern underlying all of his or her thoughts and emotions.

The easiest metaphor used to understand the different mindsets of the four body types is the weather patterns of the four seasons. Although it is possible to derive mental and emotional characteristics from the body type, this only provides for a basic and rudimentary understanding. For example, we noted in the previous chapter that the Qi in Taiyangs tends to ascend straight up to the head. From this, we get a sense that Taiyangs tend to be great thinkers. Unfortunately, we are unable to get a fuller sense of their psyches.

Comparing the constitutions to the seasons gives us a better sense of their mindsets. Taiyang mental dynamics, for example, are said to be like the spring season, when life is bursting forth. Shaoyangs' minds are like the heat of summer, full of fire and excitement. Taiyins' minds are like the fall, when nature slows down in preparation for a long winter. Finally, Shaoyins' minds are like the ice crystals of the winter, when all is still and silent.

The mental dynamics of the body types also correspond to the growth of a plant throughout the seasons. Taiyangs are comparable to the bursting energy of a sprouting plant in the spring, Shaoyangs to the blossoming of a flower during the summer, Taiyins to the bearing of fruit in autumn, and Shaoyins to the storing of energy in the roots during the winter.

A further metaphor may be found in the idea of the four elements commonly linked with the seasons: wind (spring), fire (summer), earth or mountain (fall), and water (winter). Taiyangs may be likened to the wind, the freest of the elements, which can touch the world (occasionally with devastating effect, as in tornadoes), but cannot be touched. Shaoyangs are like the uncontrollable brush fires that burn in the summer, passionate and swift. The fall is the season of the harvest, and mountains are accumulations of the earth; both represent Taiyin energy, which gathers mass to itself and sits with infinite patience and silent majesty. Finally, Shaoyins are like water, which sinks to the lowest place, in search of stillness and reflection.

As mentioned before, physical landscape exerts an effect on weather. Tall mountains can prevent storms from passing, for example, and deserts can create warm fronts that influence the weather. In the same way, our physical bodies can exert an influence over our thoughts and feelings. In this chapter, we explore this influence through that vague, gray area known as behavior. Behavior is alternatively defined as those physical habits that express our mental predispositions, or those mental habits that are determined by our anatomy and physiology. We'll address four aspects of behavior: movement, voice, sense of humor, and manner of eating.

Taiyang

Positive Traits	Negative Traits	Other
Active (not passive)	Arrogant	Masculine
Positive, idealistic, optimistic	Self-righteous, dogmatic	Revolutionary
Intelligent, creative	Stubborn, uncompromising	Outspoken
Sociable	Inflexible	Inquisitive
Heroic, brave, bold	Rebellious	
Resolute	Short-tempered	
Tenacious	Rude	
Progressive, pioneering	Impractical	
Charismatic	Careless	

Table 5.1: Taiyang Personality Traits

Crazy geniuses

Taiyangs possess the energy of spring. Spring is the season when creatures emerge from hibernation, procreate, and give birth. Taiyangs also possess the energies of wind. Thus, they are swift and constantly changing, like whirlwinds stirring the leaves. These energies combined give Taiyangs extremely creative minds, able to give birth to fresh, new ideas. Taiyangs are highly intelligent, extremely original, and naturally inquisitive. Their creativity allows them to come up with extraordinarily clever ideas. Thus, Taiyangs are frequently called geniuses. At the same time, their curiosity frequently takes them beyond ordinary life experiences into the realm of the unknown. Because of this, Taiyangs perpetually run the risk of being misunderstood by society and labeled as crazy or fools.

It is said that the difference between a genius and a fool is the thickness of a piece of paper. Because the dividing line between a so-called genius and a so-called fool is so thin, a genius may easily cross over to become a fool, and vice-versa. This can be understood by a principle of Yin-Yang theory: "When Yin reaches its extreme, it converts into Yang; when Yang reaches its extreme, it converts into Yin." That is, if you reach one extreme, you run the risk of becoming the extreme opposite. Taiyangs who do not manifest their genius may end up being perceived as fools by society, either because their work is unacceptable or incomprehensible to lay people, or because they cross over and become fools. The highest proportions of geniuses and fools are found within this body type.

Renewal and revolution

Spring is also the season of beginnings. It is the time when plants, animals, and life begin anew. As such, spring is the opportune time for the winds of change and revolution, for new beginnings. Taiyangs, infused with spring energy, are frequently the initiators of change; they are the idealistic revolutionaries with visions before their time, brave and intrepid, innovative and reforming. In business settings, Taiyangs are trailblazers in new ventures or new frontiers. Historically, many pioneers and revolutionaries were of the Taiyang constitution.

Standing out in a crowd

In social settings, Taiyangs are not afraid to initiate conversations and make new friends. Taiyangs are skilled at communication and are highly sociable. They lack fear in all activities, whether in a social, personal, or business setting. However, they are not the life-of-the-party types, or at least they do not try to be. They never show themselves off on purpose. Taiyangs stand out, not in a flashy way, but in a solid, resolute, and powerful way. Others automatically notice them, because of their exceptional energy and the way their intelligence manifests in their speech and conversation.

Springing forward

Taiyangs are explosive, dynamic characters. To understand this aspect of the Taiyang mentality, consider the energy that forces a seed to sprout during the spring season. To crack open the hard shells of seeds requires a tremendous amount of energy. This energy is actually present in the seed, but only in potential form, accumulated over the long winter season. It requires a spark or burst to ignite it. This spark is the energy of the spring season, and the energy present in the Taiyang individual. Because of this energy, plants are able to break through their hard shells and shoot up through the soil. This rising energy correlates to the extreme, rising Yang energy of this body type.

Whatever Taiyangs set their minds to, they spring after it, like a puma pouncing after its prey. They know how to go forward and attack, but do not know how to go backward and retreat. They charge into any and all challenges with little thought of failure. This bold energy makes them resolute and determined in all of their judgments, decisions, and actions. If thwarted, they always find a way to conquer any obstacles in their path. Taiyangs do not give up easily. They pursue their goals until they come to fruition. This gives them an active, brave and progressive spirit, often depicted symbolically as the mystical dragon.

Big dreamers

Taiyangs dream big, but often have difficulty bringing their aspirations to fruition. As a result, they often grow disinterested in the everyday world around them; it only serves as the resistor of their thoughts. They are constantly pondering how to rise above the world around them in order to change it.

Independence and self-centeredness

Taiyangs resemble prepubescent boys. Prepubescent boys are like the spring season in that they are non-compromising, self-righteous, and dogmatic. They perceive themselves as perfect and faultless. Taiyangs are highly outspoken, valuing their own opinion above all others, and they easily get angry at those who dare to disagree. They do not readily heed advice given to them by family, friends, or associates. Indeed, once they make up their minds, they do not listen to anyone at all.

Being independent, Taiyangs detest help from others. At times, they show disapproval or even anger when someone tries to lend them a helping hand. They'd much rather get things done on their own. This makes them poor team players because they are always thinking about what would benefit themselves more than what would most benefit the whole. Their self-importance often blinds them from considering the other person's position.

Imbalance: extreme urgency and quick temper

Like a hydrogen bomb, Taiyangs contain explosive energy that can detonate at any moment, for good or ill. This unpredictable energy can cause severe mood swings. Taiyangs can oscillate between extreme anger and extreme sadness. Their Yin energy, which is relatively weak, cannot hold down the Yang to keep it from ascending. As a result, Taiyangs tend to get angry more easily than other constitutions, sometimes for no apparent reason at all. In fact, impatience and a quick temper tend to dominate the Taiyang psyche.

Both anger and sadness are ascending emotions according to Sasang Medicine. Thus, it is no surprise that Taiyangs are also prone to deep-seated sadness. They feel severe sadness when they are unable to express themselves or follow through on their goals, and tend to take their failures much harder than others.

When the Taiyang spirit gets out of control, they become more rigid than usual, insisting on doing everything their way, and refusing to follow the orders or agendas of anyone else. In this state of mind, they are less likely to pause to think or reflect on their mistakes and deficiencies. Taiyangs are by nature not detail oriented in their approach to their affairs. This lack of caution makes them doubly prone to fail. Yet, as they are immune to self-reproach, such failure will only cause them to blame others and get angry at everyone except themselves.

Movement: stiff as a robot

Due to the weakness in their lower back and legs, Taiyangs cannot sit or stand for long periods of time, and have difficulty walking long distances. Given an option, they would prefer to drive. When resting, they usually like to lie down rather than sit or stand. When standing, they like to lean against a wall, and when sitting, they need a chair with a back to lean against. The Taiyang's mode of walking is rather light, but with a very straight posture. Some Taiyangs walk in a very awkward, stiff fashion, resembling robots.

Speech/Voice: mesmerizing speakers

Taiyangs are the Greater Yang and their manner of speech demonstrates this. First of all, they are afraid of no one, and freely talk to anyone at anytime. Although they are not generally garrulous, their speech can be audacious, haughty, and arrogant. They may speak abusively or violently, lashing out at others with the repeated use of profanity. When speaking, they often have difficulty containing themselves, and will shout quickly and recklessly, saying whatever comes to mind. If this excitability doesn't fully catch the attention of others, then the sound of their voices does. Some Taiyangs have very piercing, metallic sounding voices that tend to disquiet audiences and stifle conversations. Others project high-pitched sounds that overflow with vigor. Despite this less-than-appealing description of their speech, Taiyangs, on the whole, are charismatic public speakers who make mesmerizing and dynamic speeches. Hitler, Lenin, and Napoleon were all Taiyangs, able to leave the masses hanging upon their every word.

Sense of humor: none

The Taiyang person laughs and smiles the least. Taiyangs tend to dislike humor in general and avoid watching comedy programs and shows. They simply do not have the time to relax and enjoy themselves with a good laugh. Instead, Taiyangs are deadly serious all the time with little care for mundane matters. Their strong ambition and intensely combative spirit overshadow any humor they might have. Moreover, they have an intense, stern look that actually chases away the smiles and laughter of others. Nevertheless, when they do laugh, they laugh with vigor. For example, when they succeed in their endeavors, they laugh a great deal and fall into a state of narcissistic joy. Although their laughter may sound lighthearted, it is actually the cold laughter of a conqueror. Bertrand Russell's first impression of Lenin aptly describes the Taiyang laugh: "He laughs a great deal...his laugh seems friendly and jolly, but gradually one finds it grim."

Manner of eating: a mundane affair

Taiyangs are the least interested in eating. They consider meals interruptions in the ceaseless process of working toward their goals and ideas. When Taiyangs share meals with others, they will likely be engaged in discussions about their ideals rather than actually eating. They rarely enjoy eating, and cannot tolerate rich foods or large quantities of food. The foods that they do tend to eat include vegetable and seafood dishes. When out of balance health-wise, Taiyangs tend to drink excessive amounts of alcohol. This is extremely detrimental to their health because it aggravates their already excessive Yang and depletes their swiftly dwindling Yin.

Famous Taiyangs:

- Beethoven
- Van Gogh
- Napoleon
- Hitler
- Douglas MacArthur
- Lenin
- Batman
- Superman
- Darth Vader
- Captain James T. Kirk
- Sherlock Holmes
- The Terminator
- Rambo

Shaoyang

Positive Traits	Negative Traits	Other
Active (not passive)	Rash	Extroverted
Open-minded	Fickle	Passionate
Cooperative	Lacks perseverance	Sentimental
Straightforward	Easily angered	Impulsive
Honest	Critical	Competitive
Sharp	Belligerent	
Spirited	Aggressive	
Bright personality		
Cheerful		

Table 5.2: Shaoyang Personality Traits

Blossoming and branching

Shaoyangs manifest the energies of summer. During this season, nature is in full force, every organism actively and dynamically expressing itself. Summer is the time when leaves grow, flowers bloom, and trees branch out. Recall that Shaoyangs have the greatest physical development in their shoulder and chest region, where the heart is located. In synchrony with summer, a time of blossoming and giving forth, Shaoyangs are passionate individuals who open up their hearts to others. In essence, they have big hearts. Because they are kind-hearted and conciliatory, and honest in their dealings with others, they are generally well-liked by others.

Tender hearted

Though Shaoyangs appear strong on the outside, they are emotionally delicate on the inside. They are like adolescents in their blossoming years—their moods change frequently. They may be joyous at one moment, and suddenly experience depression when something trivial goes wrong. Although this delicacy and sensitivity can be difficult to cope with, it can also lend success in the arts.

Helping hand

As Shaoyangs have big hearts and outward, dispersing tendencies, they are constantly looking to help those in need and trouble. They go out of their way to offer themselves to others. They feel great satisfaction in helping others, making extreme sacrifices in their time and energy to do so. It is typical for Shaoyangs to take care of everyone else's business and not their own. This naturally leads to an increase in time spent in personal and business relations, but it also leads to less time spent with their families. This can result in success in the workplace, but it can also result in disharmonious family relationships.

A negative aspect of this extroversion is the Shaoyang tendency to show off and stand out in a crowd, with little or no thought to faults and weaknesses.

Don't hold back!

Shaoyangs are extremely straightforward on all matters. This is because they have stronger Yang (open/revealing) tendencies combined with weaker Yin (closed/hidden) tendencies. They do not hold back on criticism when they feel it is deserved. This is true in personal, business, and social relationships. In particular, Shaoyangs make excellent social critics. They have a strong sense of what is right and wrong. Participating in demonstrations and rallies, they often take to a cause to fight against what they see as an injustice. They perceive themselves as being righteous, and become very spirited and aggressive in their pursuit of justice, but only to a point. When the seas of opposition start to get rough, they tend to be the first to abandon ship, leaving everyone else to fend for themselves.

Restless freedom

Mentally, Shaoyangs have the tendency to move and not stay still, much like a wild stallion. They are constantly in search of change. They are endowed with an impulsive curiosity for all things. People of this body type are visually oriented. They love the adventure of travel and enjoy taking in the wide variety of scenery of faraway places. As you might expect, Shaoyangs do not like to be fixed into a pattern or forced into doing things. They prefer to live according to their own ideas and rules. They love freedom of choice, and express and experience this freedom through movement. This can, at times, lead to disorderliness and dissoluteness. But by nature, Shaoyangs cherish life and are rarely self-destructive.

Speedy and flashy

As they are always on the go, Shaoyangs are speedy and agile. They possess swift decision-making abilities and an instantaneous wit. They are thus able to adapt quickly to changing situations. In an emergency, they show extraordinary mental clarity and physical reactivity. They are sharp, quick-witted, clever, and perceptive, making them excellent conversationalists and entertaining party guests.

Leave without a trace

Shaoyangs often act out of an inner urgency. Everything must be done quickly in order to satisfy them. If a project does not proceed up to speed, then a Shaoyang will simply drop it, and start something else. This is, in fact, a habit of Shaoyangs. Comparable to deadbeat dads, Shaoyangs father countless projects. When their "children" don't "grow up" fast enough to satisfy them, they fly the coop. Shaoyangs often fail to contemplate the consequences of their actions until something goes wrong. Yet, even when they do get into trouble, they refuse to let it bother them, simply forgetting the matter and moving on. In this manner, they always remain available to start new projects, carrying no regrets from the past.

The setting sun

Initially, Shaoyangs are as passionate as a dancing flame or as eye-catching as a blossoming rose. Yet, they swiftly dissipate and die out like an extinguished flame or cut flower. In this they are similar to summer, for although it is the brightest and hottest season of the year, it is actually waning into fall. Like the last radiant rays of a setting sun, the Shaoyang energy is actually somewhat hollow, that is to say, bright on the outside but empty on the inside. Thus, the spring energies of the Taiyang body type are stronger than the Shaoyangs' in that it is energy emerging rather than declining.

This is apparent in Shaoyang personality traits. Though active and proficient when it comes to starting projects, they tend to back off or quit when faced with any dilemmas. They lack the explosive and enduring energy needed to overcome an obstacle in order to push through to completion. Despite their frequent failures however, Shaoyangs remain optimistic, cheerfully oblivious of the fact that theirs is the light of a setting sun.

Heeding the call

Shaoyangs have a talent for appointed roles. This means that they are skilled at carrying out the responsibilities given to them by their superiors. They may even be passionate about such work. These appointed roles range from everyday work to what are known as "heavenly decrees," or religious callings. Interestingly, although this is true in external affairs, it is not the case in domestic matters, such as in being a dutiful husband or wife. Also, although Shaoyangs take orders well, they do not necessarily act according to the group decision at times, and may choose to follow their own particular interpretations of what is best.

Although this seems to contradict the Shaoyang's basic need for freedom, it actually does not. As stated, Shaoyangs are externally oriented; in fact, they base their entire identity upon the impressions they make upon others. To this extent, they are more than willing to adopt the roles appointed to them, in order to establish their identities in the minds of others.

Imbalance: anxiety

In a state of imbalance, Shaoyangs may suffer from residual worry. Constant anxiety can result from leaving their projects unfinished. They always fear what might happen next. When this fear becomes acute, Shaoyangs can develop forgetfulness, which is considered a dangerous sign of ill health in Sasang Medicine.

When Shaoyangs overextend themselves in the pursuit of external achievements, failing to govern their inner spirit and their domestic affairs, then they become all heart, depending only on their feelings and emotions. In this state, they fail to prioritize their work according to importance or necessity, but instead base their actions and judgments solely upon their feelings or moods. This tendency to forgo a logical and rational approach toward their activities may at times produce erratic behavior patterns.

Movement: rapid and unbalanced

Because they have a light lower body, Shaoyangs have a very distinct mode of walking. It is rapid, and makes them appear as if they were floating or gliding. When walking in a group, they are the ones moving their way to the front of the pack. Their posture is generally rigid or straight. While walking, their trunks frequently rocks from side to side, giving their stride an unbalanced appearance. Shaoyangs also have a tendency to look around or gaze at distant things when they walk. When rushed, however, they forget to check their surroundings and stampede directly on towards their destinations.

As stated previously, Shaoyangs tend to start and finish things quickly, making them seem unsettled and unbalanced in all physical activities. They are in a constant state of turbulent movement, leading to rough and irregular actions and behaviors, and a lot of mistakes.

Speech/Voice: loud and talkative

Corresponding to their dynamic, somewhat hyperactive nature, Shaoyangs are loud and talkative, their voices crisp, high pitched, and full of strength. Although they can be well-behaved and gentle at times, they may also express aggression and fury, with a lot of cursing. In fact, they often sound as though they are arguing or demanding an explanation from others, even when they aren't.

As Shaoyangs are straightforward, they don't beat around the bush when they talk. In fact, they prefer to give their conclusions first without regard for introductory statements. They speak quickly, freely, and humorously. As they are very flexible and adaptable to circumstances, they are able to come up with speeches that can win debates, or at least woo audiences.

Shaoyangs are usually garrulous, interrupting others or meddling in their affairs, sometimes to extremes. They may occasionally play the part of the mediator, able to resolve an issue peacefully, but at other times, they revert to being the troublemakers who complicate the situation. Shaoyangs tend to talk without acting. This may lead them to lose the trust of others because their actions do not back up their speech. Another cause for mistrust is their tendency to look around as they talk, not concentrating on the person they are with. This tendency is not due to any dishonesty on their part (Shaoyangs are usually very honest); rather, it is due to their innate restlessness.

Sense of humor: light-hearted, bright, and cheerful

Shaoyangs are generally light-hearted, with bright and cheerful demeanors. They probably laugh the most among the four constitutions. They are constantly on the lookout for comedy, and are able to find it even in those things that other constitutions do not consider funny. They crack jokes easily with their friends, colleagues, and family members, as well as with their superiors and teachers. Situations or surroundings do not restrict the Shaoyangs' humorous tendencies. They often make jokes out loud inside movie theaters or restaurants. When Shaoyangs laugh, it is hearty, loud, and clear, without being decorous. This is to be expected, as Shaoyangs are usually very open and candid about themselves, revealing their inner nature to others freely.

It may seem contradictory to say that Shaoyangs are lighthearted on one hand, and belligerent and quick-tempered on the other. Yet, just as the hot summer sun encourages both the enthusiasm to have a good time and the rage to do violence, so does Shaoyang energy fuel both humor and anger.

Manner of eating: a feast for the eyes

Shaoyangs eat very quickly and are not picky about foods. Nor are they particular about their diet, although they tend to prefer cool foods such as raw salads, and ice cold drinks. Shaoyangs usually have no problems with their appetite or digestion, so they can eat and not gain much weight.

With their highly developed sense of sight, Shaoyangs tend to select foods based on appearance. When cooking (which they rarely do), they apply the same criterion, cooking foods that look great but don't necessarily taste good or have much nutritional value.

Famous Shaoyangs:	
Mozart	Arnold Schwarzenneger
Elvis Presley	James Bond
Bruce Lee	The Fonz
Elizabeth Taylor	Popeye
Jacqueline Kennedy Onassis	Pocahontas
Julie Andrews	Hans Solo
Robert DeNiro	Bart Simpson
Madonna	Peter Pan
Muhammad Ali	Bugs Bunny
Ronald Reagan	

Taiyin

Positive Traits	Negative Traits	Other
Dignified	Cowardly	Conservative
Polite	Lazy	Taciturn
Decorous	Closed-minded	Ambitious
Persevering	Stubborn	Imposing
Impartial	Covetous	Pragmatist
Optimistic	Wicked	
Benevolent	Dubious, skeptical	
Prudent		
Honest		
Humorous		
Gallant, heroic		

Table 5.3: Taiyin Personality Traits

The pragmatic harvester

Autumn is the time when nature starts to slow down from the activity of summer. It is a time for harvest and preparation for the winter ahead. Gone are the sprouting, blossoming energies of the spring and summer. During autumn, the leaves dry up, wither, and fall as the trees pull nutrients downwards. This season embodies the Taiyin energy—inward and downward, gathering and accumulating.

The Taiyin person likes to gather and harvest various things, such as food, money, property, information, and knowledge. Taiyins like stability, in concrete and substantial ways. They dislike abstract, intangible, idealistic values. Being the ultimate pragmatists, they do not engage in flights of fancy.

The slowing down of autumn energy can manifest in Taiyins' physical manner. According to Dr. Jae Ma Lee, Taiyins like to "stay still and calm and not move around." For this reason, they are often depicted symbolically as cows. They tend to focus exclusively on their present selves and the present state of things. External stimulation and competition are neither needed nor desired by Taiyins.

Finish what you started

Taiyins excel at accomplishing goals. They have a great amount of Yin, which stabilizes them, allowing them to stick to projects through to their completion. In fact, they have the most endurance, perseverance, and "stick-to-itiveness" of all the constitutions. Without complaint, they will make tremendous efforts to accomplish their goals, as they are perfectly willing and capable of sweating it out. The saying, "Success is 1 percent inspiration and 99 percent perspiration" fits them perfectly. Taiyins also refuse to quit because they abhor leaving tasks unfinished. It leaves them with an uneasy, troubled feeling.

The big man on top

Taiyins have a talent for managing big scale corporations. They are typically the bosses; they want to be the general giving the orders, rather than the foot soldier carrying them out. This is because they have a grandiose and magnanimous vision of the world, fueled by greed and grounded in pragmatism. On one hand, this causes them to dislike the blind and purposeless energy of the worker, and on the other, it gives them the fuel necessary to realize their ambitions. In another sense, one might say that the mountain-like, accumulative nature of Taiyins makes them a natural center around which others gravitate.

Taiyins tend to excel in administrative and managerial work. Taiyins take full responsibility for any failures in the workplace. As a result, they tend to be cautious and slow in their work, proceeding diligently and with full concentration. Taiyin men do not care as much for matters outside of work. When they get into financial trouble, it is their endurance and perseverance that gets them out of the hole.

The queen of the castle

Taiyin women are very family oriented, preferring to be good housewives and good mothers. Although they can be ambitious career women as well, they never shirk away from their family duties.

In Sasang Medicine, Taiyins (both male and female) are said to have a talent for domestic affairs, meaning that they have a close bond to their habitat. Even in new and unfamiliar territory, they are able to "set up the tent" and settle themselves in very well. They rather enjoy ruts and routines, and are able to remain at one location, residence, occupation or social position for a long period of time.

Able to see the big picture

The Taiyin's energetic qualities are closest to the center. As we saw in the last chapter, the Qi energy of Taiyins descends obliquely, leading to great development in the abdominal region. Because of this emphasized center, Taiyins are able to occupy a centered vantage point from which they can see in all directions. They are able to maintain an impartial attitude towards all aspects of life, and can put everyday affairs and circumstances into proper perspective. As a result, they are able to exercise prudence in all undertakings. This makes them reliable and trustworthy in the eyes of others.

A mature presence

Taiyins have the heart of middle-aged people, giving off a stable, commanding presence. No matter what their age, Taiyins give the impression of being well-behaved, mature people. This is apparent in their manner of speech, the way that they carry themselves, and even in their facial and bodily characteristics, which have a noble and dignified appearance.

Taiyins are benevolent and magnanimous, possessing a powerful sense of integrity. They are also the most decorous among all the constitutions. These qualities combined make Taiyin men true gentlemen and Taiyin women true ladies.

Taiyins can be tenacious and persistent when they are trying to convince or persuade others. However, if anyone violates their trust or faith, Taiyins break off the relationship without hesitation.

Hard to get the ball rolling

Just as nature rarely begins any new growth in the autumn, Taiyins are also hesitant to begin new projects. Although they lack the strong Yang energy necessary to start projects as Taiyangs do, once they've begun something, their tremendous Yin reserves allow them to sustain, persevere, and see projects through to completion.

Despite their good work ethic, Taiyins have a tendency to become quite lazy. As their nature is basically Yin, they tend to want to gather and conserve energy (Yin) rather than expend it in outward action (Yang). Also, they simply hold a greater mass than other constitutions, requiring more energy to move it. This laziness can develop into carelessness in all matters.

Pleasure seekers

In a state of imbalance, Taiyins may focus too much on enjoying life's pleasures, steering clear of anything that requires earnestness or a sober attitude. Taiyin men, for example, may become excessively recreational. They may socialize and dine with others, engaging in excessive eating and drinking, often followed by compulsive gambling. Or, they may lay back on the couch and watch TV for a whole day, while eating several bags of potato chips. Such addictive behaviors may last for days, sometimes to the point where they forget that they have a family or domestic responsibilities waiting for them. This irregular lifestyle jeopardizes their family life as well as their health.

Imbalance: fear

Fear dominates the minds of the Taiyins. In a state of imbalance, they are commonly disbelieving, cautious, closed-minded, and cowardly. They tend to trust only those people who are familiar to them, never venturing out to experience anything new and exciting.

Taiyins also have a tendency to be wicked and cunning due to their greedy, gathering nature, which makes them want anything and everything. At times, in order to satisfy this excessive greed, they try inappropriate and unscrupulous tactics to get what they want.

Taiyins are also naturally obstinate, wanting only to carry through on their ideas and opinions. When these behaviors become overly dominant, Taiyins develop severe palpitations, a serious condition for Taiyin types in Sasang Medicine.

When in a state of imbalance, this conservative and accumulative tendency can become excessive. Taiyins can come to focus exclusively on their inner selves, while expressing extreme reluctance to share any part of themselves—physically, mentally, or financially. They can become excessively greedy and possessive, constantly desiring to acquire more than what they have. This may make them better providers for their families, but it often destroys their social or business relationships.

Taiyins may also become very dull, slow, and foolish. Their resolve and ambition can grow weak and narrowly focused, and they may lose their otherwise broad perspective. Like a wild boar that can only see the ground inches in front of its nose, Taiyins in this state will charge forward, even though they cannot see where they are going. Pure stubbornness impels them, and even when it becomes clear that their original goal is unattainable or wrong, they will push onward without modifying their plans. When they finally run into an obstacle that simply cannot be overcome, Taiyins will grow lazy and give up. Unlike Shaoyangs, however, they will continue on with memories of failure.

Movement: slow as a cow

The movements of Taiyins are in general slower and clumsier than the other body types (unless they happen to be well-trained athletes). The Taiyin walk, for example, is slow and heavy. They usually touch the ground with their heels first, producing a stable and poised gait. On the other hand, the walking manner of some Taiyins may resemble that of a duck. Some Taiyins bend their upper bodies slightly downward as they walk. Thanks to their strong lower bodies, healthy Taiyins are blessed with tremendous endurance, allowing them to stand or walk for long periods of time.

Speech/voice: heavy and powerful

Taiyins are as stone-cold in their verbalization as they are rock-solid in their perspective. They often do not feel the necessity to speak, even when the occasion calls for them to do so. Typically, Taiyins will speak only when absolutely necessary. Of course, there are exceptions. Some Taiyins are readily able to jump into a conversation and talk in a loud voice, sometimes non-stop for hours, fueled by their surplus Yin energy. These are the so-called Heat-type Taiyins, who tend to have flushed faces and are prone to high blood pressure, obesity, and constipation.

When Taiyins in general do speak, it is usually with dignity. But at times their speech can become incoherent and illogical, especially when they are in a state of imbalance. Although they may be reticent, they often brew thoughts and ideas within, and can at times be wicked and crafty as previously mentioned. Taiyins can speak with assertiveness when talking to others. However, they tend to be the weaker opponent in debates. In general, many Taiyins have thick, husky, and muffled voices.

Make no mistake however, for some Taiyins are excellent at composing and delivering speeches. President John F. Kennedy, Martin Luther King, Jr., and Winston Churchill were Taiyins whose speeches are considered to be among the greatest of this century.

Sense of humor: either dull or nonstop

Although Taiyins generally have blunt or dull facial expressions, they generally do have a light-hearted, laughing attitude within. So when they laugh, they laugh vigorously, with a big voice. An example of the Taiyin laugh is Santa Claus's.

Nevertheless, those Taiyins who are out of balance show dull humor. This may be due to inherent weaknesses in their respiratory and circulatory systems, or possibly their innate tendency toward fear, which prevents them from seeing the humor in life.

Again, Heat-type Taiyins prove to be the exception to the rule. They can go overboard with their sense of humor. They have a great reserve of energy and are extraordinarily strong and forceful in their daily actions, including their humor. These Taiyins may even be louder and stronger than Shaoyangs in laughing or cracking jokes in public places.

Because of their light-hearted, laughing attitude within, there are some Taiyins who make great comedians, including W.C. Fields, Jay Leno, and Rosie O'Donnell.

Manner of eating: I ate the whole thing!

Taiyins eat without reserve. They do not concern themselves with the look, color, or taste of food, nor the mood or ambiance of the meal. Taiyins tend to think that these are simply extravagances. As the ultimate pragmatists, Taiyins consider quantity to be of the utmost importance. Anything and everything in large quantities will satisfy them. Thus, for many Taiyins, starting the day with just a light breakfast would be unthinkable. They must have a multi-course meal. Although they have a dignified appearance in general, when they eat, they do not necessarily follow acceptable manners. They will take big bites and gulp things down quickly. Taiyins have the most difficulty sleeping when they are hungry and need to have food in their stomachs to sleep soundly.

Famous Taiyins:

☯ Winston Churchill	☯ Jay Leno
☯ Thomas Edison	☯ Rosie O'Donnell
☯ Martin Luther King, Jr.	☯ Monica Lewinsky
☯ John F. Kennedy	☯ Roseanne
☯ Al Capone	☯ King Kong
☯ Hulk Hogan	☯ Santa Claus
☯ George Foreman	☯ Jabba the Hutt
☯ Homer Simpson	☯ Fred Flintstone

Shaoyin

Positive Traits	Negative Traits	Other
Composed	Passive, inactive	Introverted
Calm	Selfish	Conservative
Orderly	Narrow-minded	Delicate
Methodical	Jealous	Precise
Meticulous	Authoritarian	Meditative
Clean	Stubborn	Crafty
Tidy		
Modest		
Prudent		
Patient		
Perceptive		
Social		

Table 5.4: Shaoyin Personality Traits

Enduring the winter

Winter is a season characterized by stillness, as evidenced by the impression one receives when viewing a winter landscape after a snowfall. Shaoyins, like the winter, are still in that they are extremely passive, and lack initiative. In the same way that trees or plants do not show themselves outwardly in the winter, so are Shaoyins extremely introspective, avoiding any outward expressions of their thoughts and feelings. They dislike standing out in a crowd. Shaoyins prefer to stay behind the scenes and help people inconspicuously. They particularly like to help those people who show the talent and drive to become successful.

Shaoyins are prominent in one important aspect: they are patient and are able to persevere beyond the limits of endurance of other constitutions, as all living creatures must in order to survive the unforgiving winter. Shaoyins are externally weak, but internally strong. They may look soft and modest on the outside, but inside, they are firm, methodical, and precise. Because Shaoyins are very systematic, orderly, and businesslike in their approach to work, they prefer administrative or clerical work to more active or social work. Like Taiyins, Shaoyins have extraordinary patience and perseverance. They are able to sit or stand for long periods of time without complaining, and can withstand even the most difficult situations when their personal gain is concerned. Furthermore, they are strict with themselves and tend to live a regulated lifestyle.

In an orderly fashion

Shaoyins are skilled at good conduct, and can be very decorous and formal. They are modest, calm, rational, and orderly in their approach to people and matters at hand. They are also tolerant and patient, giving every individual their undivided attention. As a result, they can be adept at gathering and organizing people. Although uncomfortable when encountering people initially, Shaoyins are very friendly with time.

Shaoyin men are decorous, but usually only in formality. They are very considerate and exhibit good manners when dealing with the opposite sex. Like Taiyin men, they are family oriented and make devoted husbands. However, they can get *too* involved in family matters, and nag their spouses about minute details.

Like their male counterparts, Shaoyin women make excellent spouses. They are neat and tidy when it comes to housekeeping responsibilities. They are nurturers who like to take good care of their husbands and children.

Mind your own business

Shaoyins do not like meddling in the affairs of others and, likewise, do not care for others to meddle in their affairs. They are highly self-reliant. When they get in trouble, they firmly believe that they are responsible for themselves, and that they should be the ones to solve their problems. Consequently, they prefer to be alone when troubles or worries arise. Shaoyins also believe it is better to receive than to give. However, they will not rely on or become dependent on others without good reason. Therefore, they are often misunderstood, this being especially true of Shaoyin women.

Meditative mind

Shaoyins have a meditative mind, which in extremes can lead to self-centeredness and egotism. It is easy for them to think that all matters revolve around them. This is especially true with regard to material gains—Shaoyins in an unbalanced state often consider themselves to be beyond right and wrong, and will do almost anything surreptitiously for the sake of even the smallest gain.

Wise beyond years

Shaoyins have the heart of an elderly person; they are wise beyond their years. Also, like many grandmothers, they tend to give off an impression of being small and exquisite. This usually matches them, as Shaoyins are usually delicate and detail-oriented. Because Shaoyins plan well ahead of time with attention to detail, they thoroughly finish whatever matters they engage in.

The safe bet

Shaoyins dislike sudden change and adventure, preferring things that are stable and certain. They would rather earn less money and be on a salary than take the risk of opening up their own businesses. They naturally shy away from large-scale transactions. Shaoyins who do dare to open a business will not jump into high-risk investments and deals. They can also be indecisive, hesitating at every opportunity. They tend to focus on every little thing, such that they fail to win big in the gamble of life, settling instead for infinitesimal (but certain) gains.

The penny pincher

Taking the exact opposite approach of Shaoyangs, who act and buy on impulse, Shaoyins meticulously calculate and analyze every possible benefit or loss before they undertake any project or purchase any product. In this regard, they display sharp and quick wit (unlike the usual indecisiveness). They calculate profit and loss down to the minutest detail in their personal, social, and business affairs. They often fight over insignificant matters because they do not like to take even a little loss. Thus, they can be unreasonable and stingy at times.

The green-eyed monster

Shaoyins can easily become jealous of others. They may get stomachaches whenever someone close to them becomes rich. They may also become jealous of those who outperform them in social or business relations or even in recreation and sports. However, they do not manifest this outwardly.

Where's your messiah now?

Another negative aspect of Shaoyins is that they can turn out to be cowardly intellectuals or hypocritical opportunists. They may talk about doing something, or about why they will *not* do something, but only actually do it when a leader or messiah opens the door of opportunity for them. Thus, it is said of them that they will wait forever for their leader or messiah. At times, they can be sycophants who will say or do anything for their own profit.

Living in an uncertain world

Unlike Taiyangs, who have a tendency towards masculinity, Shaoyins display more feminine qualities. They are highly sensitive and insecure, lacking the assertiveness of the Yang types. In addition, Shaoyins are often introverted, and do not express their personal opinions publicly. Therefore, Shaoyins seem timid, with constant worried looks on their faces. They are often suspicious of others and lack the kind-hearted understanding of the other constitutions.

Obstinate and crafty

Once Shaoyins make up their minds, there is no turning back. Like the solidly frozen ice in winter, they do not budge an inch. Their stubborn nature can manifest strongly in their personal, social, and business relations. Because Shaoyins have the heart of the elderly, trying to dissuade them from their views is like trying to change the long-held political or religious beliefs of the elderly, whose opinions and life views are no longer as fluid as when they were young.

The mentality of Shaoyins is often compared to donkeys in Sasang Medicine. Because donkeys are not as fast as horses or as strong as cows, they often try to use their wits or craftiness to achieve their objectives. So it is for Shaoyins who are not fast like Shaoyangs or strong like Taiyins. Instead of speed or strength, Shaoyins use their cleverness to perform their duties.

Seething on the inside

When difficulties arise, Shaoyins easily fall into indolence due to their passive Yin nature. This may completely overshadow their orderly and systematic approach to matters. Shaoyins can also keep negative emotions within themselves for very long periods of time. Although they do not often get angry, when they do, they tend to hold grudges. Likewise, when their feelings get hurt, it is difficult for them to let them go. When a Shaoyin person finds a fault or weakness in others, be wary: Shaoyins never forget.

Imbalance: chronic worrier

Although they have an apparent calmness about them, Shaoyins always feel uneasy, insecure, and apprehensive on the inside, worrying constantly over trivial matters. They are like water with a still surface concealing the turbulent unseen currents. Worrying causes some Shaoyins to become extremely hasty in their actions. Physically, worry often leads to indigestion and/or a stifling sensation in the chest. According to Sasang Medicine, when Shaoyins gain full control over their apprehension, their digestive systems become stronger, allowing them to regain their health.

Movement: quiet and gentle

The Shaoyin manner of walking is natural and quiet, much like the flight of a butterfly. Some Shaoyins walk with their feet digging into the ground. Other Shaoyins walk with their bodies bent forward. Shaoyins' overall movements are gentle, elegant, and graceful, much like their temperament. They look stable whether standing, sitting, or walking. Some Shaoyins are very introverted, creating movements that are cautious or unsure, whereas others appear to be in a big hurry, creating movements similar to that of the Shaoyang type. Like their Taiyin counterparts, Shaoyins can stand and walk for long periods of time. In fact, many Shaoyins are very good runners due to their strong hip and leg development.

Speech/Voice: quiet yet persuasive

Shaoyins are eloquent speakers who, at times, choose to sit quietly with a smile on their faces instead of participating in a discussion. At times, their silence may alienate them from others, and their inscrutable smiles may in fact be masking their true thoughts or intentions. Shaoyins speak quietly, calmly, and poetically. Their speech is orderly, intelligent, and carefully crafted—Shaoyins definitely qualify as smooth talkers. When they speak, they possess an uncanny charm, which often enchants a person of the opposite sex. At times, they speak as though they are whispering to someone, and can mumble without clearly stating their thoughts. Shaoyins can usually find greater success speaking with people they know well or in small gatherings—public speech is not their forte. However, there have been some calm, gentle, yet extremely influential and powerful speakers of this body type throughout history, including Gandhi, Mother Teresa, and Abraham Lincoln.

Sense of Humor: shy

When they are in a familiar surrounding among people they know well, Shaoyins have no problem giggling, laughing, or smiling. But in an unfamiliar atmosphere, Shaoyins' innate tendencies show up. Shaoyins generally do not smile or laugh much, and often lack a sense of humor.

When they do laugh, it is in a low tone. Moreover, it is unnatural, awkward, or done with pretense. They might smile with embarrassment, or blush out of nervousness at a joke, or laugh, but add a look of contempt. More often than not, they do not laugh at all, instead showing a subtle smile with their eyes. Many times, their smiles are delayed and not spontaneous. One explanation for this is that Shaoyins are generally more timid, cautious, and unsettled than the other body types, tending toward digestive and nervous problems. Picture the innocent yet sensual smile of Marilyn Monroe or the nervous laugh of Woody Allen.

Manner of eating: picky, fastidious, and slow

Among the constitutions, Shaoyins are the most picky and fastidious about the foods that they eat. It is hard to please Shaoyins' tastes when cooking for them. They tend to eat at a slower pace, chewing thoroughly. This is in part due to their meticulous tendencies. Also, as their sense of taste is well developed, they like to savor the taste and flavor of the foods that they eat. They have an excessive fondness and greed for foods they like. Due to the constitutional weakness of their digestive system, they have problems eating large quantities of food, or foods and drinks that are cold (such as raw salads and iced drinks), for which they pay the price with indigestion, diarrhea, gas, or other digestive ailments. Their clean and neat tendencies show up in every facet of their dining experience, from how they prepare food to how they set the table—Shaoyins' meals go from A to Z, including dessert and toothpicks. Even though they are picky about food, they still like diversity, as long as each dish is appealing to both the eye and palate. There are many Shaoyin women who are excellent cooks, and for some Shaoyin men, cooking becomes their hobby.

Famous Shaoyins:

- Ghandi
- Mother Teresa
- Albert Einstein
- Abraham Lincoln
- Marilyn Monroe
- Meg Ryan
- Woody Allen
- Al Pacino
- Cain (TV's Kung Fu Series)
- Texas Ranger
- Charlie Brown
- Casper the Friendly Ghost
- Cinderella
- Snow White
- Olive Oyl
- ET

Chapter 6

Turbulence: Your Predisposition Towards Illness

Excess Yin will beget a disease of Yang; excess Yang
will beget a disease of Yin.
—*Yellow Emperor's Inner Classic*

No matter where you travel, you are likely to encounter some turbulence. This turbulence comes in many forms. If you are traveling by plane, you will certainly encounter air turbulence, however mild it may be. On a ship, you will meet water turbulence in the form of waves. Even when you travel by car, you will run into rush-hour traffic or bumpy, uneven roads. Nevertheless, you must maintain your plane, ship, or car, and keep your course if you are to reach your destination.

Similarly, in your quest for balanced health, turbulence is inevitable. No matter how healthy or strong you may be, your inherent energetic tilt creates your turbulence. This turbulence may come in the form of a physical or mental disease or distress. Obviously, if you are more balanced within your given body type, then you will likely encounter less turbulence, and will be better able to weather any turbulence that does happen to arise. In order to make your journey as pleasant as possible, you need to take a good look at your body type, and then note the conditions and diseases you are predisposed to.

Sasang Medicine actually considers disease manifestation to be the third crucial element in determining one's body type, after the body and the mind. This is because disease is defined in Sasang Medicine as an unbalanced, disharmonious state of Yin and Yang, and the specific nature of this imbalance reflects an individual's inherent energetic tilt, the origin of one's body type.

What this implies, of course, is that different constitutions are susceptible to different diseases. It also implies that different body types may manifest the same disease due to different causative factors, and with different appearances. Let us take hypertension as an example. Hypertension occurs frequently in both Taiyins and Shaoyangs. However, hypertension in Taiyins results from their surplus Yin (excessive mass) and their poor circulation, whereas in Shaoyangs, it results from the excessive rising of Yang energy and their weak Kidneys. Thus, Taiyin hypertension would be associated with sluggishness, while Shaoyang hypertension would be associated with hyperactivity.

Not only does the pathological state differ with each body type, so does the healthy state, defined as relative balance. What is indicative of health for one body type may be a symptom of imbalance or disease for another body type. For example, a sign of health for the Taiyin body type is spontaneous sweating. However, spontaneous sweating is a sign of imbalance for the Shaoyin type, because it indicates a lack of Yang energy.

The goal of Sasang Medicine is to harmonize the Yin and Yang within each body type instead of treating or eliminating the specific entity that brought about the disease. If relative Yin-Yang harmony is established, then the body will be strengthened, so that it may fight the disease and expel it on its own.

The following sections describe the states of health, mild imbalance, and serious imbalance for each body type. The healthy state refers to the ideal condition for a body type, in which a person is physiologically functioning at an optimal level, given his or her basic energetic tilt of Yin-Yang. This state should be maintained through daily cultivation to prevent the onset of imbalance and turbulence. The state of mild imbalance refers to a slight deviation from the normal physiological functioning of a given body type. If an individual is sensitive to the signs of mild imbalance, then he or she may rebalance easily through dietary modification, herbs, acupuncture, or Qi Gong exercises. The state of serious imbalance refers to a great tilt in the balance of Yin-Yang, such that the disease may be critical or chronic, and difficult to cure or recover from. In acute conditions, strong herbs and more drastic treatments may be necessary. For chronic conditions, long-term treatment with tonic herbs and acupuncture, combined with serious dietary modifications, Qi Gong, and longer periods of rest, may be required for full recuperation.

Regardless of what level of health you are at, it is important that you cultivate your body, mind, and spirit. The more serious your problem or illness, the more you need self-cultivation.

Taiyang

Common Conditions in Taiyangs	
Excessive saliva or foaming from the mouth	Vomiting (Fan Wei)
	Esophageal disorders or cancer
Lower back pain	Stomach disorders or cancer
Lower body weakness or paralysis	Bone marrow disease
Jie Yi syndrome	Brain disorders
Dysphagia (Ye Ge)	Infertility

Healthy state

Taiyangs are typically healthy individuals. Being the greater Yang body type, they possess a great amount of Yang energy. In other words, their Qi, which is Yang energy, is exuberant. Thus, Taiyangs are generally energetic and active, which prevents them from getting sick. Even when they do fall ill, they tend to recover quickly.

As stated above, each body type possesses different signs for health and disease. In the case of the Taiyangs, for instance, a large amount of urine without associated pain, urgency or difficulty is a sign of good health, whereas it may be a sign of pathology in other body types. Urination indicates that energy is moving downward within the body, rather than accumulating solely in the upper regions. Accordingly, the more frequently Taiyangs urinate, the better their health. In fact, frequent urination is the most important prerequisite for health in the Taiyang body type. It follows that a sudden difficulty in urination may indicate the presence of disease in Taiyangs. If difficult urination is the first noticeable symptom when you start to become sick, then you may be of the Taiyang body type.

Another sign of good health in Taiyangs is the condition of the stools. If the stool is slippery, thick, and large in quantity, then it indicates that the Yang energy is neither excessively drying nor excessively rising, thus indicating good health. But if the stool is dry and difficult to eliminate, then this indicates that there is heat build up and that the energy is not properly descending.

Lastly, there should be no palpable masses below the epigastric region. If a small mass is apparent but disappears quickly, then the ailment may be considered to be mild. If the mass is large and will not disappear quickly, the disease may be considered serious.

Mild imbalance

Recall that Taiyangs possess strong Lungs and weak Livers. The outwardly dispersing tendencies of the Lungs are associated with mental and emotional qualities like arrogance, dogmatism, rudeness, and a short temper. Thus, excesses of these types of behaviors may reflect hyperactivity in the Lungs. When further unbalanced, Taiyangs may be unable to restrain themselves and will plow forward with a complete lack of regard for consequences. They simply become overly macho, aggressive, and unyielding.

If Taiyangs get extremely angry or excessively saddened, an emotion which later turns into anger, they weaken the Liver's ability to gather in and consolidate energy and essential substances. Ingesting too much alcohol, a habit that unbalanced Taiyangs are prone to indulge in, will also impair the Liver's proper functioning. Eating foods that are hot, spicy, greasy, and hard to digest, meanwhile, will weaken the esophagus, stomach, and Liver, leading to diseases in the digestive organs as well as the overall body. All of these factors (anger, sadness, or a desire for alcohol and hot, spicy, greasy foods) are both causes and signs of imbalance.

Another sign of mild imbalance in Taiyangs is frequent saliva or foam coming out of the mouth. This condition is said to occur due to a depletion of Qi and blood. At this point, treatment is necessary.

As the body type with the greatest amount of Yang, Taiyangs possess the greatest Yang dynamics within the body, taking the form of rising tendencies. Although Taiyangs generally have excellent circulation throughout the entire body, these rising tendencies cause energy to concentrate in the upper body. Because too much of this energy goes upward, and not enough goes downward, Taiyangs tend to have weaker lower bodies. Therefore, they commonly suffer from lower body problems such as lower back pain or lower body weakness.

A common condition found in Taiyangs is the Jie Yi syndrome, an unusual disease manifestation identified by the founder of Sasang Medicine, Dr. Jae Ma Lee. There is no western equivalent for this syndrome. In this syndrome, the individual experiences tremendous fatigue and weakness in the lower body, making it difficult to walk. Taiyangs with this problem can become so tired that they dislike moving or talking. As the Jie Yi syndrome progresses, the individual's body gets thinner. Generally, paralysis, swelling, pain, chills, or fever do not accompany this syndrome.

Serious imbalance

In severe cases of lower body weakness, Taiyangs may develop paralysis of the legs and lower body. Also, as the reproductive organs are located within the lower half of the body, that is, within the lower abdominal cavity, Taiyang women may develop weak uteruses leading to infertility. Taiyang men may suffer from sexual problems such as impotence. For these reasons, Taiyangs need to strengthen their lower bodies through regular exercise and dietary modification.

The fiery nature of Taiyang energy creates a rapid, burning internal environment within the body. This causes internal dryness within Taiyangs. If dryness becomes excessive, then blood and other Yin substances within the body become depleted. At this stage, Taiyangs will fall ill. The psychological sign of this dryness is a feeling of urgency. Thus, when Taiyangs feel more urgent than usual, they should be careful, as this indicates that their bodies are becoming more Yang (dry). If dryness is allowed to progress, the lack of blood and Yin substances may result in the development of bone marrow disease.

The internal dryness can also cause serious digestive problems such as dysphagia (Ye Ge) and vomiting (Fan Wei). Both dysphagia and vomiting in Taiyangs are serious signs of dryness and rising Yang energy due to the inability of deficient Yin energy to hold things down.

A person with dysphagia has difficulty swallowing food. When Taiyangs experience dysphagia, they usually do not have other symptoms such as high fever, abdominal pain, borborygmus, diarrhea, or dysentery. If these symptoms are present along with dysphagia, then sufficient vitality is left in the body to overcome the condition.

In Taiyangs, vomiting is closely related to dysphagia. Vomiting may occur immediately after swallowing food, or after several hours. Usually, those that vomit more frequently than others are of the Taiyang body type.

In Taiyangs, vomiting frequently occurs in combination with stools that are dry and scant. If vomiting is accompanied by the sensation of a cool breeze blowing in the esophageal region, then this indicates an urgent and dangerous condition for Taiyangs requiring immediate treatment.

On the whole, it is fairly easy to distinguish Taiyangs from the other body types due to their distinctive symptoms. Jie Yi syndrome, dysphagia, and vomiting are the most frequently occurring conditions for unbalanced Taiyangs. When dysphagia and vomiting occur together with Jie Yi syndrome, it is the most serious stage of disease for Taiyangs. One occurring without the other is obviously less serious. Among the three, Jie Yi syndrome is the least serious. Dr. Lee himself suffered from all three diseases for nearly seven years until discovering Sasang Medicine.

Shaoyangs

Common Conditions in Shaoyangs	
Constipation	Vomiting blood
Urinary disturbance	Sexual disorders
Acute or chronic kidney disorders	Infertility
Habitual lower back pain	Osteoporosis
Knee weakness	Pulmonary tuberculosis
Hypertension	

Healthy state

The Shaoyang types have a strong Spleen and weak Kidneys. According to Sasang Medicine, the Spleen is responsible for the fire (Yang) energy or warmth in the body, and the Kidneys are responsible for the water (Yin) or cooling energy. Thus, this constitution has more fire than water. Their bodies are typically hot (Yang), especially in the head and chest regions. They also tend to have warm hands and feet.

Being a Yang body type, Shaoyangs also have a strong amount of Yang energy. Physically, their strong Yang gives Shaoyangs plenty of energy to get things moving, manifesting with their ability to digest food quickly and easily. Internally, their metabolism is so rapid that energy is quickly used up without being stored. This is the reason why they are generally thin and do not easily gain weight.

Bowel movements are of prime importance for gauging the health of Shaoyangs because it shows that the fire (Yang) and water (Yin) within their body is harmonized. Shaoyangs are in good health when their bowel movements are smooth, slippery, and regular. The stools should be dry initially and somewhat loose and easily eliminated toward the end. When Shaoyangs are sick, a large quantity of loose stool once or twice per day indicates that they are healing and well on the way back to a balanced state of health. The illness should cease shortly thereafter.

Mild imbalance

Like a blazing, ravaging fire, diseases tend to progress rapidly in Shaoyangs. Thus, it is important to catch the key symptoms at the initial stage of any disease for Shaoyangs, especially when headaches or constipation are present.

The first sign of imbalance in Shaoyangs is constipation. Constipation is not as important a symptom for other body types, but for Shaoyangs it is a primary sign of disharmony. For Shaoyangs, constipation indicates that their water (Yin) is depleted and their fire (Yang) is in excess. Because their body type is innately deficient in Yin and excessive in Yang, constipation, even when there are no other symptoms present, foreshadows a greater imbalance yet to surface. As the progression of disease in Shaoyangs is rapid, one should take curative measures without hesitation. A warning sign of imminent constipation is an absence of bowel movement for more than a day or frequent diarrhea (three to five times in a day) in small amounts.

Shaoyangs also tend to have voracious appetites due to their excessive Yang energy. Fortunately, they do not gain weight because their internal heat metabolizes food rapidly. However, this intense heat may easily cause rashes when foods improper for their body type are ingested. For example, foods that are hot and spicy, like garlic and ginger, can cause Shaoyangs to break out in rashes, with itching, redness, and heat.

Other consequences of excessive heat in Shaoyangs are the tendency to develop a flushed face, stifling heat sensations in the chest, and insomnia when they are mentally stressed. They also tend to feel more irritable and restless than other body types after catching a cold or flu.

Weak sexual energy is also more pronounced in Shaoyangs than with other body types. Shaoyangs possess congenitally weak Kidneys so they tend to experience a sharp decline in sexual energy. According to Sasang

Medicine, an intimate relationship exists between the Kidneys and the sexual organs and reproductive system. When the Kidneys are weak, sexual energy is lowered. Hence, Shaoyang men tend to have low levels of sexual energy because of their constitutional Kidney weakness. Although many Shaoyang men seem to be sexually strong and active because their Yang energy gets activated and excited easily, they still lack endurance due to their insufficient Yin energy. In this, they are much like a struck match—the flame is hot, but the wick is short. Sexually overactive Shaoyang men can quickly weaken their Kidneys and develop problems in the genito-urinary systems, such as urinary difficulty, or nocturnal emissions. Shaoyangs' weak Kidney energy also may make them prone to sexually transmitted diseases. In addition, Shaoyangs often develop urination problems due to heat, such as urinary tract infection.

Shaoyangs have weak lower bodies, though not as pronounced as with Taiyangs. Recall that their energy is concentrated in the Yang regions of the body, that is, the chest and shoulder regions. Thus, energy fails to accumulate in the lower regions of the body. Weakness in the waist and lower body may result in lower back pain and arthritis of the knees.

Serious imbalance

A sign of a major disease in Shaoyangs occurs when, after several days of constipation, the chest feels hot, congested, and painful. This combination of symptoms is unique to the Shaoyang constitution. It indicates a congestion of excess heat in the body, a condition warranting prompt attention. Failure to treat this problem can lead to what is known as a "collapse of Yin," a very serious condition.

As a result of their excessive fire and weak Kidneys, Shaoyangs are also susceptible to hypertension. Also, Kidney weakness manifests in a weak reproductive energy. This is not only restricted to a low sexual endurance in men. In women, this weakness manifests as difficulties in conceiving, maintaining a pregnancy, and having multiple births more than Yin body types. Taiyangs, however, experience much greater problems in these respects.

Kidneys are said to rule the bones in Sasang Medicine. Therefore Shaoyangs are susceptible to osteoporosis and poor posture in old age. In their younger years, activity prevents the bone degeneration. With age, however, physical activity and overall metabolism slows down; this is when the Shaoyangs' inherent bone weakness starts to manifest.

Shaoyangs are also susceptible to pulmonary tuberculosis as a result of their deficient Yin and excess Yang. Symptoms appear in Shaoyangs as a flushed face, low-grade fever, and a heat sensation in their palms, soles, and chest. They also cough up blood, develop a thirst for cold drinks, and experience night sweats.

Footsteps on the path

A thin, 69-year-old woman named Judy K. came to see me with chief complaints of lower back pain, and a shooting pain that radiated down her left leg, all the way down to her foot. She had been suffering from these afflictions for two months. Judy said that the pain persisted throughout the day, but would grow particularly intense in the afternoon and at night. She had been taking the usual over-the-counter remedies, but had experienced no significant relief.

When Judy went to see a Western medical doctor, the X-ray exam revealed osteoporosis in her hip and spine. The doctor recommended that she take female hormones to prevent further degeneration of her bones. Although she desperately desired to alleviate the pain of her condition, she feared the possible side effects of the hormones. She came to me looking for a safer alternative.

Upon inquiring about her past medical history, I discovered that Judy had been on high blood pressure medication for the past eight years, and had suffered from frequent bouts of dizziness and headaches. With the medication, her blood pressure remained at the borderline (140/90), occasionally going up a good deal more, especially when under stress.

Judy told me that she had suffered from constipation (a bowel movement once every four to five days!) all of her life. She also revealed that she had been very active at her church, and that, before her pains began, she had been exercising two to three times a week at the local health club. She said that she was generally a very happy person, although she got angry and frustrated at times. She usually woke up early in the morning, performing her activities swiftly (she could not stand it otherwise). She also expressed that she loved meeting and talking to new people. Her tongue was red and dry, with minor cracks, and very little coating. Her pulse was thready, wiry, and slightly rapid. (In traditional Eastern medicine, examination of the tongue and pulse are two of the most important tools used in diagnosis. Though they do not play a great part in differentiating the constitutions of Sasang Medicine, they nevertheless provide accurate assessment of the present state of health and prognosis of a patient.)

Interpretation

I had already recognized Judy as a Shaoyang by the way she had walked into the office: her gait was quick, light, and floating, with gliding steps, even with her pain. As I asked her questions, I confirmed my initial impression by taking careful note of her facial features: she had the glittering eyes and narrow, protruding forehead typical of Shaoyang body types. I also noted that she was very cheerful and in high spirits, despite the fact that she was probably experiencing a great deal of pain. Judy was garrulous as she talked, describing her symptoms and problems with what could only be described as enthusiasm. Shaoyangs tend to keep a youthful appearance and energy even in the later years of life.

Her lower back and sciatic pain, according to Sasang Medicine, results from weakness in the Kidneys. Recall that the lower back region is the domain of the Kidneys. So when Kidneys develop weakness, one of the chief complaints that Shaoyangs can have is lower back pain.

According to Sasang Medicine, osteoporosis is most common in the Shaoyang types due to the close relationship between the bones and Kidneys. Because the Kidneys rule the bones, they must be strengthened before improvement can be made in the skeletal system. This is the key to treating such conditions as osteoporosis.

Hypertension is another condition frequently observed in the Shaoyang body type. Shaoyangs are particularly prone to hypertension because of the weakness in their Kidneys. The Kidneys are the source of Yin energy in the body. As they are weak in the Shaoyang types, their deficient Yin energy is unable to hold the excess Yang energy down; this Yang energy rises, causing hypertension. This condition is aggravated when Shaoyangs are under stress and tension. When under emotional pressure, their constitutional Yang bodies easily become congested and hot, leading to anxiety, irritability, and restlessness. As with osteoporosis, it is imperative to consider the role played by the Kidneys (the source of Yin energy) in the treatment of hypertension in Shaoyangs. The treatment (for both osteoporosis and hypertension) in this patient thus focused on building up the Kidney Yin.

Also, as Shaoyangs have a lot of internal heat with fluid dryness, they tend to be constipated. Recall that the primary requisite for health in the Shaoyang type is a regular bowel movement, and that one of the first signs of imbalance is constipation. Thus, constipation must be addressed whenever treating this constitution.

Treatment and recommendation

True to her Shaoyang nature, Judy seemed to be in a hurry to get a treatment, not bothering to hear my explanations. I advised her that the first thing she needed to do to improve her condition was loosen up a bit and slow things down—especially her mind. As Shaoyangs are prone to quick sadness and deep anger (two emotions that cause the energy to ascend), I instructed her to not hold in any anger, and to be careful of any sudden sadness that she experienced. I explained to her that both of these emotions injure the Kidneys, which in Sasang Medicine are related to the bones. I also explained that, although people of any constitution could get osteoporosis, Shaoyangs often experience an acutely accelerated progression of the condition.

I outlined the importance of meditation in daily life, and instructed Judy to constantly center her awareness on the Dan Tian (a spot approximately three inches below the navel). I also gave her several Qi Gong exercises, with a special emphasis on those designed to strengthen the Kidneys. (For further explanations on Qi Gong, see Chapter 9.)

The herbal formula that I prescribed for Judy was a constitutional formula called Shi Er Wei Di Huang Tang (Twelve-Ingredient Rehmannia Decoction), which includes cooked rehmannia, cornus fruit, and alismatis. This formula strengthens the Kidneys in Shaoyang types. With acupuncture treatments twice a week and an herbal formula ingested daily, Judy's lower back and sciatic pain stopped. She was back in shape in six weeks and her blood pressure had dropped to 110/80. After visiting her doctor, she was told to reduce her blood pressure medication by one half. She was also elated to find that the constipation that she had suffered from all of her life had disappeared altogether. She now had a bowel movement once a day.

To maintain her newfound health, I prescribed a famous formula called Liu Wei Di Huang Wan (Six-Ingredient Rehmannia Pill) to Judy, and recommended that she come in once a month for a check-up. Subsequent monthly exams over the next six months revealed that her blood pressure had stabilized and that she was living a normal life. She was exercising five days a week without pain and happily reported that her Western medical check-up revealed no further degeneration in her bones.

Taiyin

Common Conditions in Taiyins	
Diabetes	Pulmonary tuberculosis
Hypertension, arteriosclerosis	Constipation
Hepatitis	Bronchitis
Heart disease	Dysentery
Cirrhosis	Asthma
Jaundice	Rashes
Stroke	Irritable bowel syndrome
Gallbladder disorder	Allergies
Hypotension	Neurasthenia
Enteritis	Intestinal cancer
Appendicitis	Hemorrhoids

Healthy state

A sweaty Taiyin is a healthy Taiyin. In other body types, sweating is a sign of weakness or possible illness. But for Taiyins, sweating is the foundation of health. They must "sweat it out" to prevent their bodies from falling out of balance. It is important to remember that bowel movements and urination are not the only processes of waste removal in the body. Sweating is also another way the body secretes wastes and toxins. Since Taiyins accumulate so much waste in the body due to their slow metabolism and excess eating and drinking, they must eliminate as much as they can on a daily basis. Therefore, it is imperative for Taiyins to exercise regularly.

No matter where the sweat appears on Taiyins, as long as the beads are thick, it shows vitality. If the beads of sweat are small and disappear quickly, then their vital energy may be in a weak state. Taiyins typically feel refreshed and vitalized after sweating, whereas Shaoyins become tired or may develop a mild fever after sweating. Thus, those who feel comfortable sweating profusely with little exertion or while eating cool foods in the winter may be considered to be healthy Taiyins.

Taiyins commonly feel that visits to the doctor are unnecessary. They will usually weather minor illnesses, such as the common cold, flu, or digestive complaints, without bothering to get a check up.

Mild imbalance

Taiyins begin to fall out of balance if the skin becomes firm, the pores close, and sweating stops. When sweating does not occur in Taiyins, it indicates that other symptoms will eventually appear. The body may progress into a more serious illness.

The lack of circulation to the superficial regions of the body, especially the skin, combined with the Taiyin tendency to accumulate toxins, make individuals of this type more prone to developing skin disorders. Some of the commonly occurring skin disorders in this body type are eczema, boils, psoriasis, and rashes. Taiyins also frequently complain that their hands and feet get cracked or chapped easily during the winter season.

Being the greater Yin body type, Taiyins possess a great amount of Yin substance in their body. This Yin energy manifests as an inward, gathering tendency. This means that Taiyins tend to gather and hold energy inside, creating an accumulation of Yin substances in the body. These Yin substances include retained fluids, fatty tissues, mucus, and other unmetabolized pathological substances. Their accumulation results in a body that is more often than not on the obese side. Taiyins tend to have a large appetite, which exacerbates their condition, resulting in a general slowing of their physiological processes or metabolism.

Because Taiyins have a large appetite and are not physically active, they can easily develop constipation. However, diarrhea constitutes a greater problem for this constitution than frequent constipation. Taiyins may also complain of pain in the eyes. This usually manifests as pain and itching of the eyes, or a general pulling sensation at the corners of the eyelids, which leaves them with a feeling of fatigue. Taiyins may easily catch colds and flu because of the weakness in their Lungs. They may also suffer from hay fever, sinusitis, and bronchitis.

As far as mental or emotional signs of imbalance are concerned, Taiyins need to be cautious about excessive greed. This greed can cause heat conditions in their Liver and dryness in their Lungs, leading to Liver and Lung diseases. Since the spirit is easily disturbed whenever there is a buildup of heat in the body due to a stagnation of substance, Taiyins may easily develop fearful minds, palpitations, insomnia, and forgetfulness.

Serious imbalance

Illnesses do not manifest easily in younger Taiyins because their blood circulation is relatively active. However, when they reach middle age, chronic debilitating diseases develop more frequently in Taiyins than in any other body type. This is due to the slowing down of their already slow metabolism. Examples of chronic debilitating diseases that Taiyins are prone to include liver disorders, such as hepatitis and cirrhosis, and circulatory and geriatric diseases, such as hypertension, stroke, heart disease, and diabetes.

Weakness in their Lungs predisposes Taiyins to many diseases of the respiratory system as previously mentioned. One disorder that many Taiyins suffer from is acute and chronic asthma. Some other respiratory illnesses that befall Taiyins are emphysema, pneumonia, and pulmonary tuberculosis.

Taiyins also tend to suffer from palpitations more frequently than other body types due to their weak circulatory and respiratory systems. When palpitations continue, combined with symptoms of a stagnant feeling in the intestines and absence of sweating, it indicates that a disease has developed.

Taiyins usually do not respond to minor external stimuli. Thus, they look slow and tranquil. But when shocked with an intense stimulation, they may easily develop a nervous disorder such as neurasthenia, a condition in which a person suffers from anxiety, nervousness, irritability, and depression, together with unexplainable chronic fatigue and lassitude.

A serious state of imbalance occurs when Taiyins develop diarrhea with a sensation of fullness in the mid-abdominal region. They may develop an uncomfortable feeling, as though their midsections are clogged up by a fog.

Also, when Taiyins feel anxious, their bowel movements may fluctuate from diarrhea to constipation, with an uncomfortable sensation in the lower abdomen. This is similar to the irritable bowel syndrome in Western medicine, which is a disorder of the gastrointestinal tract marked by pain in the abdomen, constipation, or diarrhea, or alternating constipation and diarrhea. In Sasang Medicine, if this syndrome occurs after a period of absence of sweating, it is considered a sign of a more serious illness.

Footsteps on the path

Barbara N., who was 72 years of age, was brought into my clinic by her daughter. Barbara spoke in a low, muffled voice: "I have been having this cough for the past eight years. It occurs throughout the day and is generally worse in the evening. Every time I cough, my chest hurts. I've had frequent episodes of bronchitis, but I've never been diagnosed as having asthma," she said. Barbara also said that she had difficulty breathing, and that she would have a sudden large amount of clear mucous accompanying her cough once or twice a day. Even while she spoke, she was coughing, and needed to use tissues. With a look of desperation, she confessed, "I just don't know what to do." She was reaching out for some immediate help.

Barbara said that she had tried all types of Western medication to suppress her cough, but to no avail. Along with her main complaint (the coughing), she revealed that she suffered from bladder incontinence, and that she had to wake up frequently during the night to go to the bathroom. She also said that she felt very tired all the time, and that she suffered from frequent bouts of depression.

During the course of the interview, I noticed that Barbara and her daughter kept arguing with each other as to what was going on with her. I could see that both of them were under a lot of stress. Barbara later told me that she worries constantly about her daughter, who recently went through a bitter divorce.

Barbara's other symptoms included ulcers in her stomach and esophagus, with frequent gas and bloating. She also suffered from lower back pain. Because of all of the Western medications she was taking, she experienced side effects such as a dry mouth and diarrhea.

Her medical history revealed that she had had two small strokes in the past eight months or so—she wasn't sure when. The cause for her stroke was her high blood pressure. To add to her grim situation, she also had high cholesterol.

Physically, Barbara weighed 175 pounds, at the height of only 5'4". She had a typical Taiyin large potbelly with a thick, stocky frame. She looked heavyset, with most of her weight concentrated in her abdomen and waist region; this gave her a very commanding presence. Although every feature on her face was large, her nervous, doe-like eyes were particularly prominent. She also had very solid, thick skin.

I could sense during the diagnostic interview that Barbara was very pessimistic about her condition, and apprehensive about the whole process of seeing me. She said that she constantly worried about everything, from her financial difficulties to her daughter's marital situation. She also said that she was an anxious person, who was fearful and easily stressed. Recently, she noticed that she was depressed, angry, and even sarcastic about her condition.

All of her symptoms—physical, mental and emotional—worsened after losing her husband. He had passed away four years ago after suffering for more than two years from lung cancer. She had lived with him for over 40 years.

At the time of her visit, Barbara was seeing four specialists: an internist, a pulmonologist, a gastroenterologist, and a psychiatrist. As a result of seeing so many specialists, her list of medications was overwhelming— she actually brought her pills in a supermarket-sized bag! These included bladder control pills, hormone replacement pills, blood thinners (for stroke prevention), blood pressure and cholesterol pills, anti-depressants, pills to stop acid reflux, and pills to stop post-nasal drip. To top off her intake of medications, she took high doses of vitamins such as A, B-complex, C, E, and a few other over the counter herbal supplements, like gingko, echinacea, and American ginseng.

When I asked her about her diet, she said that her favorite foods were chocolate and dairy products, including cheese, yogurt, and ice cream. She said that she ate frequently between meals and ate even when she was not feeling hungry. In addition, she said that whenever she ate, she would eat to fullness. She drank one cup of coffee per day and had cravings for white flour products and sugar. Otherwise, she had a fairly balanced diet, with whole grains, and fresh and cooked fruits and vegetables.

Interpretation

It was very easy to diagnose Barbara based on her bodily appearance, personality, and disease manifestations. Barbara's cough, her chief complaint, revealed the Taiyin constitutional weakness of her Lungs.

Barbara exemplifies what can happen when the body and mind are not properly cared for. She embodies the kind of ailments that Taiyins are the most susceptible to—obesity, high blood pressure, high cholesterol, and strokes. These ailments do not occur overnight. Rather, they are the results of years of abuse to the body and mind. As Taiyins tend to accumulate energy and mass instead of letting it out and circulating it (due to the weakness of their Lungs), they develop various problems in their circulatory, hormonal, and nervous systems, resulting in many adult-onset ailments.

Furthermore, when Taiyins are shocked, they experience great difficulty recovering from it. They develop palpitations, and the emotional anxiety, worry, and fear that is left in the wake of such traumatic events can continue to cycle within them for a long time. The devastating emotional trauma of losing her husband of more than 40 years no doubt played a significant role in damaging Barbara's health. When this was combined with additional stress (particularly from her daughter), a poor diet, lack of exercise, and other unbalanced daily habits, many pathological changes resulted.

Treatment and recommendation

I first addressed Barbara's diet. I explained the importance of eating only to 75 percent of her capacity, so as to give her stomach ample room to digest the food. I told her to reduce consumption of dairy products, as they tend to form excessive phlegm in the body. Dairy products are appropriate for Taiyin body types. However, only whole milk that has not been pasteurized, homogenized, or skimmed, or other like products are acceptable, and even then, only in small amounts. I also counseled Barbara to reduce her intake of sweets and chocolates.

Because Barbara was interested in learning more about the proper diet for her body type, I suggested that she increase her intake of legumes and nuts (peanuts, walnuts, chestnuts, pine nuts, gingko nuts, pistachios, etc.), as they are very helpful in balancing her body type. For coughing, pears are frequently used, and plums and apples are also helpful. I also suggested that she increase her intake of pumpkins, radishes, asparagus, and various sprouts, as these can help to strengthen her weak Lungs.

Along with these diet guidelines, I recommended some Qi Gong breathing exercises in a sitting position to calm and balance her mind and emotions. I advised her to perform the exercises for five minutes twice daily, and throughout the day in short spurts. As for regular exercise, I suggested that she start walking a little bit, as she tended to stay indoors watching TV for long hours. She was to start with 10 minutes of walking daily, and build up slowly over the next two months to 30 minutes of walking, five to six times per week. I explained to her that Taiyins have a tendency to "sit back and take it easy," aggravating several of their health problems, so she needed to move around as much as she was able to.

I then outlined a program of acupuncture and herbal treatments for her to follow. As her condition was chronic in nature, I told her in advance that it was going to take some time for her to notice improvements in her condition. However, there was an immediate improvement in her cough and an increased sense of calm in her after two sessions. I administered acupuncture treatments twice a week, combined with a daily dose of herbal medicines for the next three months, at which time she was released from my care.

Because Barbara conscientiously followed the program, with strict adherence to the dietary and exercise guidelines, at the end of these three months, she was pleased that she had made sufficient progress in various aspects of her health. She had no recurrence of cough, her chief compliant, for several weeks. Her incontinence was less frequent and she did not have to wake up so much at night to use the bathroom. Her overall energy level improved, and she felt more stable emotionally. With increased energy and a sense of calm, Barbara gained more confidence. She was also delighted that she dropped several pounds. She resolved to stay on the dietary and exercise guidelines. A subsequent follow-up exam a month later showed no recurrence of the cough. Barbara was well on her way to recovering her health and peace of mind.

Shaoyin

Common Conditions in Shaoyins	
Poor appetite	Sinusitis
Chronic fatigue	Prolapse of stomach
Indigestion	Rhinorrhea
Cold hands and feet	Plum pit syndrome
Habitual abdominal pain	Melancholy
Cold body	Tonsillitis
Chronic diarrhea	Depression
Allergic rhinitis	Jaundice
Chronic dysentery	

Healthy state

Shaoyins are in good health as long as they have no problems with digestion. If they fall ill, Shaoyins can recover readily when their appetite and digestion are functioning properly. When the appetite and digestion become weakened, Shaoyins immediately feel uncomfortable. Firm stools are also indicative of health in Shaoyins.

Another sign of good health in Shaoyins is the absence of spontaneous sweating and sighing, and the ability to eat and drink cold foods and liquids. They are also in good health when their hands and feet do not get cold easily, and they are able to tolerate cold weather well.

Mild imbalance

Signs of imbalance for Shaoyins stand in direct contrast to disease symptoms in Shaoyangs. Shaoyin illnesses are considered to be caused by cold, whereas Shaoyang diseases mainly result from heat. Due to the lack of fire (Yang) energy and excess water (Yin) energy, Shaoyins tend to have cold hands, feet, and bodies, weak tolerance for cold weather, low energy, and frequent sighing. The coldness worsens with excessive sweating, such as from too much exercise.

The body is falling out of balance when there is spontaneous sweating, which is sweating without exertion or with mild exertion. This imbalance stems from a constitutional weakness in their Yang energy; weakened Yang energy leads to spontaneous sweating. The greater the amount of sweat, the greater the weakness in Yang energy. This is in direct contrast to the Taiyins, who exhibit good health when there is plenty of sweating. Shaoyins should be cautious when they experience cold, fatigue, and excessive sweating, as their bodies are spinning out of balance.

Many diseases develop as a result of Shaoyins' constitutionally weak Spleen and Stomach. People who constantly have stomach disorders throughout their lives are usually Shaoyins. Shaoyins suffer frequently from poor appetite and indigestion, which results in malnutrition and chronic fatigue. In this state, Shaoyins lack energy in their voice, tiring quickly after just a few minutes of talking. Many people with gloomy facial expressions due to indigestion and/or constant abdominal pain may be of the Shaoyin type. It is interesting to note that the majority of people who suffer from seasickness are Shaoyins.

When Shaoyins overeat cold, raw foods, they readily get diarrhea. The same holds true for iced drinks, sodas, and cold alcoholic beverages, such as beer. The weakness in their digestive and immune systems due to deficient Yang energy makes Shaoyins susceptible to various allergies, especially hay fever, and sinus problems, such as acute and chronic sinusitis. Although Taiyins also have problems with allergies due to their weak Lungs, Shaoyins tend to have it worse.

Because Shaoyins are strong in Yin but weak in Yang, they have a natural tendency towards stagnation, both with regard to their bodies and their minds. Mental stagnation makes them extremely narrow-minded and scrupulous, as well as chronically apprehensive and nervous. This mentality can easily lead to melancholy or depression in this constitution. Due to such emotional depression, Shaoyins are susceptible to what is called the "plum pit" syndrome. In this syndrome, a person feels as if the pit of a plum were stuck in his or her throat even though there is no actual presence of a mass. This is not considered a serious state of imbalance for Shaoyins.

Serious imbalance

Shaoyins who are in good health must be careful even if they only experience diarrhea two or three times a month. As this indicates a weakening of the digestive fire or Yang energy, it should not be taken lightly. When diarrhea occurs more than four to five times in one day or continues for three consecutive days, this is a serious state of imbalance. At the other end of the spectrum, three to four bowel movements with dry stool in one day is also a cause for concern. When the diarrhea does not stop and the lower abdomen feels cold as ice, it is a symptom of major illness for Shaoyins.

When the weakness of Yang energy worsens, there is a lack of energy to hold organs in proper places. This results in prolapsed organs. So for Shaoyins, compared to the other constitutions, there are more frequent occurrences of prolapsed organs of stomach, uterus, intestines, rectum, and so on.

Though Taiyins have much more difficulty eliminating toxins from their bodies, Shaoyins, too, can have difficulty as well. Due to the lack of Yang energy, substances can stagnate, accumulate, and turn into stones. So Shaoyins can have trouble with developing gall and kidney stones.

Shaoyins tend to have poor overall health. They frequently get minor ailments and illnesses, which never seem to disappear. As a result, Shaoyins often complain and worry about their constant state of ill health, and will pay frequent visits to the doctor. On the other hand, Shaoyins rarely develop serious illnesses, and they tend to possess longevity. One possible reason for this is that their prudent and meticulous nature allows them to be aware of their weaknesses and exercise caution regarding their health (not overeating or overexerting, for example). Another reason is that Shaoyins possess inherently strong Kidneys. The Kidneys are believed to be the foundation of health in Eastern medicine.

Footsteps on the path

Jennifer S. is a 20-year-old college student who was referred to me by her father for her vomiting. She had been vomiting continuously for two and a half months, and had just been released from the hospital a week ago. When she initially checked into the hospital, a CT scan had been performed, and the doctors found that she had a 7-centimeter tumor (ganglion neuroma) near the spine in her upper back. However, they felt that this tumor was not related to the vomiting. Jennifer was subsequently released from the hospital after three days. However, she checked back into the hospital the very next day because of her continuing nausea and vomiting. This time, she stayed in the hospital for three weeks straight, until surgery was performed to remove the tumor from her back. She was released a few days after the surgery, but had to be readmitted a few more times, until her final stay in the hospital a week before she came to see me. From her second admission to her final release, the doctors at the hospital had performed just about every test available, including blood tests, X-rays, MRIs, CT scan, sigmoidscopy, EGD (endoscopy), a pelvic exam, and a gastric emptying radionuclide scan. Nevertheless, all the test results had returned negative.

Her vomiting occurred at any time. "Every time I vomit, it hurts the stitches" where the surgery was done, she said. She added, "Sometimes the vomiting can go on for hours, but once the food is out, it feels okay." In general, her vomiting occurred right after eating. All foods would come up except soups (but even easily digested soups were occasionally rejected by her system). At times, even in the absence of food, she would experience dry retching.

Doctors had prescribed popular antacids for her condition. She was also prescribed a heavy dose of post-surgery antibiotics that caused severe diarrhea for several days.

Jennifer's past medical history revealed that her vomiting had started about three years earlier, and had occurred in two month intervals for a day or two ever since. As a result of this problem, she had completely lost her appetite, and had lost 20 pounds within the last two months. She experienced no other pains elsewhere in her body, except for a stiff neck, which she had noticed recently.

Jennifer's other symptoms included tremendous fatigue, a dry mouth with a desire for cold drinks, sweaty hands, and easy bruising and bleeding. Palpitations also accompanied her condition. She also noted that she caught colds two to five times a year. Her menstruation was irregular, lasting seven days, heavy with clots and a lot of cramping. Although she used to be constipated, her bowel movements at the time were normal.

Her tongue was pale in color with tooth marks, a thin, greasy, white coating, and a lot of red points/spots. Her pulse was very rapid (110 beats per minute) but weak, and soft in the right second position.

Interpretation

Physically, Jennifer was small in stature at 5' and weighed only 90 pounds. She had a quiet demeanor, with a calm, gentle voice typical of Shaoyin types (and partially due, no doubt, to the tremendous suffering she had undergone as a result of her condition). When asked about her emotional state and personality, she replied that she was generally calm, although she could get nervous, envious, or easily hurt. She also noted that she tended to be detail oriented and tidy. These characteristics exemplify her Shaoyin nature.

Jennifer's pale tongue with tooth marks and greasy, white coating indicated a weakness of the Spleen Qi and a retention of dampness, while the red points revealed a prior buildup of heat from stress. The rapid and weak pulse reflected heat due to deficiency, and its softness, the weakness of the Spleen.

The signs and symptoms, along with her facial and bodily figure and emotional disposition, revealed her to be of the Shaoyin body type. In this body type, there is a constitutional weakness in the digestive system. Jennifer's digestive system was further weakened by the stresses of daily living, and the transition of going from high school to college. In addition, when inquired about her diet, she revealed that she ate many greasy foods, including hamburgers, pizzas, and fried chicken, with carbonated drinks. She also frequently ate snacks in between meals, and always ate to fullness. Without a doubt, these bad dietary habits also played a major role in weakening her digestive system.

Treatment and recommendations

The first thing that I did with Jennifer was to get her to relax by deepening her breath. I taught her a simple breathing exercise (mentioned in Chapter 9) effective for this purpose. I then proceeded to treat her with a constitutional acupuncture therapy, placing particular emphasis on strengthening her digestive system (Spleen) and increasing the Yang energy in her body. I also prescribed a simple formula called Xiang Sha Yang Wei Tang (Cyperus and Cluster Nourishing the Stomach Formula), commonly used for her body type and condition. Furthermore, I made strong recommendations regarding her diet. Among other things, I encouraged her to include more ginger and rice porridges, and reduce cold drinks (see Chapter 7). In addition, I recommended that she eliminate all snacks, keep her meals regular, and eat only in moderate amounts.

I asked Jennifer how she felt on her second visit. "I didn't vomit even once. I have been eating well," she replied. "I can even keep the herbs down," she added jokingly. Her overall energy level had improved, and she felt great.

On her third visit, she reported that she was doing very well, with no problems of nausea and vomiting. She ate well, and her energy continued to improve.

On her fourth visit, she still showed no vomiting. Her energy level continued to rise, and she reported that she had gained six pounds since the first treatment. Her diet had also improved, and she was eating less junk food than before.

In each subsequent visit, I noticed small increments in her health and vitality. Her eyes began to sparkle with more energy and her voice became stronger. I released Jennifer after a total of 10 visits. She returned for a check-up three months later, and was pleased to report that none of her former distressing symptoms had returned. She was enjoying life again! She is now doing very well, and her previous debilitating condition of vomiting is all but forgotten.

Part II

Destination: Health

Chapter 7

Food for Your Body Type

What is food to one, is to others bitter poison.
—Lucretius, *De Rerum Natura*

It is said that food is your best medicine. According to Sasang Medicine, a healthy, well-balanced diet can be as effective as medications or dietary supplements as a preventive measure against disease. Poor dietary habits, on the other hand, have been associated with many illnesses, such as stroke, diabetes, coronary heart disease, hypertension, and cancer.

Sasang Medicine views food as an important means to balance disharmonies within your body. Every food possesses a distinctive energetic quality that either flows with or against your body type. Just as different machines require different fuels, so too do dietary needs vary from person to person. For example, some people benefit from the consumption of spicy foods, others do not. Thus, it is important that you match the substances that you ingest with your body type, whether they are foods, dietary supplements, or herbs. Otherwise, you will run inefficiently and perhaps even break down. Sasang Medicine assists you in this selection process by specifying the foods that are appropriate and inappropriate for your body type.

What Is a Balanced Diet?

There is no such thing as good or bad food. Foods that help one person may not necessarily be good for others. It follows that there is no standard, uniform diet for everyone at all times and for all situations. There are only specific diets, congruent with particular constitutions and levels of health at particular times. Of utmost importance is the practice of eating a well-balanced diet with proper emphasis on those foods appropriate to your particular constitution. To do this, you must remain flexible and open. Let your natural instincts be your guide. As most of us require some basic assistance, the following serves as a general guideline.

A balanced diet should:

- ❧ Be simple, yet comprehensive and holistic.
- ❧ Serve as the basic foundation to help you overcome physical, mental, emotional, and even spiritual imbalances.
- ❧ Help you maximize vitality so that you feel more energetic, balanced, in tune, lighter, and happier.
- ❧ Enhance and support your physical, mental, and spiritual disciplines.
- ❧ Clear the body of wastes and toxins and help to maintain proper and natural body weight.
- ❧ Help correct imbalances in your body type, strengthening what is weak, and normalizing what is excessively strong.
- ❧ Prevent and remedy diseases.
- ❧ Enhance both Eastern and Western medical treatments.

Following the direction of the Middle Path, you should avoid extremes in your diet, such as all-liquid diets, all-protein diets, brown-rice-only diets, and so forth. Over a period of time, these extreme methods can damage your body. It is also of paramount importance that you not make sudden, drastic changes in your diet. In addition, no matter how appropriate the foods you eat may be, you should never limit yourself to only a few foods.

Whatever dietary regimen you choose to follow, never become overly attached to it or excessively contemplate it. Do not become a food fanatic, worrying about what to eat every moment of your life. Keep the following maxim in mind: "Eat to live; don't live to eat."

Questions to Ask Yourself When Selecting Foods

When you select foods, you should first consider your body type. Then ask yourself the following questions:

1. What type of food does my body generally crave? What type of food gives me the most satisfaction, physically and mentally? Why? For example, why would I crave burgers or ice cream?

2. What foods are most or least beneficial to my body type? How can I modify my dietary habits to enhance my constitution and my overall sense of well being?

3. After eating, carefully note how your body responds to those foods. Generally, if you eat certain foods and feel full, uncomfortable, dull, bloated, hyperactive, heavy, sleepy, etc., afterward, then those foods may not match your body type. Also, remember to check out the ingredients and the way that the food is prepared.

4. Last but most important, trust your body. Let your natural instinct be your guide rather than overly rationalizing about your dietary needs.

Diets for Your Body Type

By eating foods appropriate to our body type, we regulate and balance our internal organs. Those organs in a state of excess are suppressed, and those organs in a state of deficiency are strengthened. This creates an overall Yin-Yang balance within the body.

In Sasang nutrition, the main area of concern is the Yin and Yang nature of various foods and its interaction with an individual's constitution. Simply stated, a Yang body type should consume Yin-type foods, and a Yin body type should consume Yang-type foods. For example, Shaoyins generally have a cold constitution, so they need warmer foods. Shaoyangs, on the other hand, have a hot constitution, so they require cooler foods.

Sasang nutrition considers the taste and temperature of foods to be the most important factors to keep in mind when selecting an appropriate diet. Take, for example, beef, chicken, and pork. When analyzed quantitatively, chicken has the highest percentage of protein, then beef, and finally pork. In Sasang nutrition, the overall thermal natures of these meats are considered: chicken is considered to be the hottest, pork is the coldest, and beef is neutral to warm. Thus, chicken is best for Shaoyins, pork is best for Shaoyangs, and beef is best for Taiyins.

Remember that these are not fixed rules. Try to gradually incorporate foods that match your body type into your daily dietary regimen. The more unbalanced or sick you are, the more attention you should pay to correcting your diet. As long as you keep a Middle Path approach to your diet, you will be fine.

Taiyangs

Appropriate foods

- ☯ Grains/legumes: buckwheat.
- ☯ Meat/Poultry: none.
- ☯ Sea foods: shellfish (oyster, abalone, mussel, wreath shell), crabs, mackerel, sea cucumber, sea squirt, prussian carp, small octopus, octopus, squid.
- ☯ Vegetables: celery, pine needles, Chinese cabbage, cucumber, lettuce, burdock root.
- ☯ Fruits: grapes, wild grapes, persimmons, cherries, Chinese quince, pine pollen, kiwi.

Inappropriate foods

- ☯ Avoid or reduce hot and stimulating spices and foods such as red and black pepper, ginger (both fresh and dried), onion, cinnamon, garlic, fennel, green onion, chives, turmeric, mustard, etc. Also avoid all meats and poultry, greasy foods, honey, ginseng, hard liquor, and coffee.

General guidelines

- ☯ Taiyangs should avoid high-calorie, high-fat, high-protein, or highly concentrated foods, such as protein powder supplements. Taiyangs have difficulty gathering, absorbing, and storing energy due to their weak Livers, so they are not able to properly extract and assimilate nutrients from these foods. Also, all of these foods can build up heat in the body that is detrimental to Taiyangs' health. They should also carefully limit alcohol intake because alcohol builds heat. Taiyangs have an urgent nature, and any foods that build heat can exacerbate this mental tendency.
- ☯ Taiyangs should avoid stimulating, greasy foods. Any excessive amount of meat or poultry, as well as fried, broiled, or grilled foods must be avoided. In addition, hot and spicy foods should be eliminated from the diet.

❧ In general, Taiyangs tend to have difficulty keeping foods down, again due to weak Livers. Eating an excessive amount of meat will usually result in digestive upset, causing symptoms such as nausea or vomiting. The addition of alcohol to such meals only exacerbates the problem by making it even more difficult to swallow foods down or by causing an almost immediate, violent rejection of the meal. If this sort of eating pattern persists, then the Taiyang stomach will weaken, and emaciation may result.

❧ Energy in Taiyangs tends to move most rapidly in an upward direction. To counter this, Taiyangs need to eat foods that can help them to remain calm. They should favor foods that are bland or plain, and that can nourish the Liver and the Yin aspects of the body. Certain seafood, fruits, and green vegetables are especially well suited for Taiyangs.

Shaoyangs

Appropriate foods

❧ Grains/legumes: barley, aduki beans, mung beans, kidney beans.

❧ Meat/poultry: pork, duck, egg.

❧ Sea foods: oyster, sea cucumber, sea squirt, abalone, halibut, squid, small octopus, octopus, crab, crayfish, swellfish, mackerel, mussel, soft-shelled turtle, snake fish, flatfish.

❧ Vegetables: Chinese cabbage, cucumber, lettuce, burdock root, eggplant, spinach, celery, hops.

❧ Fruits: musk melon, strawberries, raspberries, blackberries, blueberries, bananas, coconut, cantaloupe, pineapple, persimmon, avocados.

❧ Others: Ling Zhi mushroom, peppermint.

Inappropriate foods

❧ Avoid or reduce hot, stimulating spices and foods like red and black pepper, ginger (both fresh and dried), onion, cinnamon, garlic, fennel, green onion, turmeric, mustard, etc. Other inappropriate foods include chicken, turkey, lamb, honey, ginseng, hard liquor, wine, and coffee.

General guidelines

☙ Shaoyangs have a Yang (heat) constitution like Taiyangs, so foods that are hot and/or spicy such as chicken, lamb, and various spices are not recommended for them. Also, foods that have been treated by fire (heated or boiled) should be reduced. Most illnesses and health problems in Shaoyangs are caused by excessive heat that in turn causes Yin deficiency. Therefore, foods that are cool, cold, or bland, or that nourish the Yin are especially good for them. Fruits and leafy or stalk/stem vegetables should be eaten in large quantities. Fish and shellfish are also beneficial.

☙ Because Shaoyangs have a strong digestive "fire" or metabolism, they usually have no problems with appetite or digestion. They are able to eat a large quantity and a wide variety of foods without gaining much weight. However, although their digestive system is continually hyperactive, their eliminating function is weak, causing them to become easily constipated. Consuming fiber-rich, cooling vegetables and fruits, and reducing fried and spicy foods will alleviate and improve this condition.

☙ Unlike Taiyangs, who cannot tolerate greasy foods, Shaoyangs can ingest greasy foods without much difficulty. However, since oils tend to build up heat in the body, moderation is essential.

☙ Because most problems in Shaoyangs stem from heat or fire, they should avoid honey, coffee, and other stimulants. Coffee can easily excite Shaoyangs, making them nervous. They may also experience palpitations, insomnia, acid indigestion, or a "high" feeling, as if intoxicated.

☙ When mentally stressed, Shaoyangs easily become flushed and restless, experiencing such symptoms as chest congestion and insomnia. At such times, eating something cool and nourishing to aid the Yin aspect of the body, like bananas or strawberries, will help to calm them down. Also, peppermint, green, or cassia-seed teas are great for soothing the agitated nerves of Shaoyangs (see Chapter 8).

☙ Hot, spicy, stimulating foods can easily cause acid indigestion, and, at times, diarrhea (instead of the usual constipation) in the Shaoyang constitution. Although young, healthy Shaoyangs are able to eat hot, spicy foods, such as mustard, chili peppers, or hot sauces without much difficulty, older Shaoyangs should reduce or avoid them.

Taiyins

Appropriate foods

- ☯ Grains/legumes: wheat, brown rice, oats, soybeans, tofu, millet, Job's tears, lentils, beans, peas, peanuts.
- ☯ Meat/poultry/dairy: beef, butter, cheese, yogurt, and cow's milk. If you are vegetarian, you can omit all the food in this group.
- ☯ Sea foods: agar-agar, algae, brown seaweed, carp, cod, eel, fish liver oil, kelp, laver, salmon, sea hair-tail, spawn of a pollack, tuna, other sea weeds and marine products.
- ☯ Vegetables: alfalfa sprouts, asparagus, bamboo shoots, bean sprouts, bracken, broad bellflower, broccoli, carrots, cauliflower, dandelion, lotus root, mushrooms (all types except Ling Zhi), pumpkin, radish, squash, sweet potatoes, taro, tomatoes, turnips, yams.
- ☯ Fruits/nuts: almonds, apricots, cantaloupes, chestnuts, gingko nuts, honeydew melons, mangoes, papayas, pears, pine nuts, pistachios, plums, umeboshi salt plums, walnuts, watermelon. All types of nuts are good for Taiyins.

Inappropriate foods

- ☯ Foods or supplements that build excessive heat, such as chicken or chicken soup, mutton, ginseng, or honey, should be avoided, as they can dry up essential fluids and ignite the stagnant substances within Taiyins. Pork is also not recommended.

General guidelines

- ☯ Taiyins are born with a strong digestive system. They can eat just about anything without much difficulty. They are also able to absorb and detoxify a variety of harmful substances, due to the strength of their digestive system. Unfortunately, these abilities often cause Taiyins to grow overconfident, leading to dietary abuses. They have increased affinity for alcoholic beverages, coffee, and cigarettes. The consequences of these abuses may not be immediately apparent, but they begin to take their toll as Taiyins grow older and their bodies weaken.

☯ Because their cast-iron digestive system allows them to enjoy both wide varieties and large quantities of food, many Taiyins easily become over-weight. When under stress, Taiyins eat constantly, without experiencing the feeling of fullness common in the other constitutions. It is not uncommon for a Taiyin to gain several pounds a day. Being overweight can easily lead to fatigue because Taiyins do not have enough energy to properly sustain themselves. As digestion requires even more energy, having a meal can cause even more fatigue. Taiyins tend to rest by lying down after meals, a position that promotes further weight gain. To begin to lose weight, Taiyins should restrict their intake of processed sugar and rich, salty foods. An excessive intake of salt, of course, can easily lead to fluid retention in Taiyins.

☯ Whether consuming foods or herbal supplements, Taiyins should always follow a two-pronged, somewhat paradoxical approach. This involves eating foods to help eliminate dampness, excess accumulation of "improper water," while simultaneously consuming foods that help to moisten the body, especially the Lungs. In actuality, there are two kinds of water. Turbid or unclear water (dampness) must be eliminated from the body because it cannot be metabolized and used for physiological functioning; pure or clear water, on the other hand, is needed by the body to moisten tissues and body organs, especially the constitutionally weak Lungs of the Taiyin. Taiyins should also try to improve their overall circulation and watch out for obesity. These are the key elements by which Taiyins can maintain health in daily life.

☯ For Taiyins, it is best not to eat foods that are extremely cold or extremely hot. Because Taiyins tend to have sluggish Qi and blood circulation, it is important that they consume foods that spread the energy throughout the body and promote sweating. Foods that help to promote bowel movement and urination are also a must for Taiyins.

☯ Due to their weak circulatory system, Taiyins tend to suffer from hypertension, stroke, heart attacks, and edema more than any other constitution. Therefore, foods that are known to cause these disorders should be avoided.

☯ Root vegetables are good for Taiyins, and radishes are one of the best root vegetables that may be ingested in large amounts. Radishes will help to tone up the Taiyins' digestive and respiratory systems, and can also rid the body of excessive phlegm and body weight. For Taiyins, eating radishes frequently can help them to avoid the common cold, flu, and other respiratory infections.

🌀 For palpitations and/or a stuffy feeling in the chest, Taiyins should try eating lotus root or taking powdered lotus seed as a tea, as they can nourish their mind and help calm them down. Taiyins tend to have weak respiratory systems, but by eating fruits like pears, plums, and apricots, and nuts such as gingko and walnut, they can strengthen these deficiencies. Although it is not used as a food here in the United States, broad bellflower or balloon flower (platycodon) root is one of the best foods for strengthening the weak lungs of Taiyins. In Korea, it is frequently used as a vegetable side dish. You can purchase broad bellflower at a local Asian market or herb shop, and eat it steamed.

🌀 All varieties of nuts are good for Taiyins. It would seem at first glance that Taiyins should avoid nuts since they are high in calories and oily in nature. In reality, however, they are actually high in protein and contain essential fatty acids (unsaturated fatty acids) that are missing in meat and dairy products. Nuts will actually help Taiyins with the dispersing of energy and moistening of dryness.

🌀 Although Taiyins enjoy eating a variety of meats, the best for them is beef. Its sweet taste and neutral to warm thermal nature can strengthen their energy and blood, while mitigating the dryness that occurs inside the body, especially in the Lungs. Nevertheless, the ingestion of beef should be balanced with foods from other groups and not be the sole basis of their diet.

🌀 Other foods that are excellent for Taiyins are marine products—fish, seafood, and sea vegetables.

Shaoyins

Appropriate foods

🌀 Grains: glutinous rice, rice, hulled millet, glutinous millet.

🌀 Meat/poultry/dairy: chicken, turkey, mutton, goat's milk.

🌀 Sea foods: Alaskan pollack, catfish, cod, eel, red snapper, yellow corvina, sea hair-tail, anchovy, croaker, loach, tuna.

🌀 Vegetables: potatoes, cabbage, crown daisy, carrots, onion, garlic, ginger, leek, scallion, red pepper, green pepper, black pepper, mustard, tomatoes.

🌀 Fruits: apples, oranges, Mandarin oranges, tangerines, lemons, peaches, dates, mangoes, nectarines, pomegranates, hawthorn berry.

🌀 Others: honey, ketchup, royal jelly, bee pollen, ginseng, cocoa.

Inappropriate foods

    ☙ Shaoyins should reduce or avoid foods that are either cold or damp-producing. Aduki beans, bananas, barley, beer, buckwheat, chestnut, Chinese cabbage, cold milk, green beans, ice cream, musk melon, pear, persimmons, pork, squid, walnut, watermelon, and wheat products, especially noodles, all fall under these categories.

General guidelines

☙ Shaoyins have a highly developed sense of taste, and with good reason. Of the four constitutions, they have one of the weakest digestive systems. Thus, it is important that they eat their foods slowly and selectively. If they obey their bodily cravings, they tend to instinctively know what types of foods are good for them. They usually remember any foods that they disliked or that may have given them problems, such as an upset stomach or diarrhea. As a general rule, they should avoid eating foods that are either cold in temperature or difficult to digest, such as pork, wheat products, unripe fruits, or cold milk. They should also restrict the quantity and variety of food that they eat in one sitting.

☙ It is absolutely imperative that Shaoyins remain calm during meal times. Emotional excitation of any kind can easily upset their entire digestive system.

☙ Due to their weak digestive system and generally cold body, cold foods and drinks such as raw salads, cold sandwiches, ice cream, yogurt, sodas, or beer will easily cause diarrhea and abdominal pain in Shaoyins. Cold fruits, especially those common in the summertime, such as watermelons and cantaloupes, will create similar problems. Cold foods require a greater expenditure of calories (heat) in order to raise them to body temperature, where digestion may occur. Thus, it is best for Shaoyins to eat well-cooked, soft foods that are easily digested. Also, it is a good idea for them to sip warm water with meals rather than drinking ice water or cold beverages of any kind. Hot, hearty soups are better than cold, raw salads for them.

☙ Shaoyins must be especially careful about drinking cold beverages and foods in the summertime. In hot weather, the external part of the body becomes much warmer, while the inside becomes much colder. This occurs in order to balance the overall temperature of the body.

Shaoyins, who are already internally cold by nature, will suffer from digestive disturbances if they ingest cold drinks or foods in hot weather.

☯ Foods that are cool or cold in nature may be cooked, stir fried, roasted, baked, steamed, sautéed, etc. in order to heat them up and assist the digestive processes of Shaoyins. Fruits, meanwhile, should be cooked or dried and eaten in moderate amounts. Consumption of cold fruits like bananas, persimmons, and kiwis should definitely be limited.

☯ The majority of available spices and flavorings are excellent for Shaoyins because they help to stimulate digestive juices, facilitate digestion, and warm up the body. One of the most important spices for Shaoyins is ginger, which can be used raw or dried. Ginger not only facilitates digestion, but also warms up the entire body. Cinnamon is another spice that may be used frequently by Shaoyins, along with fennel, nutmeg, cardamom, and black peppers. One word of caution is necessary, however: Shaoyins should not overindulge in the usage of spices, as anything in excess will overstimulate their delicate digestive system, resulting in diarrhea, foul-smelling stools, and/or abdominal pain.

Chapter 8

Teas

Thank God for tea! What would the world do without tea?
How did it exist? I am glad I was not born before tea.
—Sidney Smith

Many people drink tea for its taste. Some people prefer sweet teas, some prefer bitter teas, and some prefer a more savory taste. Whatever your preference may be, it is best that you follow it. Through this preference, your body is letting you know what it needs to maintain, regulate, and heal itself. You should, however, couple your basic instincts with an understanding of the action the tea will have on your health because you should drink tea in accordance with your body type.

Sasang Medicine traditionally integrates teas into its treatment regimens. As tea is such a common and accessible drink around the world, it is ideal as a medium for the promotion of balance, health, and longevity.

Many of the teas mentioned in this chapter may be found at your local supermarket or health food store. Others need to be purchased at an Asian market or herb shop.

There are several ways to prepare tea. The simplest way involves placing the herb in a cup, filling the cup with hot water, and allowing it to steep for 10 to 20 minutes. The same herb may be reused one to two more times.

A stronger tea may be prepared by adding roots, fruits, or seeds (with dosages indicated in this chapter) to one and a half cups of water, then boiling the water down to one cup. Start with the minimum indicated dosage, increasing gradually according to your taste and condition. Drink two to three cups of this tea per day, or as recommended by your physician or herbal practitioner.

Taiyang

Teas for Taiyangs: Chinese quince
                      Acanthopanax root bark
                      Pine needles

Chinese quince

Also known as chaenomelas fruit, this herb has a sour taste and a slightly warm temperature. This herb concentrates its action on the Liver and the Stomach, and is especially effective when a Taiyang person is tired or has no desire to work or play. It is one of the best herbs to stop vomiting (a serious condition for Taiyangs). It can also treat other digestive complaints, such as abdominal pain, indigestion, and diarrhea. Another major function of Chinese quince is to strengthen tendons and bones, especially in the lower body. Thus, it can benefit Taiyangs, who easily develop weaknesses in their lower back and legs. In addition to its strengthening effect, Chinese quince is also known for its ability to relax the tendons and other connective tissues, so it is used to stop neuralgia, rheumatic pain, and cramps in the calf. Dosage: 5 to 12 grams.

Acanthopanax root bark

Acanthopanax is a root bark that has a pungent and bitter taste and a warm temperature. It strengthens the Liver and Kidneys, organ systems that tend to be weak in Taiyangs. It also strengthens the muscles, bones, and tendons, particularly in the lower back and legs. It dispels rheumatic arthritis and is an excellent herb for the elderly and for children who experience difficulty in lower body movements. This herb is also a diuretic that can eliminate edema and ease difficulties in urination (remember that frequent lengthy urination is great for Taiyangs). Dosage: 5 to 15 grams.

Pine needles

This famous tea is said to have been used by the immortals of the East. It is said to regulate and harmonize all the internal organs. It has been traditionally used for people suffering from stress, insomnia, and a stuffy feeling in the chest. It is helpful for people suffering from hypertension, edema, scurvy, hair loss, arthritis, and skin disorders such as tinea and scabies. It is also commonly used for epidemic encephalitis, flu, chronic tracheitis, and the prevention of stroke. Taiyangs can benefit from regular ingestion of this herb as it helps to strengthen the bones and the legs while promoting urination.

Another part of the pine tree, called knotty pinewood, is commonly used for treating leg weakness in Taiyangs. It is indicated for arthritis, rheumatic pain, and traumatic injury. Dosage: 12 to 20 grams for pine needles and 9 to 15 grams for knotty pinewood.

Shaoyang

Teas for Shaoyangs: Peppermint
Barley
Green tea

Peppermint

This herb is pungent in taste and cool in temperature. It also possesses an aromatic quality. It is typically used for common colds and influenza and is very good for sore throats, red eyes, and headaches. It is also used to treat skin problems like rashes and measles. Peppermint eliminates stagnation in the Liver (a common syndrome in Eastern medicine), which manifests with such symptoms as irascibility, pain in the chest or flanks, and gynecological problems like PMS. Remember that Shaoyangs have a lot of heat in the upper body, particularly in the Stomach and chest regions. Thus, this herb is excellent for Shaoyangs because it is effective in clearing excessive heat in the Stomach, chest, and head regions. Dosage: 2 to 10 grams.

Barley (ungerminated)

Barley is sweet in taste and cool in temperature. Because of its high fiber content and cool temperature, barley can help people suffering from constipation, particularly Shaoyangs, who are prone to this condition. It can help stop thirst and induce urination. Barley tea may be taken hot or cold depending on the weather. It is one of the most frequently consumed beverages in Korea, and is especially good for the Shaoyang type. Dosage: 5 to 15 grams.

Green tea

Green tea is made from the unfermented, "unsweated" leaf of the tea plant. It is an excellent substitute for coffee. The caffeine found in green tea, called theophylline, is milder than that found in coffee, allowing you to sleep at night. Green tea is also nearly impossible to get addicted to, unlike coffee. Green tea improves overall bodily metabolism, relieves fatigue, and improves concentration and memory. People who are under emotional stress or who are involved in heavy study can drink green tea to help them settle down, relax, and focus. According to recent scientific research, green tea also helps to lower cholesterol, control hypertension and diabetes, and improve the metabolism of fat. Regular consumption of green tea may thus help to counter the effects of greasy, fatty foods. In addition, researchers have discovered a compound in green tea called ECGC, which can inhibit the breakdown of healthy tissue. ECGC also has an anti-tumor effect and thus helps in cancer prevention. Green tea's slightly bitter taste, cool temperature, and descending, calming properties make it excellent for Shaoyang types. Taiyins may also drink this tea to benefit, as it may help them to lose excess weight. Dosage: two cups daily.

Taiyin

Teas for Taiyins: Job's tears (coix seed)
Kudzu (pueraria root)
Schizandra fruit

Job's tears or coix seed

This seed has a sweet, bland taste and a cool temperature. It is an excellent herb for removing excessive water in Taiyins, and can help to treat edema, ascites, or difficult urination. It is also effective for strengthening the digestive system and eliminating food stagnation. It can also strengthen the Lungs, which tend to be weak in Taiyins. As a general tonic, it greatly aids in the recovery from fatigue. Specific uses for this herb include treatment of such conditions as beriberi, diarrhea, neuralgia, rheumatic arthritis, and diabetes. It is also effective for tinea of the foot and abscesses in the lungs or intestines. When taken for a long time, it has a beautifying effect, and can reduce freckles, liver spots, and pimples. Dosage: 5 to 15 grams.

Kudzu or pueraria root

This herb has a sweet, pungent taste and a cool temperature. It is commonly used in the treatment of colds and flu. It is excellent for hangovers, headaches, and stiffness and pain in the neck and shoulders. It is also very good for building up essential fluids, thus, it is appropriate for Taiyins, who tend toward internal dryness, especially in their Lungs. This herb can also induce sweating, important for maintaining health and balance in Taiyins. Kudzu can also effectively treat the constipation that many Taiyins suffer from. Kudzu tea is used in the treatment of diabetes, hypertension, heart disease, and measles, among other things. Dosage: 10 to 20 grams.

Schizandra fruit

This herb contains all five flavors, as its Chinese name, Wu Wei Zi ("a seed with five flavors"), implies. Its main flavor is sour, and it has a warm temperature. Schizandra increases energy and vitality and helps to stop excessive sweating and seminal emission. In addition, schizandra contains substances that stimulate the brain waves, ridding the mind of sleepiness and memory loss, especially when due to excess exertion. It also strengthens weakened eyesight, and is an excellent herb for people who work late into the night, or for students studying late for their exams. According to Sasang Medicine, this herb targets the Lungs (which are constitutionally weak in Taiyin types), strengthening and moistening them. Another beneficial effect for Taiyins is schizandra's spirit-calming effect. On the whole, schizandra is used for a variety of symptoms and diseases, including cough, asthma, thirst, excessive sweating, palpitation, insomnia, dream-disturbed sleep, chronic diarrhea, diabetes, neurasthenia, forgetfulness, and summer heat. Dosage: 5 to 15 grams.

Shaoyin

Teas for Shaoyins: Ginseng
                       Ginger (fresh or dried)
                       Cinnamon (bark or twig)

Ginseng (Asian ginseng)

This root is sweet and slightly bitter, with a slightly warm temperature. Its main effect lies in strengthening the Qi of the whole body, especially that of the digestive and respiratory systems. Ginseng soothes and
calms the mind, and acts to lower physiological stress. It also has a profound effect on the endocrine system. Ginseng reduces cholesterol and
can prevent and help treat both high and low blood pressure and diabetes.
It also works well for neuralgia, rheumatism, and arthritic conditions. Ginseng is an excellent herb for aiding the recovery from fatigue. According
to recent research, it can also prevent and treat many types of cancers.

(Note, however, that although ginseng can treat high blood pressure,
it is inadvisable to take it if your systolic pressure is over 180 mmHg. Also,
avoid ginseng if you are of an excess-type constitution with such heat signs
as fever, thirst, irritability, restlessness, flushed face, red eyes, coarse breathing, skin rashes and dark urine. Consult with your practitioner if you notice any of the above symptoms, or if you develop others like insomnia or
heart palpitations after ingesting ginseng.)

Ginseng is the best and most important herb for Shaoyins because it
can strengthen the Qi of the whole body, particularly that of the Spleen—
the weak organ system of Shaoyins. See the next section for further details
on this important herb. Dosage: 3 to 9 grams. Note: for Shaoyins, a combination of ginseng, dates, ginger, and honey in a tea makes a superb tonic
for the whole body.

Ginger (fresh or dried)

This commonly used culinary herb has a pungent taste and a warm
temperature. It helps to warm up the whole body and improve circulation
and metabolism. Ginger concentrates its action on the digestive system,
where it improves overall digestion, and stops vomiting, diarrhea, abdominal fullness, and pain. These actions make it particularly appropriate for
Shaoyins, who tend to have weak digestive systems (Spleen) and who tend

to be cold and lacking in energy. Ginger may also help people with low blood pressure and can help in the prevention and treatment of common colds and vaginal discharge. Ginger is commonly used in cooking to detoxify many types of seafood. Anyone who eats sushi regularly is familiar with pickled ginger, which serves to offset the nature of the cold, raw foods and aid in digestion.

Dried ginger is warmer than fresh ginger, and has the additional function of reviving a person suffering from shock or collapse with such symptoms as extreme coldness in the abdomen and limbs. Do not use dried ginger if you are pregnant. Dosage: 3 to 9 grams for both fresh and dried ginger.

Cinnamon (bark and twig)

Cinnamon bark has a pungent, sweet flavor and a hot temperature. It is one of the best herbs for Shaoyins because its warming nature can balance the cold nature of the Shaoyin constitution. The major action of cinnamon lies in its ability to warm and strengthen the Yang energy of the whole body, especially in the digestive system. It can effectively treat digestive complaints such as a loss of appetite, vomiting, and diarrhea. Since cinnamon warms up the entire body, it can help those with cold limbs, edema, excess watery or white phlegm, and difficult urination. Pains due to cold, including stomach, hypochondriac, or menstrual pain, are effectively treated with this herb. Cinnamon bark may also be used for resuscitation.

Cinnamon twig is less warming than the bark, and does not affect the digestive system much. However, it is able to improve the blood and energy circulation throughout the body. It is used for a wide array of symptoms, ranging from common colds (due to its mild sweat inducing action), palpitations, and edema, to various pains, including chest pain, painful urination, and arthritic pain. It is also commonly used in the treatment of such gynecological conditions as absence of menstruation, irregular and painful menstruation, fibroid tumors, and ovarian cysts.

For Shaoyins, drinking hot cinnamon tea can help prevent colds. Use 5 grams of bark or 15 grams of twig with five to 10 dates and three grams of fresh ginger. Decoct in two cups of water down to one cup. You can add some honey or other sweeteners. Do not use cinnamon bark or twig if you are pregnant. Dosage: 2 to 5 grams for bark and 3 to 15 grams for twig.

Asian vs. American Ginseng: Which Is Right for You?

The pharmaceutical name for ginseng is panax ginseng. The word panax means cure-all, from the Latin word panacea. Ginseng, meanwhile, can be translated as "the human plant," as its appearance resembles that of a human. It has also been called "the essence of man" or "the dose of immortality." As these names suggest, ginseng promotes longevity. Ancient Eastern folk tales attribute immortality to wild ginseng roots in particular, which explains why they often cost tens of thousands of dollars. Wild ginseng is considered so precious that emperors of the East have been known to pay fortunes to acquire it.

Today, ginseng is the most commonly used herb in the world. Although several varieties of ginseng exist, they can be mainly divided into Asian and American categories. Among the Asian types of ginseng, there are Korean and Chinese varieties, which can be further divided into red ginseng (steamed) and white ginseng (dried). Herbs considered to be milder forms of ginseng, though they are not from the same family, include codonopsis root (Dang Shen) and pseudo-stellaria root (Tai Zi Shen).

(Note: There is another variety of ginseng called Siberian ginseng [eleutherococcus senticosus], a relatively recent discovery by Soviet scientists, that belongs to a genus in the ginseng family, but is of a different strain than panax. It is also an adaptagen and is used to increase overall energy, strengthen both digestive and circulatory systems, and calm the nerves. Indications for this herb include stress, poor appetite, impotence, bronchitis, chronic lung ailments, arthritis, lower back pain, and knee pain. Siberian ginseng is considered to be one of the best herbs for insomnia. A modern Western medical study has shown that it lowers blood pressure and cholesterol levels.)

Historically, ginseng has been used as a sexual stimulant, and in Asia is considered the number one aphrodisiac, as well as an overall body tonic. According to traditional and modern research, ginseng does not just improve sexual performance. It also strengthens vital energy, calms the mind and nerves, tones the skin and muscles, clears the eyes, improves memory, increases tolerance to a variety of stresses, and strengthens the function of visceral organs, particularly the Lungs and the Spleen. In all, ginseng strengthens the digestive, respiratory, genito-urinary, and cardiovascular systems, affecting the endocrine and immune systems as well. Because its effects are all encompassing, ginseng is especially well suited for people who are weak, debilitated, and in convalescence. Taken over a period of time, it can be of tremendous benefit to the whole body.

American ginseng (panax quinquefolius), which is grown in the hardwood forests of northeastern North America, is said to have been discovered by Jesuit missionaries in the 1700s. Since 1715, it has been harvested and exported to all areas of the world, especially Asia. Although both Asian and American ginseng are Qi tonics and both help to build up body fluids, American ginseng is more cooling in nature, and so benefits the Yin aspect of the body more. Like its Asian counterpart, it extends endurance, boosts the immune system, and reduces stress. It also helps to synchronize and harmonize the functions of all the internal organs, thus relieving undue internal stress.

Western medicine categorizes all varieties of ginseng as adaptogens, substances that normalize bodily function by making the body more efficient at utilizing other substances and eliminating toxins. Therefore, all varieties of ginseng are considered relatively safe for people of all ages.

Although both Asian and American ginseng are effective in treating a variety of ailments, Sasang Medicine incorporates the important factor of body type into the use of ginseng. Korean and Chinese ginseng, especially the red types, are more appropriate for the Shaoyin constitution. Because Shaoyins lack Yang energy, the strong Yang action of the Korean and Chinese ginseng is well suited for them. Codonopsis and pseudostellaria are also suitable for Shaoyins, as both herbs focus on strengthening the Qi of the Spleen or the digestive system. They can be beneficial to Taiyin body types as well due to their abilities to produce fluids and strengthen the Lungs.

All forms of ginseng, especially the Korean and Chinese varieties, are ill suited for Shaoyangs because they strengthen the Qi or Yang energy of the digestive system. Remember that Shaoyangs generally do not lack Yang energy in this area. If Shaoyangs were to take ginseng, they might suffer from some of the following side effects: irritability, insomnia, red eyes, palpitations, flushed face, overall flushed feeling, skin rashes, and headaches. These side effects result from excessive heat buildup. Taiyins may also notice some of these symptoms when taking Korean or Chinese varieties of ginseng. If any of these symptoms arise, then American ginseng or other herbs more appropriate for the constitution should be used.

For Taiyins, there is another type of Shen herb (ginseng in Chinese is called Ren Shen) that does not belong to the ginseng family. It is called Sha Shen (Dud Duk in Korean), or glenia root, and is commonly eaten in Korea as a vegetable side dish. It is a Yin tonic that strengthens and harmonizes the Lungs, benefits the Stomach, and produces fluids. It is commonly used for dry or chronic cough, and for convalescence, especially after a fever-producing disease. Glenia root is most appropriate for Taiyins because it strengthens their weak Lungs without drying up the interior of the body. Remember that Taiyins easily experience dryness in the interior of the body even though they retain excessive water.

For Taiyangs, no variety of ginseng is satisfactory.

The following chart lists the various types of ginseng commonly used, as well as the herbs that are similar to them in name or in actions, and the type of constitution they are appropriate for.

Herb	Taste & Temperature	General Function	Body Type
White ginseng (Ren Shen)	Sweet, slightly bitter, slightly warm	General Qi tonic	Shaoyin
Red ginseng (Hong Shen)	Sweet, slightly bitter, very warm	Strong Qi tonic	Shaoyin
American ginseng (Si Yang Shen)	Sweet, slightly bitter, cool	Qi and Yin tonic	Shaoyin Taiyin
Codonopsis root (Dang Shen)	Sweet, neutral	Mild Qi tonic	Shaoyin Taiyin
Pseudo-stellaria root(Tai Zi Shen)	Sweet, slightly bitter, neutral	Mild Qi tonic	Shaoyin Taiyin
Glenia root (Sha Shen)	Sweet, cool	Yin tonic	Taiyin

The usage of ginseng does not depend on whether you are a man or woman. Rather, it depends on your body type and the condition that you are trying to treat. These factors will determine the type and the dosage that a person should take.

To demonstrate the power of ginseng for the Shaoyin constitution, I would like to present the following case study related to me by Dr. David Lee, a senior colleague of mine:

While interning at a major university hospital in Korea, Dr. Lee met a 25-year-old woman who had been hospitalized for anorexia nervosa. In order to lose weight, this patient had bought commercial diet pills. After taking these pills, she began to have serious bouts of diarrhea, which made her lose a considerable amount of weight. Although she was 5'7" tall, at the time of her hospitalization, she only weighed 77 pounds. Dr. Lee said that she was so thin, fragile, and emaciated that she resembled a mummy more than a human being. She had no flesh on her skull-like face, and her hipbones stuck out noticeably, since there was absolutely no flesh in her waist and hips. It seemed as though she was just a skeleton, with thin skin stretched over her bones.

Diet pills are very damaging to the stomach and intestines, as they reduce the appetite, stop nutrient absorption, and create diarrhea. Those with strong digestive systems, such as Taiyins or Shaoyangs, generally have no problem with taking such pills. Shaoyins, however, have a constitutional weakness in their digestive system, so such pills take a tremendous toll on their bodies. For this Shaoyin patient with anorexia nervosa, who could neither eat (even if she desired to do so), nor digest and absorb food even if she managed to eat, diet pills aggravated an already serious imbalance, leading her to the gate of death.

Though the hospital in which Dr. Lee did his clinical observation was one of the most advanced in the country, with access to the latest in medical equipment and drugs, there was little that the Western doctors could do for this patient. She was given antidepressants and appetite stimulants intravenously. Still, she could not eat. The doctors then decided to feed her canned nutritional supplements through a feeding tube, but she still could neither digest nor assimilate any nutrients, as her digestive system was extremely weak. Her weight continued to drop, and she began to have convulsions due to the sudden drop in her blood sodium level (which occurred despite the fact that she received sufficient amounts of electrolytes intravenously).

The prognosis for patients with severe anorexia nervosa is generally not good. One study reported that 25 percent of patients afflicted with this grave disorder die of "sudden death syndrome" due to electrolyte imbalance in their blood.

The director of the hospital told the patient's parents that there was not much more that could be done, advising them to take her home once her condition stabilized. But her parents could not take her home. The hospital staff was at a loss because they simply did not know what to do with her.

Dr. Lee had recently finished Western medical school (he was already a doctor of Oriental medicine), and was observing as a Western medical intern. But he could not stand idly by. In Korea, when someone is very thin and weak, they are usually advised to take tonic herbal formulas to help increase their appetite and allow them to gain weight. Knowing this well, many teenage girls don't take these formulas, because they do not want to gain weight.

Dr. Lee managed to convince the hospital doctors of the efficacy of tonic herbs. Dr. Lee told the residents that he would convince her parents and give her ginseng (which can strengthen the digestive system of Shaoyins) through the feeding tube. As per Dr. Lee's instruction, her parents made a decoction of several ginseng roots at home and brought it to the hospital. Dr. Lee administered three doses of the decoction per day through the tube. After one day of administering the ginseng, the patient's state of mind became clear and her eyes became bright. She repeatedly said that she wanted to eat some food. When she was given yogurt, she ate it without any hesitation. A little later she was given some rice porridge, which she had no problem eating. Several hours later, she actually tried some solid food. The chief physician was full of smiles, and said, "In the future, when we have any patient with anorexia nervosa, I will personally advise them to take ginseng." A month later, the patient was released from the hospital, in normal health.

Chapter 9

Exercise, Meditation, and Qi Gong

Gather your Qi and make it soft; can you be like a baby?
—Lao Tzu

The sage breathes with his heels;
the commoners breathe with their throats.
—Chuang Tzu, Taoist philosopher

The journey toward optimal health requires more than looking at a map. We must walk the walk. In other words, we must actualize ourselves and our journey through real physical motion. It is not enough for us to maintain a healthy diet or drink herbal teas as though we were plants, needing only a few basics to grow. On the contrary, movement is one of the most important tools in balancing our Yin-Yang energies.

Exercise is vital, because we are dynamic creatures. We need to move because we were made to move. If we do not, then we not only deny ourselves the benefit and pleasure of movement, but we actually encourage our own stagnation, decay, and destruction. An old adage clearly expresses this idea: "A used door never squeaks and running water never goes stale." If we do not use our bodies through exercise, then we are asking for time and disease to have their way with us.

Just as important as the fitness of our bodies is the fitness of our minds and spirits. Thus, the exercises we perform should not only balance out our bodies, but our minds and spirits as well. Meditation and breath control are designed to develop balance between our bodies and minds, and facilitate the cultivation of spirit. Qi Gong (a system of energy cultivation exercises) combines basic movements with breath control.

In this chapter, we will discuss these varied forms of exercise. We begin with general comments concerning physical exercise. Then, we discuss the merits of Qi Gong and meditation (both sitting and standing). The final section provides specific advice for each constitution concerning exercise, including a couple of appropriate Qi Gong exercises. These Qi Gong exercises were adapted from the popular "Eight Brocade Exercises," the introductory series of movements used in most Qi Gong schools.

Please remember that the basic objective of this book is the realization of balance of the Middle Path. Although a given body type may be naturally skilled in certain sports, these will either not be addressed, or addressed incidentally. Instead, emphasis will be given to exercises that address a given constitution's weaknesses and deficiencies, so that individuals may realize well-rounded health.

Physical Exercise-General Comments

Yang types are more dynamic, urgent, active, and restless. They need to slow down a little. Calming and relaxing exercises, like Qi Gong, Tai Chi, and Yoga are ideal for them. The still postures (both sitting and standing) used in meditation and Qi Gong are excellent for them.

Yin types, on the other hand, are more passive, calm, lazy, and inactive. Thus, their exercises should be more dynamic. Between the two Yin types, Taiyins need more intense, heavy, and prolonged physical training, so as to burn off calories and fats and get their metabolism going. They must incorporate a lot of aerobic exercises into their exercise regimen in order to strengthen their weak hearts and lungs. Shaoyins, on the other hand, need to do milder exercises for shorter periods of time, so as not to sweat excessively and damage their frail Yang energy.

Whether you are of a Yin or Yang body type, you need to perform exercises for your entire body. However, as Yin types have less energy going to the upper body, they must focus on doing exercises that develop muscular strength and endurance in the upper body. The opposite is true for Yang types, who need to perform more exercises for their lower bodies.

Breathing Exercises

Don't forget to breathe! Although breathing goes on without our knowing it, our level of relaxation and awareness can determine its quality. The practice of being aware of the breath is therefore vital. Imagine how much gas exchange is lost when we go through just one day breathing shallowly or quickly. Yet many people do just that, day in and day out! Because breathing is so important (and so neglected), we will discuss it in some detail.

Sitting postures

1. Sit on a firm chair close to the edge of the seat (Fig.9.1). This will help to keep your spine aligned. The angle between the torso and legs should be 90 degrees. The bend at the knees should also be 90 degrees. You may also sit on the floor with your legs crossed (as in the lotus position, Fig. 9.3), or kneel with your knees slightly open (approximately two to three fist widths, Fig. 9.4). The important thing is that you keep your posture (your spine) as straight as possible. Keep yourself relaxed; it's important that you not be stiff.

2. Your knees and feet should be two fist widths apart. Toes should point either straight ahead or slightly inward to "lock in" the Qi (Fig. 9.2).

3. Place your hands on your knees. Other hand positions may also be used. One popular method involves crossing your hands with the thumbs interlocked, and placing your hands at the Dan Tian, or Cinnabar Field. This is the main energy center of the body, and is the area located approximately two to three inches below the navel (Fig. 9.5).

4. Relax your elbows and shoulders completely.

5. Align your ears and shoulders, and your nose and navel.

6. Tuck your chin in and imagine that there is a string attached to the top of your head that is pulling your body straight up toward the ceiling.

7. Close your eyes halfway and look either at the tip of your nose or one yard in front of you. Do not cross your eyes or excessively strain them.

8. Touch the tip of your tongue to the roof of your mouth.

9. Try to concentrate on the Dan Tian, the area where it is believed that your mind and body meet. It is the center of your being and the source of your strength, both mental and physical.

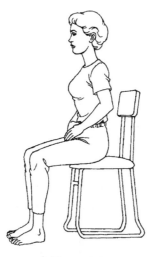

Figure 9.1

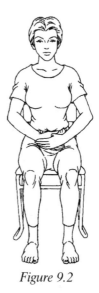

Figure 9.2

Figure 9.3

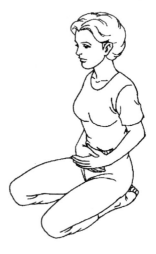

Figure 9.4

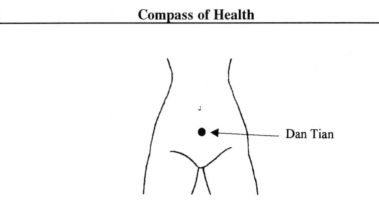

Figure 9.5

Standing posture

1. Stand naturally with your feet slightly wider than shoulder width apart (Fig. 9.6). Keep your toes pointing straight ahead. Keep your knees slightly bent, aligned with your toes to the point where you can just see your big toe. If you have difficulties bending this much then straighten your legs a little more (but the knees must stay bent). Keep your back straight, as in the sitting meditation. This is the horse stance, used extensively in Qi Gong and many forms of martial arts, including Tai Chi. The horse stance can be twice as wide as the shoulder width.

2. Your arms are in front of your chest, bent slightly at the elbows at about two-thirds of the full arm's length. Imagine that you are hugging a tree or a large beach ball (Fig. 9.7). Fingers are loosely held and elbows are slightly bent. Arms and shoulders should be completely relaxed. After a few minutes in this position, you should be able to feel tingling and/or heat sensations in your hands. This is the sensation of Qi being activated.

3. The position of your head, tongue, and chin are the same as in the sitting meditation. Try to ground yourself, feeling your soles pressing deep down into the floor. Concentrate on your Dan Tian. Instead of looking at the tip of your nose or on the ground, look straight ahead, but do not focus your eyes on anything. Simply maintain a relaxed gaze.

4. Practice the following method of breath control in either the sitting or standing meditation posture.

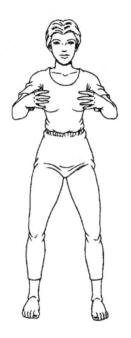

Figure 9.6   *Figure 9.7*

Breath control

By regulating the depth and speed of the breath, one increases the efficiency of the breathing process. Oxygen intake is increased, providing more energy to power the body's vital processes. The benefits of proper breathing are not limited to metabolic functions, however. Through proper breath control, you can control your Qi and your mind. As the breath and Qi are tied to the spirit, when you regulate your breath, you are actually manifesting your true Self. If breath is likened to a thread, then the Self is a tapestry. The manner and speed with which you breathe determines how well your tapestry is woven. Generally speaking, the state of your breathing reflects the state of your mind. If you breathe fast and shallow, for example, then your thoughts tend to be fast and shallow. Breathe deep and slow, and your mind will become profound and gentle.

Notice any thoughts that appear in your mind, and then release them and allow them to flow, just as you would observe a drifting cloud in the sky. Once they have passed, gently refocus your mind on proper posture and breathing. You may also visualize the breath as a stream of light flowing in and out through the body, cleansing and purifying everything in its path.

First take two or three deep breaths, exhaling fully and forcefully through the mouth to eliminate any stale air trapped in your lungs. Then slowly breathe in while expanding your lower abdomen to the count of four. Then slowly breathe out while contracting your lower abdomen to a count of four. Focus on breathing rhythmically. Try not to move your chest (it will move slightly); instead, only your lower abdomen should move. Inhalation must be done through the nose; exhalation can be done either through the nose or the mouth. This is to ensure that Qi is properly extracted from the air. You may drop the tongue from the upper palate while exhaling. Once you become comfortable with the inhalation and exhalation, try to add a pause between each breath. To summarize: inhale to a count of four, then pause for a count of two; exhale to a count of four, and then pause again for a count of two.

As you become more proficient with this breathing exercise, you can increase the length of time of inhalation and exhalation and the pauses between them. You may also try to vary the rhythm. Many ratios of rhythms or cycles exist, such as 4:16:8:4 (inhalation; pause; exhalation; pause) or 4:7:8 (inhalation; pause; exhalation). The most important thing is to try not to hold the breath forcibly, because this can put excessive strain on the body. People with hypertension must be especially careful about holding their breath after inhalation, as blood can forcibly rush upward to the head. This is the reason for keeping the retention short at the beginning. At no time should you hold your breath more than necessary—the internal pressure buildup can be dangerous.

Perform this simple breathing exercise for three to five minutes twice a day, in the morning after you wake up and in the evening before you go to bed. You can also practice this exercise at any time during the day (except immediately after meals). Though simple, if practiced regularly and conscientiously, this exercise can greatly benefit the health of your mind and body.

Meditation

Meditation confers several benefits. Physical benefits are well known and well documented, especially regarding regulation of heart rate and blood pressure. Psychologically and spiritually, meditation helps us to deepen our awareness of the universe within us and around us, and to expand our consciousness. Simultaneously, it helps us to focus our awareness upon the ever-fleeting, ever-returning point that we call the present moment. In short, meditation balances body and mind, and promotes health and longevity. Thus, all constitutional types should meditate on a daily basis.

There are many techniques of meditation, including guided imagery, chanting, or "just sitting." I will briefly discuss three simple types of meditation here. One type involves the use of a mantra (a word or sound) repeated silently. Another involves counting your breaths. The last type of meditation involves focusing awareness on certain points on the body.

After you finish the breathing exercises mentioned above (which are themselves forms of meditation), practice meditating in the sitting position. Repeat words or sounds that either have meaning (such as tranquility, peace, or serenity), or do not (like the word one). Words with religious connotations are fine. Experiment with several words, sounds or phrases until you find one that is comfortable for you. As an example, you can repeat the word "calm" as you inhale and "relax" as you exhale. When you exhale, try to put a slight smile on your face. Repeat this process for a specific amount of time (in the beginning, try for three to five minutes). Gradually increase the time to 20 or 30 minutes twice a day.

Counting the breath is another meditation method used frequently in Zen Buddhism to help beginners to yoke their restless minds. When you exhale, count your breath, starting from one. When you have reached the count of 10, count back down to one again. Repeat, going from one to 10, and from 10 to one, until your allotted time is up. If you get distracted by your thoughts or emotions, and lose track of what number you were on, just go back to one and start over. Don't get caught up in your feelings of frustration or anger if you find yourself repeatedly losing your count; consider your feelings to be another distraction, and restart your count. Although it may seem like a boring and pointless exercise, it is effective in training you to focus your mind and remain aware of the present moment.

The last meditation technique that I would like to mention involves focusing on specific acupuncture points. The first point is called the Dan Tian, as previously mentioned, which is located within your lower abdomen, just below the navel (Fig. 9.5). The other point, called Kidney 1 (K-1), is located on the soles of the feet, about one-third of the distance from the base of the second toe to the heel (Fig. 9.8). There is a groove there that you can easily feel when you flex your toes. Every time you inhale, focus your awareness on your Dan Tian, and every time that you exhale, focus your awareness on the points on the soles of your feet. As with the other meditation techniques, you should repeat this for a set amount of time.

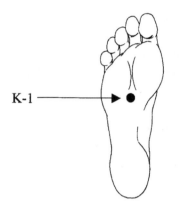

Figure 9.8

Exercise and Qi Gong for Every Body Type

This section provides specific advice for each of the four body types. Build your exercise regimen around the general guidelines, and perform the Qi Gong exercises for your body type, and you will be on the path towards health and balance.

Before you begin practicing the Qi Gong exercises, you should keep a few principles in mind:

- ❧ It is important that you practice these exercises at least once a day, preferably in the morning, right after you wake up. Don't practice right after or right before eating.

- ❧ Take off all jewelry, eyeglasses, watches, and so on, and wear loose, comfortable clothing to free up the flow of energy. Loosen your body by performing some gentle stretches if you like.

- ❧ Avoid listening to loud music or watching TV as you practice. It is important that you not be distracted when doing Qi Gong. Be mindful, paying particular attention to your breathing and posture. Remember to keep the tongue at the roof of your mouth throughout the exercise.

- ❧ Maintain a relaxed attitude; don't exert unnecessary force. Keep your breath and your movements slow, smooth, and soft, and your mind calm and quiet.

☯ Try to practice outdoors if you can, in close proximity to nature. The ocean, a mountain, or a park with many trees are ideal locales. If you must practice indoors, make sure the room is well ventilated.

☯ After completing any exercise, it is ideal to rub your palms together, and "wash" your face with the warmth you generate in them. Then, relax in either the sitting or standing position for a few minutes.

☯ Most of the Qi Gong exercises begin in Ready Stance (also known as the beginning position), depicted in figure 9.9. In this stance, you stand naturally, with your feet shoulder width apart (toes pointing straight ahead), and with your arms hanging naturally at your sides. The knees are bent slightly. Look straight ahead. As in the sitting and standing meditation exercises, keep a straight posture, and focus on your Dan Tian.

General guidelines for Taiyangs

☯ Exercise the lower body. Taiyangs should concentrate on lower body exercises (as much as their leg strength permits). Walking, jogging, cycling, stair stepping, hiking, skiing, and aerobic exercises involving the lower body are all beneficial. Controlled weight training exercises and calisthenics for the lower body are also good for encouraging development of Taiyangs' weak legs. Squats, leg presses, calf raises, leg extensions, and hamstring curls should be emphasized during a weight training session. Whatever you do, you should try to exercise your lower body for at least 20 to 30 minutes four to five times a week.

☯ Exercises that combine soft and gentle movements with regulated breathing, such as Tai Chi, Qi Gong, or Yoga, are also well suited to Taiyangs. These Yin-type exercises develop softness, foster inner serenity, and promote flexibility (qualities that Taiyangs need).

☯ Maintain a good posture. By doing so, Taiyangs will benefit their weak lower backs.

☯ Try to limit exercises that hang your body upside down for long periods of time, as in the Yoga headstand or shoulder stand posture.

Figure 9.9

☯ Remember: The key to Taiyang health is to slow down and keep
    still. One of the best ways to achieve this is to practice holding
    the standing meditation position described above for a few min-
    utes each day (for at least five minutes).

Qi Gong exercise 1: Toe Raise

   1. Start off in the beginning stance with your arms at your side
       (Fig. 9.10). Slowly rise up on your toes as high as you can,
       then pause for a count of two (Fig. 9.11).
   2. Then come down as gently and slowly as you can back to
       beginning position.

   Breathing: Inhale as you rise up and exhale as you sink down.
   Perform 10 repetitions of this exercise.

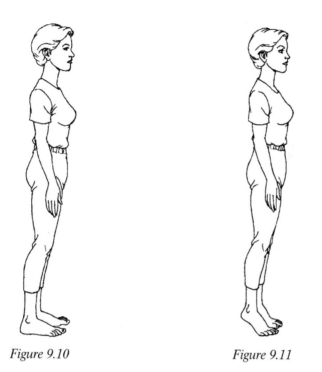

Figure 9.10   Figure 9.11

General Benefits: This exercise is good for relaxing physical and mental tension. It smooths the circulation of Qi and blood throughout the body, especially to the legs. It can also help people balance and center their bodies and minds. This exercise benefits the spine and also builds bone marrow, which Taiyangs lack when they are seriously unbalanced.

The calming, relaxing, and centering effect induced by this exercise can be of tremendous benefit to Taiyangs. Remember that Taiyangs have the most amount of energy rising up in their bodies. Because the focus of this exercise is in the lowest part of the body, it can counter and regulate that ascending energy.

Qi Gong exercise 2: Waist and Head Turn

1. Place your hands on your waist and open your legs wide to assume a horse stance (Fig. 9.12). Turn your head and torso slowly to the left. First turn your body from the waist as far as it will go, and then turn your head as far as it will go (Fig. 9.13). Hold this position for a count of two.

2.   Return your body back to the center slowly. Repeat on the
     other side.

Breathing: Inhale as you turn to either side and exhale as you return
to the center.

Perform 10 repetitions of this exercise to both sides.

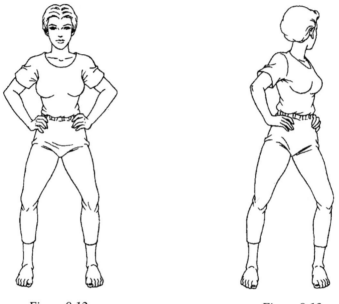

Figure 9.12   *Figure 9.13*

General Benefits: This exercise stimulates blood circulation to the
head and neck, thereby reducing tension in those areas while strengthening the waist region. It basically helps to clear the sensory organs (especially the eyes) and the whole head, and revitalizes the entire nervous system. The turning of the waist is said to regulate and strengthen the Liver.

As this exercise focuses on the Liver, and helps to bring energy down
from the head and neck, it is excellent for Taiyangs.

General guidelines for Shaoyangs

☯   Shaoyangs should concentrate on movements that exercise
    the lower back, especially those involving twisting and
    bending. Such movements help to strengthen both the lower
    back and the Kidneys. Other exercises beneficial for
    Shaoyangs include walking, running, cycling, stair stepping,

hiking, cross-country skiing, and aerobics. Exercises that take place either in cold outdoor weather (skiing, snowboarding) or in water (swimming, scuba diving, snorkeling, water skiing) are also excellent for this hot constitution.

❧ Like Taiyangs, Shaoyangs should engage in soft, quiet, gentle movement exercises like Tai Chi, Qi Gong, and Yoga. This will help to calm their excessive Yang energy, and nourish their deficient Yin energy.

❧ Shaoyangs may show their natural abilities and skills in competitive athletics. However, they have a tendency to get too emotionally involved in such sports. If any sport causes you to become overly angry and emotional, try to reduce participation, or eliminate it altogether in favor of another sport.

❧ Shaoyangs should relax the tension in their chest and shoulders, and correct their manner of walking by slowing their pace.

❧ Practice kneeling for 10 minutes a day. Kneeling is an excellent way to bring energy down to your center and strengthen your knees.

❧ Practice the horse stance. It is tremendously effective in strengthening the Kidneys as well as descending the energy to the lower part of the body.

❧ To help with your concentration, practice archery, bowling, and billiards. These exercises will enhance your ability to focus and develop your patience. The sport of fishing is also good for building patience.

❧ As with Taiyangs, limit any exercises that suspend your body for long periods of time (such as the Yoga headstand or shoulder stand posture).

❧ When weight training, concentrate on exercises that strengthen the lower body, such as squats, leg presses, calf raises, leg extensions, and hamstring curls.

Qi Gong exercise 1: Whole Body Twist

1. Place your hands on your waist and open your legs wide to assume a horse stance (Fig. 9.14). Slowly bend and rotate your upper body toward the left (Fig. 9.15), continue to

rotate your body to the right side, and then come back to the center. Make a large scooping motion with your upper body, leading with your head around to the left and returning (counterclockwise) back to the starting position.

2. Repeat to the right in a clockwise motion. Throughout this exercise, it is important to concentrate on the soles of your feet.

Breathing: Exhale as you bend and rotate your upper body to each side and inhale as you lift the upper body back to the beginning position.

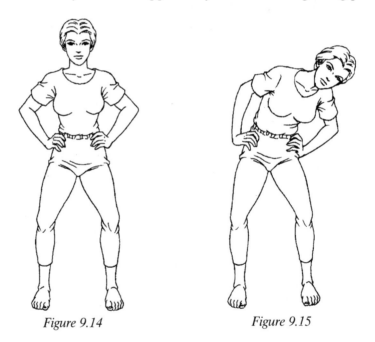

Figure 9.14   *Figure 9.15*

Perform 10 repetitions of this exercise on each side.

General Benefits: This exercise is said to eliminate excess physical or mental strain on the nervous system, which does not improve with rest. Thus, it is excellent for relaxing the whole body. This exercise can also lower blood pressure. The main focus of this exercise is to bring energy down to the lower back and legs.

Shaoyangs have "hot" bodies. Their energy is centered in the upper body (chest region). This exercise brings that heat energy down, while calming irritability and restlessness. It also strengthens the lower back and legs, regions where Shaoyangs tend to be weak.

Qi Gong exercise 2: Bending and Holding Feet

1. Start from the beginning position. First bring both hands to your lower back with your thumb in front and fingers supporting your low back (Fig. 9.16). Bend backwards slowly as far as you can. Do not overstrain. Then slowly bend forward and down, while the palms of your hands rub the buttocks and the back of the legs down to the heels. Let your head hang between your two legs and rotate both palms so that your hands grasp your toes (Fig. 9.17). If you cannot reach your toes, just go as far as you can with your hands on the back of your legs. Hold this position for a count of two.

2. Now rub the inner legs as you straighten upward back to the beginning position. When both hands reach the lower abdomen, slide them to the small of your back and repeat the exercise.

Breathing: Exhale bending forward and inhale straightening upward and bending back.

Perform 10 repetitions of this exercise.

Figure 9.16

Figure 9.17

General Benefits: This exercise targets the Kidneys and waist. It will strengthen the muscles in the back and waist, the region said to be under the domain of the Kidneys in Eastern medicine. Deficient Kidneys causes weakness and chronic soreness or pain of the lower back.

A word of caution: elderly and weak persons should be careful and gradually work their way into a fully bent position. Those who suffer from hypertension or arteriosclerosis should be careful not to lower their heads too much during this exercise.

Footsteps on the path

Jisun L. is a 32-year-old woman who came to my clinic complaining of an unremitting headache that she had been suffering from for two months. She also complained of a feeling of fullness and pain in the chest, insomnia, red eyes, tongue ulcers, a flushed feeling in the face, and emotional instability. She had been using over the counter painkillers, but had experienced little improvement in her symptoms.

Jisun is an immigrant from China who came to the United States three years ago after divorcing her husband. For the past year, she has been working as a massage therapist in a health spa, a place where she does not have to speak much English to work. She works overtime every day, and has only one day off each week. She experiences constant stress, both from the clients' complaints and negative comments and from the physical demands of working long hours in rooms that are stuffy and hot, with little fresh air due to their proximity to the sauna and steam rooms. She often feels frustrated with her work, but knows that she must endure it in order to survive in this country.

Jisun has practically no social life. This is not due to her long work hours; rather, it is a consequence of her inability to speak English. As a result, she feels as though she does not have a true friend to talk to. Not having a car only adds to this feeling of isolation. In all, she feels as though her freedom has been strained by her inability to adapt to her new culture. She often feels very homesick and misses the five-year-old child she had to leave behind, particularly after the Chinese New Year.

Even in her present physical and emotional state, she managed to hold a full smile, cheerfully asking questions regarding her condition throughout the course of her interview.

Interpretation

After careful observation of Jisun's signs and symptoms, appearance, demeanor, and manner of speech, I diagnosed her as a Shaoyang type with an excessive build up of internal heat. Jisun was clearly aggravated by her work and new culture and missing her home and family. Excess heat had built up in her Spleen and Stomach due to this emotional stress and had congested the upper part of her body, creating her chief complaint, persistent headaches.

Treatment and recommendation

In a condition like Jisun's, acupuncture and herbal treatments work well. But it is the stress of life that Jisun faces daily that is at the root of her imbalance. Thus, there is a need for active participation by the patient in order to speedily and fully recover from her condition, as well as to prevent its recurrence. Meditation and Qi Gong exercises serve this purpose well. They are absolutely essential whenever stress is involved in creating an illness. Therefore, I prescribed a routine for Jisun to follow in the morning, evening, and in between her massages.

The first thing I recommended was to have Jisun practice kneeling for 10 minutes twice a day, once upon awakening in the morning and again at night before she went to bed. The practice of kneeling helps to center and calm the energy, which Jisun needed. Kneeling before bedtime would help her sleep soundly. Another exercise I advised her to practice was the horse stance. This exercise focuses energy down low and helps to strengthen Kidneys, the weak organ in Shaoyangs. I told Jisun to hold this pose five minutes twice a day and anytime she has a break between her patients. When these two movements are combined with breathing exercises, they can immediately settle and ground Shaoyangs. I also gave the two Qi Gong movement exercises as mentioned above in the Shaoyang guidelines.

Remember that Shaoyangs are the people who need to be calmed and slowed down. As their energies are centered in their upper bodies, they have a definite need for the energy to come down to their center, the Dan Tian. Thus meditation and Qi Gong are indispensable tools. After I instructed her in the clinic, Jisun began to feel centered and relaxed almost immediately.

Along with meditation and Qi Gong instructions, I prescribed an herbal formula called Liang Ge San Huo Tang (Cool the Diaphragm and Dispel Fire Decoction) that cools her heat and nourishes Yin. I also recommended once a week acupuncture therapy. The level of her pain diminished, and the flushed sensation in her face began to subside after one week of treatment. After one month on this regimen, almost all of her symptoms disappeared. Each and every day, Jisun noticed a subtle difference in how she reacted to her stress. She did not get angry easily (so she did not have to keep her emotion inside and boil over). She felt more relaxed and "centered" and felt so good about herself that she resolved to make the best of her situation and learn English in her spare time. Jisun discovered new joy in her situation, and hope for her future.

General guidelines for Taiyins

- Exercise regularly. It is absolutely important for Taiyins to incorporate sufficient amounts of exercise (at least to the extent that they sweat profusely) into their daily routines. Whenever Taiyins feel tired or heavy, they should do some form of exercise. Taking a brisk walk, riding a stationary bike, running on a treadmill, swimming, or doing mild aerobic exercises are all fine. Whatever form of exercise is adopted, it is important that the breathing deepens and the circulation gets going as a result. If Taiyins cannot exercise, then they should at least go to a sauna to sweat.

- Get plenty of fresh air. Although everyone needs to get as much fresh air as possible, Taiyins in particular need it to balance out their constitutional Lung weakness. Waking up early and exercising outdoors in the fresh air, especially near trees or the ocean, will be of tremendous benefit to them. Tai Chi or Qi Gong exercises in particular are good for strengthening their Lungs. Outdoor sports such as fishing, golf, or hiking can also be helpful.

- Of the four body types, Taiyins respond best to heavy, intense, prolonged physical exercises. The reason for this is that Taiyins have a lot of energy in reserve and only high, extended levels of exertion can release this energy. A moderate amount of physical exercise is also the best remedy for Taiyins' fatigue, stress, fear, and depression. To this end, exercises such as calisthenics and weight training are ideal. Many Taiyins are overweight, and this type of exercise regimen will also help them to lose weight. Be sure to warm up and cool down properly to prevent injury.

- Other types of physical exercises that Taiyins can participate in with great benefit are racquet sports such as badminton, racquetball, squash, ping-pong, and tennis.
- Taiyins should try to keep their necks in straight, comfortable alignment with the rest of their bodies. They should also try to remove all the tension from their abdomens.
- Yoga positions that suspend a person in an upside-down position for a short period of time (such as shoulder stands, plows, and headstands) are excellent for Taiyins. Talk to a qualified Yoga instructor for instructions on the proper way to perform these exercises before engaging in them yourself.
- Exercises that involve bouncing movements, such as jumping on a trampoline, are excellent for Taiyins. Bouncing movements help activate the dormant energy in their bodies, thereby putting zip and bounce back into the lives of Taiyins. A word of caution: those that have knee or lower back problems must practice caution.

Qi Gong exercise 1: Drawing the Bow

1. Assume the horse stance, and maintain it throughout the entire exercise. Raise your hands and cross them at the wrist at chest level with the right hand in front of the left hand (Fig. 9.18).
2. Extend your left arm out to the left with the forefinger pointing up and the other fingers bent, and your palm pushing away from you. Follow your left hand with your eyes. At the same time, clench your right hand into a fist and pull it back (keeping it level with the right shoulder) as though you were drawing a bow back (Fig. 9.19). As you stretch your arms apart, bend your legs slightly to lower your stance. Maintain this position for a count of two. Then, return to the original crossed arm position, this time with your left hand in front of your right hand. Repeat the exercise on the opposite side.

Breathing: Inhale as you extend your arms into bow. Exhale as you return to crossed arm position.

Perform 10 repetitions of this exercise on each side.

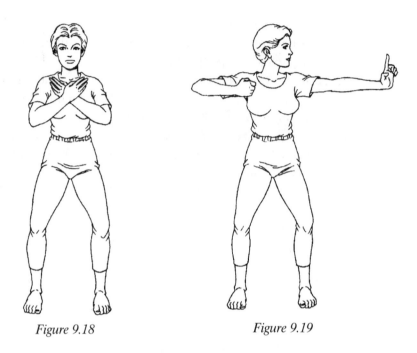

Figure 9.18   Figure 9.19

General Benefits: This exercise increases lung capacity. It also promotes circulation, especially in the head and neck regions, and strengthens the chest, shoulder, and arm muscles.

As this exercise centers its activity on the Lungs, Taiyins will derive the most benefit from it. The improved breathing and increased overall circulation derived from this exercise will help increase energy as well as move stagnant and dormant energy, bringing them back to balanced health.

Qi Gong exercise 2: Dynamic Punch

1. Stand in a horse stance. Make a fist with both hands and bring them to your waist with the palms upward (Fig. 9.20).
2. Look to your left as you punch to the left, with your fist in a horizontal position, palm down (Fig. 9.21). Then bring the fist back to the waist and repeat to the right side with the right fist (in horizontal position). Return to the starting position.
3. Punch with the left hand straight in front of you, with your fist in a vertical position (Fig. 9.22), with the thumb on top. Bring your fist back and repeat with the right fist (in vertical position). Punch out slowly, but forcibly. It is important in this exercise to hold the eyes wide open, glaring fiercely at an imaginary opponent.

Breathing: Exhale as you punch to the side and front, and inhale as you bring your fist back to the waist.

Perform 10 repetitions of this exercise (total of 40 punches).

Figure 9.20   *Figure 9.21*

Figure 9.22

General Benefits: This exercise regulates the breathing and increases the vitality of the whole body, building energy and strength. It also improves concentration and promotes the smooth circulation of Qi and blood throughout the body. Furthermore, it helps to release pent-up anger, thereby relieving stress.

This movement assists overall bodily circulation, especially through the dispersal of stagnant energy in the Liver. This makes it excellent for Taiyins. As things move slowly within Taiyins, energy easily stagnates and transforms into internal heat, resulting in emotional imbalances. This exercise releases and disperses that heat and energy, helping to restore Taiyins to a balanced state.

Footsteps on the path

Allen E. first came to me in 1991 with a bout of flu that he had been suffering from for 10 days. The flu aggravated his wheezing and asthma attacks, which he had to endure for the past 25 years, since the age of six. In addition to the asthma, Allen suffered constantly from allergies. Allen had been using several bronchodilator inhalers regularly (about five to six times per day) to relieve his symptoms.

Since moving from New York to California one year ago, Allen had noticed a worsening of both his asthma and his allergies. He had also noticed that the asthma tended to be worse during the night, with physical exercise, or in damp weather and dusty environments, and that inhalation was more difficult than exhalation.

His asthma limited his performance in his job as a part time warehouse manager, and also prevented him from enjoying the physical exercises (weight training and running) that he loved so much. Allen described his energy level as being below average during the daytime, worse during his asthma attacks, and very low at night (especially with an asthma attack).

Allen's other physical symptoms included some digestive problems with belching and gas, an occasional bitter taste in his mouth, and palpitations. Because of his allergies, Allen's sinuses frequently clogged up, with itching and dripping. Allen had had pneumonia three times in his life. His family history revealed that his father had also suffered from asthma all his life. His diet was also very poor, with a lot of fast food, and irregular mealtime hours.

"I've been suffering with this asthma for so long that I simply feel out of sync with my body and mind," Allen said, in a deep-toned, dispirited voice and a thick New York accent. "I don't feel as though I have any control over my life anymore." Allen stated that, emotionally, he was under a great deal of stress. Aside from his part time job, Allen worked hard to make it as an actor, but had experienced much frustration, anger, and sadness in his attempts. He was also a newlywed, and was experiencing some tension with his wife. Allen mentioned to me that he preferred to take things slow, enjoyed routine, and disliked leaving things unfinished, whether at work or at home.

Examination of Allen's tongue revealed that it was red in color, with a geographic coat and many deep cracks and tooth marks. His overall pulse was irregular and thin; weak on the right side and wiry on the left.

Interpretation

Allen appeared a bit apprehensive and irritated, which is a typical out-of-balance state for a Taiyin. Several of his statements, including his preference for a more relaxed pace, revealed him to be a Taiyin. Allen had a stocky build and a well-balanced physique, with a concentration of energy and weight in the lower part of his body. Although many Taiyins are overweight or pot-bellied, several have Allen's well-proportioned, heavyset body. In any case, all Taiyins share the low center of gravity that gives them a very stable appearance.

Allen's red and cracked tongue revealed a severe drying up of bodily fluids due to a build up of internal heat. This heat was due in part to the constitutional factors of Lung weakness and an overly strong Liver. These factors were further aggravated by the elements of his diet and lifestyle, particularly his stress. His pulse revealed stagnancy and weakness of Qi energy, and depletion of essential fluids in the body. Although Taiyins generally have a fair amount of Qi energy, the extreme constitutional weakness in the Lungs, combined with other factors, led to a swift depletion of Allen's Qi.

Allen's digestive problems resulted from the stagnancy in his Liver, which affected his stomach. The bitter taste in his mouth indicated a build-up of heat in his body, while his palpitations (a common symptom in Taiyins) resulted from the constitutional weakness in his circulatory system.

In all, Allen needed to get his Lungs strengthened and his Liver regulated. Once the Lungs begin to disperse and distribute energy throughout the body, and the Liver lets go of its tendency towards excessive accumulation, then the body can return to a state of balance.

Treatment and recommendation

In Allen's case, the inherent weakness in the Lungs (a Taiyin predisposition) led to a weakness in his immune and respiratory systems, resulting in his allergies and asthma. This condition was further aggravated by the stress of his family life and job. Therefore, the treatment principle involved strengthening the Lungs and regulating the Liver.

In addition to constitutional acupuncture, herbal formulas, and a dietary regimen specific to his body type, I outlined a comprehensive program of meditation and Qi Gong exercises for Allen. The reason for this is twofold. One is to help increase overall energy, the other is to calm him down from his stress. There is simply nothing better than meditation and Qi Gong for this purpose. Because his asthmatic condition worsened with physical exercise, I recommended to Allen to begin and end his exercise program with Qi Gong and meditation for 10 minutes. This would help regulate his constitutional imbalance and increase his lung capacity so that he can better tolerate physical stress. It would also help him cool and calm down afterwards. Remember that Taiyins, due to their surplus mass, eventually end up with short supply of Qi or energy. Meditation and Qi Gong can rapidly build a good supply of Qi and get things moving in their bodies.

Due to Allen's stress, heat had built up. This dries up fluids (Yin) in the body and can create even more difficulty for Lungs to function properly. By calming the mind and body, the heat disperses and Lungs become moistened so that they can properly disperse energy throughout the body.

After one week, Allen returned and reported that he no longer had any flu symptoms and that his sinuses had cleared up without any discharge. He still experienced chest congestion and occasional sneezing, but was happy to report that he had had to use his inhaler only once per day for the past three days. He said, "I can breathe and smell a lot better, and my breathing seems calmer."

Gradually over the next eight months (with bi-weekly acupuncture treatments and daily herbal medicines with daily Qi Gong and meditation), his condition improved, such that he had to use the inhaler only about once every two weeks. His allergic attacks had also grown very infrequent, revealing that his constitution had become more balanced through the regular treatments, dietary and lifestyle changes, and Qi Gong. This transformation showed up on his tongue, which looked more normal. Many of the deep cracks had disappeared, leaving only a few minor cracks, and the tongue color had changed from red to pink (normal). The tooth marks (indicative of weak Qi) had reduced, and his tongue coating was much more even, rather than being geographic. His pulse also showed an improvement, with less irregularity and more strength. At this point, we stopped the acupuncture treatments and only herbal supplements were prescribed to maintain his improved condition. Allen found renewed strength through the combination of my therapy and his diligence in performing Qi Gong exercises and regulating his lifestyle.

General guidelines for Shaoyins

- Avoid sweating excessively. Yang energy (which Shaoyins tend to lack) is lost through the sweat. Exercise should be done in moderation (moderate exercises for short duration). Prolonged strenuous activities and saunas should be avoided.

- Shaoyins may also find value in Tai Chi, Qi Gong, and Yoga for their calming and relaxing effects. The slow, controlled movements, combined with the regulation of the breath, will teach Shaoyins to calm down and dissolve their apprehension and anxiety. Casual strolls in a peaceful surrounding, such as a beach or park, may also accomplish this.

- On the other hand, Shaoyins should involve themselves in more aggressive activities in order to balance their passive tendencies. Competitive sports like basketball, football, or volleyball are excellent for this purpose. Again, all of these exercises should be practiced in moderation. Shaoyins should also try to exercise as much as possible outdoors.

- Maintain a good posture. Shaoyins should practice sitting, standing, and walking with a good, upright posture. They should also practice fixing their gazes at faraway places. This will help them to see the big picture rather than just the fragments before their feet.

- Just as for Taiyins, bouncing on a trampoline is excellent for Shaoyins, as it helps them to develop a spring in their actions.

- Practice shoulder stands, plows, and even headstands, if you are able to, for a few minutes on a daily basis. Meet with a qualified Yoga instructor for the proper instructions on the performance of these exercises. These exercises will help the flow of energy and blood to the upper body and reverse the pull of gravity that causes Shaoyins to droop and sag.

☯   In addition to a general exercise program for the whole body, Shaoyins should include a few more exercises for the upper body to balance out their constitution. Calisthenics and controlled weight training are excellent for this purpose. Extra focus should be given to exercises for the upper body, such as push-ups, dips, pull-ups, bench presses, shoulder presses, pull-downs, arm curls, and so on. Remember, though, that everything must be done in moderation.

Qi Gong exercise 1: Supporting Heaven

1.   Start with the beginning position. First scoop and bring your hands to the front of the legs. The fingers of each hand point toward each other, close but not touching, and the palm faces upward (Fig. 9.23). Continue to raise your hands. As your hands pass the front of the chest, the fingers become interlocked (as though forming a bowl). The hands rotate right in front of the chest until the palms face upward. Continue stretching your arms up over your head until they are fully straightened (Fig. 9.24). Hold this position for a count of two.

2.   Now separate your fingers and bring both palms outward and down to the sides (Fig. 9.25), ending at the beginning position. Try to make the movement slow and continuous without any jerky motions.

Breathing: Inhale as your hands rise up and exhale as your hands come back down.

Perform 10 repetitions of this exercise.

General Benefits: Because this exercise is accompanied by deep breathing with the arms raised, it strengthens the lungs and heart, while increasing overall bodily energy. It also stretches the entire body, helping to align and correct your posture. This exercise also massages and tones the internal organs.

Shaoyins' energy tends to stagnate in the lower parts of their bodies, with not enough Yang energy rising to the upper body. Thus, many of them have drooping postures. This movement counters this tendency by straightening the posture and allowing the Yang energy to rise up to the sky. Shaoyins are also full of mental anxiety and pent-up emotions. The deep breathing practiced in this exercise will help to alleviate this mental condition.

Figure 9.23   *Figure 9.24*

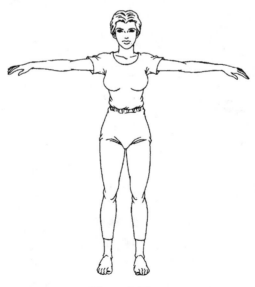

Figure 9.25

Qi Gong exercise 2: Alternate Raising of Hands

1.   Start out in the beginning position. Raise both hands to the front of the stomach with the palms facing upward (Fig. 9.26).

2.   Separate the hands. Move the left hand up and the right hand down until your left arm straightens with the palm pushing up and the fingers pointing to the right, and your right arm straightens with the palm pushing straight down and the fingers pointing forward (Fig. 9.27). Try to lengthen and stretch both arms as much as you can, without tensing your muscles. Hold this position for a count of two.

3.   Return to the original position. Then, switch your arms so that your left palm pushes up, and your right palm pushes down. This is a continuous movement. Try to make it smooth without any jerky motions.

Breathing: Inhale as you lift and separate your hands, and exhale when your hands come back down to your center.

Perform 10 repetitions of this exercise to each side.

Figure 9.26   Figure 9.27

General Benefits: This exercise strengthens the Spleen and the Stomach, and the entire digestive system. Regular practice of this exercise will reduce flatulence, acid indigestion, abdominal distention, and other digestive problems.

This exercise is ideal for Shaoyins, as it strengthens their weak digestive systems. It also can reduce stress and calm the Shaoyin's habitually nervous mind.

Footsteps on the path

Susan P. was diagnosed with fibromyalgia back in 1990. She suffers from pain all over her body, especially in her neck, shoulders, back, and arms. Occasionally, she suffers from hip pain as well. Susan is a former professor at a major university, and currently writes children's stories. Unfortunately, the pain is sometimes so severe that she must wear wrist braces to help relieve it and support her wrists when she works on her computer. The anti-inflammatory medications prescribed by her doctor do not seem to help.

Susan is 49 years of age, and is currently going through menopause. She experiences frequent night sweats, and notices hot flashes several times during the day. She also gets a low-grade fever in the afternoon and in the evening. Nevertheless, she constantly suffers from cold hands and feet; when receiving acupuncture treatments, she must cover her feet, even when the room is warm.

Susan's energy level is usually low. Her digestive system often gives her problems, in the form of constant loose stools and occasional diarrhea. She has also been suffering from frequent sinus infections (three times in a six-month period) ever since she had pneumonia five years ago. She also suffers from allergies (hay fever), for which she has been taking a popular decongestant.

Susan has a small, oval face, with small, lackluster eyes, nose, and mouth. Her overall facial features express a gentleness and softness. She has a calm demeanor with a quiet, soft, gentle voice. She has more development in her lower body, and a weaker upper body. Her gait when walking is gentle and natural, "like a floating butterfly," as described in Sasang medical texts.

When I inquired about her diet, she said that she liked hot, spicy foods and that chicken was her favorite meat dish. She had a well-rounded diet that included plenty of vegetables and whole grains. She did not smoke nor drink, and only used coffee sparingly.

Emotionally, Susan said that she is generally a gentle, quiet, and even timid person, with a proper, prudent personality. She is thorough, meticulous, and patient with her work, and is able to sit for long hours at the computer, making certain she gets things right. She does not like to make mistakes, pondering carefully over every decision. Perhaps as a natural consequence, she prefers living a low-key life, consisting of comfortable routines. It is unsurprising that one of the main reasons she stopped teaching at the university was her dislike of the limelight, and the stresses involved in making regular presentations before large audiences.

Susan feels frequent frustration (she notices that she sighs quite often), which occasionally leads to bouts of anger. She also has difficulty staying asleep at night.

Interpretation

Susan is a characteristic Shaoyin, with her ladder-like bodily figure and her fine-tuned, yet gentle and timid mentality. Many of Susan's signs and symptoms are also characteristic of the Shaoyin type, including her digestive disturbances (loose stools), and her cold hands and feet. Her liking for hot, spicy foods is also commonly seen in Shaoyins, as these foods help stimulate digestion.

The fibromyalgia syndrome can be triggered by various causes, including stress (physical as well as mental), traumatic injury, being exposed to weather factors, such as dampness or cold, and certain infections. Other factors include inadequate sleep and occasionally rheumatoid arthritis or a related disorder. In Susan's case, it was mainly due to her stress and her inability to deal with that stress.

Shaoyins have plenty of Yin in reserve, but they tend to lack Yang energy. This lack manifests itself in Susan as a low energy level, digestive disturbances, and allergies. Menopause, meanwhile, is generally caused by a lack of both Yin and Yang energies in the Kidneys, as well as an imbalance between Ying (nourishing) and Wei (protective) energies. As Shaoyin types are generally weak in Wei energy, they have trouble fending off external influences, like dampness and cold. When this constitutional weakness is combined with poor digestion and the mental stress often found in Shaoyins, disruptions in the flow of energy in soft tissues (including muscles, tendons, and ligaments)—fibromyalgia—may easily result.

Treatment and recommendation

The treatment calls for tonifying both the Yin and Yang of the Kidneys, and harmonizing the Ying and Wei energies. For Shaoyins, more focus is paid to strengthening the Yang and the Wei energetic aspect.

In addition to these herbal and dietary guidelines, I gave Susan constitutional acupuncture treatments to further strengthen her Spleen and Yang energy. I also put her on a regimen of daily Qi Gong exercises specific to her body type to improve the Qi and blood circulation throughout her body. Because Susan didn't do much in terms of physical exercise, incorporation of Qi Gong into her daily routine was absolutely essential. I advised her to practice Qi Gong exercises several times daily to help improve her condition.

Qi Gong is an absolutely essential practice for Shaoyins. Because it is mild and non-strenuous, it suits the delicate, low-energy Shaoyin constitution well. Qi Gong also boosts energy and calms the nervous Shaoyin mind. It helps Shaoyins let go of pent-up emotions, (as expressed in their frequent sighing) and makes their pessimistic thought patterns more optimistic.

To address the constitutional weakness in her digestive system, I also taught Susan some abdominal massage techniques (a form of Qi Gong therapy).

Susan almost immediately started making improvements with this comprehensive treatment regimen. She noticed a reduction in her pain and stiffness, as well as an increase in her energy level. Her limbs felt warmer, too. Susan was initially treated twice a week for several months, and then once a week for a total of six months, during which time her symptoms stabilized. The number of treatments was then reduced, and she had a maintenance treatment once every three weeks for several months. She now only experiences occasional pain of mild intensity and comes in occasionally for a treatment.

Fluctuations in treatment occasionally occurred whenever Susan strayed from a good diet (eating heavily, or eating too much spicy food), or when her emotional state was unbalanced. These difficulties are typical of Shaoyins, and should be addressed before real improvement can be made.

Chapter 10

Centering the Mind

If a person has a lot of desire, then he will have a hard time maintaining his mind, and will only find difficulty in whatever he pursues.
—Mencius

Simplicity, diligence, self-control, and integrity allow one to live one's natural life span.
—Dr. Jae Ma Lee

Sasang Medicine is primarily designed to isolate the root cause of a patient's illness rather than provide symptomatic cures. In other words, Sasang Medicine does not merely treat the disease, but aims to balance your mental attitude and cultivate your spirit. This helps the body set itself on the right path for healing.

The following sections give practical advice regarding which lifestyle patterns each body type should pay close attention to, and accordingly, what each type can do to maintain and improve health and prevent disease. Again, whatever disease or problem you may have, Sasang Medicine does not limit its treatment to just treating the physical body, but puts greater emphasis on controlling and regulating your mental and emotional tendencies in order to achieve total health.

The road to health begins with a better understanding of yourself. Seek to become aware of your strengths and weaknesses and then make appropriate plans to correct and balance your body type.

Taiyang

- Pay special attention to controlling anger and releasing sorrow, as these are often the root cause of imbalance in body and mind for Taiyangs.

- Loosen the hold on anger as quickly as possible and do not sustain sorrow for any long period of time. Both anger and sadness have upward energetic tendencies. Thus, these emotions are particularly harmful for Taiyangs. One of the best ways to settle this energy is to practice both sitting and standing meditations, with an emphasis on breathing and on grounding yourself.

- Try to keep calm and composed at all times. By doing so, the Taiyang's constitutionally weak Liver will be protected from damage and may even be strengthened. The founder of Sasang Medicine, Dr. Jae Ma Lee, said:

  "Due to his temperament, the Taiyang person always tends to move forward and does not have a tendency to move back. The emotional character of the Taiyangs tends to be masculine and not feminine." He also said, "The Taiyang person always has a rash personality. If he can slow down his pace, his Liver blood will become regulated."

  Thus, Taiyangs must always remember to take one step back and calm their urgency.

- Take the time to sufficiently study and plan projects before beginning them. Taiyangs tend to be overly confident with regards to their business and social affairs, to the point of being negligent of crucial details. This negligence causes them to encounter unforeseen difficulties that they are unprepared to deal with. When their plans are frustrated, Taiyangs immediately become angry and even violent, blaming everyone but themselves for their failures.

- Be flexible. Taiyangs must learn to adapt to change and to the people around them. In order to improve their interpersonal relationships, Taiyangs should refrain from criticizing, attacking, and fault-finding, and should instead seek to understand the feelings of others. Taiyangs should also reduce their egotistical, uncompromising, dogmatic tendencies, as well as their voracious ambition for success. It is only in this manner that Taiyangs can remain healthy, balanced, and capable of true contributions to society.

❧ When Taiyangs become excessively angry and lament more than usual, it must be considered a warning signal that they are severely unbalanced. Appropriate precautions, including meditation, dietary and lifestyle changes, and treatments to strengthen the Liver, should be taken immediately.

Shaoyang

❧ Dr. Lee wrote, "The Shaoyang person always suffers from anxiety. If he calms his mind, he can be stable and harmonize his life with the Way. If he is too anxious, his mind will be chained." Look within, and still your anxious mind. Observe your thoughts and emotions, and let them go. In this way, you can gradually reduce the impulsive, urgent, and argumentative aspects of your Shaoyang nature.

❧ Be vigilant over your emotions, especially your sadness and anger. These two emotions can wreak havoc on Shaoyangs' health. The energies of both emotions rise upward and have the potential to seriously damage the Shaoyang's innately weak Kidneys.

❧ Practice meditation. Among all the constitutions, Shaoyangs benefit the most from daily meditation. Because the Shaoyang temperament is like a dynamic ball of fire, their energy tends to rise upward and outward. Sitting meditation will counter this tendency by bringing the energy down to the center of the body (Dan Tian), where it belongs. Try to sit for half an hour, especially at the beginning of the day, and carefully ponder the tasks that lie ahead of you.

❧ Tenacity and perseverance are the traits most needed by Shaoyangs. Shaoyangs must learn to finish whatever they start. Even though they may not profit from finishing a project, they should still cultivate the discipline to see it through to completion.

❧ Learn to be frugal. To counter their extravagance, Shaoyangs must learn to live well-ordered lives that allow for plenty of introspection and careful attention to their families.

❧ If you are a Shaoyang, pay more attention to your inner self and to domestic affairs. This will help you to settle your anxious mind. In addition, Shaoyangs must learn to be less impulsive and sentimental and more centered or grounded.

❧ If you feel as though you are being pursued, easily excited, or more anxious and urgent than usual, consider it a warning sign and get proper treatment immediately. If this condition worsens, it can easily lead to forgetfulness, a dangerous development for Shaoyangs, indicating further weakening of their constitutionally deficient Kidneys and Yin energy.

Footsteps on the path

Elizabeth M. is a 39-year-old housewife with two children. When she first visited my office, she was accompanied by a friend, and was constantly talking to her and giggling. She struck me as being very cheerful and sociable. She also seemed extremely curious, wanting to know when we could start the treatment: "I'm ready for a treatment!" she cried repeatedly. Within the first few minutes of her interview, I had already learned a great deal about this gregarious woman.

Elizabeth told me that she loved to travel by herself, and that she had actually roamed Latin America alone in her 20s before she married. We slowly focused the interview upon the specific reason for her visit. I learned that her chief complaint was a digestive disturbance (she suffered from a burning pain, bloating, and gas). She also had had gastric ulcers in the past, but a recent examination proved normal. She had been given Western medicine for her prior ulcers, which she took for her current ailments. As they proved ineffective, and as she did not want to become dependent on them in any case, she came to me.

Despite her stomach pain, she maintained an excellent appetite and constantly craved food. She loved eating cold, raw foods, and had a special preference for raw salads. As she often felt thirsty, Elizabeth liked to drink a lot of soda; it seemed to cool her down and help her with her bloating and gas. She also liked iced tea, as well as a bottle of beer every day. When asked about stimulants, she said that she enjoyed coffee, drinking two to three cups per day. She also revealed that she was a smoker, averaging about a pack a day.

Some of Elizabeth's other symptoms included constipation, night sweats, headache, and irritability. Her tongue was red, with peeling in the middle, and her pulse was wiry, thready, and rapid.

Physically, Elizabeth had a high level of energy, frequently feeling "hyper" or restless in her daily life. She was typically under a great deal of stress, always trying to do too much at once. Emotionally, she said, she often felt impatient, and added that she was fairly aggressive by nature. She also considered herself to be very passionate and outspoken. She said, "I am never afraid to talk to strangers and I don't usually hold things back. I usually let people know how I feel." On the negative side, she said that she was overly fickle and extravagant, and often neglected basic domestic duties in favor of partying.

Interpretation

I diagnosed Elizabeth as a Shaoyang type. It was clear from her daily diet and habits, as well as her emotions, that she was holding a great deal of heat in her body. People of the Shaoyang constitution are born with a strong Spleen and weak Kidneys, and this fundamental imbalance often leads to an abundance of heat. This heat tends to build up rapidly in Shaoyangs, as they lack the water or Yin energy needed to "cool off." In Elizabeth's case, the stomach pain resulted from an excessive amount of heat congesting the energies of her Spleen and Stomach.

I explained to Elizabeth that the main cause for the buildup of heat in her body type was her hectic life and its resultant emotional distress. In addition, I told her that the consumption of stimulants like coffee and cigarettes allowed the heat to build up with greater rapidity, resulting in such physical symptoms as a thirst for cold drinks, an insatiable appetite for cold and raw foods, constipation, night sweats, and headaches. It also resulted in such mental symptoms as impatience, irritability, restlessness, and overall hyperactivity. Elizabeth's tongue and pulse also confirmed this buildup of heat.

Treatment and recommendation

My first recommendation to Elizabeth was, "Take things easy and cool it." I told her she needed to slow down her pace a little and try to concentrate on the tasks at hand. When Shaoyangs focus on the little things, it grounds them, and keeps their energy from dissipating in ineffective, inefficient ways. When I say that it "grounds" them, I mean it nourishes their deficient Kidneys, the roots of their bodies. I also recommended that Elizabeth soften up her speech, behavior, and movements. Shaoyangs have a tendency towards aggressive energy, which, if left unchecked, can not only cause problems like arguments and fights, but also lead to health problems as well. I also told her that she needed to see things through, no matter how difficult or unpleasant they were. Shaoyangs, with their fickle nature, tend to shirk their responsibilities at the drop of a hat when a difficulty or something more interesting comes along. This sort of irresponsibility prevents Shaoyangs from reflecting on their often wasteful lifestyles.

Although I teach breathing and meditation exercises to almost all of the patients that I treat, with Shaoyangs, I emphasize these practices even more. The centering and calming effects of these practices are precisely what Shaoyangs need every day. I told Elizabeth to start her day with 10 minutes of mediation, and encouraged her to slowly build up to 30 minutes within a month. I also encouraged her to eat more foods that correctly matched her body type. These included grains (like barley), vegetables (like eggplants, cucumbers, and celery), fruits (like bananas, strawberries, and pineapples), and seafood (like abalone, crab, squid, and oysters). These foods help to nourish the depleted Yin, and cool heat.

The treatment principle that I applied to Elizabeth was to Clear Heat and Nourish Yin (which is the basic treatment principle for people of this body type). Along with constitutional acupuncture, I gave her a formula intended to address her weaknesses. It is called Di Huang Bai Hu Tang (White Tiger Decoction with Rehmannia), and it helps to build Yin, cool heat, and relieve constipation.

Gradually, over several months of regular acupuncture and herbal treatments, along with modifications in her diet and daily living habits, Elizabeth's stomach pain stopped. More importantly, however, she said that she felt calmer and more centered. She felt that by controlling her emotions and meditating, she had gained control over her restlessness and her temper and had discovered joy in both her inner self and her domestic chores. She had regained full charge of her health.

Taiyin

- Be very cautious about becoming excessively joyful or pleased. Taiyins are prone to fluctuations of pleasure and joy, and these emotions have the potential to damage their innately weak Lungs if they are not properly controlled. As both of these emotions cause the body's energy to descend, when they become excessive, the Lungs are unable to perform the function of raising and dispersing energy.

- Release the fear of starting something new. Most Taiyins are afraid of new beginnings and hold their fears inside of themselves. When this fear becomes great, they become incapable of doing anything. To prevent this, Taiyins must learn to eliminate their fear of starting new projects. If they do not, then they will never truly progress in life. Once Taiyins shift their attention away from themselves, and onto others, they are able to overcome many of their fears. This coincidentally tends to make them more morally upright, in the sense that they shift from selfish motives to more altruistic ones. Once this is accomplished, Taiyins are able to work at their optimum level, with persistence and patience, gradually earning the trust and confidence of those around them.

- Learn to meditate. Again, I cannot emphasize enough the importance of meditation in balancing each constitution. Although it may seem as though meditation is an introspective act, something that Taiyins typically would not need, it is actually one of the most effective means to settling Taiyins' fears. Meditation actually helps Taiyins to see the big picture, allowing them to become more balanced.

- Stay active. As long as Taiyins are actively pursuing their goals, they will succeed, whether it is in the personal, social, business, political, or financial sphere. Taiyins are the most inertial of the four body types. When in motion, they are steady and unstoppable, but when they are still, it is extremely difficult to start them moving again.

- Be careful of overindulging in recreational activities. Taiyins tend to get too much pleasure out of them. They must be careful not to over-indulge in these activities in order to keep healthy.

- Taiyins must improve their interpersonal relationships by becoming less selfish, obstinate, closed-minded, suspicious, and greedy. In other words, they should reduce their tendency to dominate and look down upon other people. At the same time, they should try to be flexible and understanding and strive to listen to the opinions of others carefully. Also, they must develop their moral integrity so that they can properly distinguish between what is good for the whole and what will only be of benefit to themselves.

- It is important for Taiyins to reduce their tendency to over-accumulate possessions. Taiyins by nature tend to store and save without letting go or dispersing. As a result, they easily become stuck in the never-ending quest to acquire and maintain material wealth, status, knowledge, love, and energy. Dr. Lee offered Taiyins the following warning on this matter: "If Taiyins totally become immersed in the maintenance of their domestic affairs, they will become overly avaricious."

    ● Follow the wise old saying, "Variety is the spice of life." Taiyins on the whole tend to find comfort only in the present state of things. They must come to the realization that theirs is not the only world. Taiyins should read, listen, and travel more so that they can reach out to the world and avoid becoming a frog stuck in a well.

    ● A key to longevity for Taiyins lies in settling their fearful minds by paying less attention to their own personal problems, and more attention to outside matters. In other words, they should reduce their excessive egotistical desires and practice more altruistic deeds.

Footsteps on the path

David K. is a 53-year-old high-ranking executive at a steel mill. He had been suffering from high blood pressure for three years. This was essential, or primary hypertension, meaning that it was of unknown cause.

Since his diagnosis, David had been taking a high blood pressure medication three times per day. The side effects from the drug included weakness, dizziness, skin rashes, and edema of his face. These side effects influenced his decision to stop taking the medication and try alternative forms of treatment. He simply said, "I am sick and tired of being medicated."

Aside from his main complaint, David was also overweight (200 pounds at 5'7") and wanted to lose about 20 pounds. He had a heavy frame with a large, stereotypical Taiyin potbelly. Actually, everything about him was big. He had a round, puffy face, a reddish complexion, big, round eyes that were doe-like, and a big round nose. He said that his eyes tended to become red easily and were at times painful.

When he related his work and daily habits to me, David basically described what I knew to be the lifestyle of a high energy, out-of-balance Taiyin. He said, "I have a lot of energy and am constantly restless. I work from 5:30 a.m. until 7 p.m., six days a week. I sleep only five hours a day. I've been like this for more than 10 years." Due to his busy schedule, an "excuse" he said, he did absolutely no exercise, but on a positive note, he did not smoke.

After a pause, he added, "I am constantly under stress. I have to make many important decisions and have to stay alert for any mistakes made by my employees, as well as new business opportunities." He suffered from usual amounts of frustration in his work. He also admitted to having a temper that he always tries to disguise with a kind and gentle smile, never expressing it outwardly.

David had a typically hearty Taiyin appetite and ate abundantly from the four food groups, including a lot of meat. When I asked him how he was able to wake up so early and remain alert for such long hours, he replied that he drank a minimum of six cups of coffee and two glasses of wine per day. He felt thirsty, with a desire to drink cold water. Although he tended towards constipation, he had no problems with digestion or urination. He had noticed a slight decrease in memory and concentration in recent years. He also suffered from migraines one to two days a week.

When I examined his tongue, it was reddish purple with a crack in the center and a slight yellow coat. His pulse was wiry and full, and slightly rapid.

Interpretation

It was very easy to diagnose David, as he exemplifies a Taiyin with a lot of heat. It was clear that his mode of overworking, sedentary lifestyle, obesity, and excessive stress had all contributed to his high blood pressure. His coffee intake also played a big part in his problem.

When I first told David about the imbalance in his Liver, he was in-credulous (a typical reaction for Taiyins). I explained to him the relation-ship between the Liver imbalance and his high blood pressure, and hesi-tantly went on to tell him that the root cause of his problem was his ten-dency toward excessive greed. Surprised and almost offended to hear my explanation of the source of his problem, David asked how greed had any-thing to do with his illness. I explained that there are four constitutional types according to Sasang Medicine and that his body type belonged to the Taiyin group, a constitution having the innate tendency to gather and store excessive amounts of energies and mass.

In Taiyins, habitual patterns can manifest as accumulations of food, money, and other material things, as well as intangibles such as knowledge and information. It is this compulsion to collect that causes energy and matter to stagnate and impede circulation. When the Liver's nature to accumulate is in excess, its energy becomes stagnant and the Lungs' duty to disperse energy is weakened. The most effective treatment for David, aside from acupuncture or herbal medicine, was for him to control his mental and emotional states.

Taiyins in general have an immense amount of energy and can outlast all other constitutions. In the workplace, this gives them tremendous en-durance and persistence. However, when they do not take care of them-selves in all areas, including proper diet and lifestyle management, the fuel can run out or become stuck and stagnant. As work becomes more stressful and they do not find a proper way to vent this stress, they tend to become heated up inside. This can cause headaches, red eyes, thirst, and constipation. This is exactly what happened to David. His tongue and pulse also manifested signs of heat.

Thus, to maintain a healthy life, it is best for Taiyins to let go of their greed and reduce their selfishness. They must concentrate on releasing and stop gathering in and overloading themselves.

Treatment and recommendation

Because of David's apprehension about the treatment, I took additional time to thoroughly explain what I was going to do, giving him a comprehensive lecture on the principles of Sasang Medicine. He felt more at ease after my explanation, and resolved to commit time and effort to the treatment and to making changes in his lifestyle and diet.

I put David on a regimen of twice-weekly acupuncture treatments and daily doses of herbal medicine. After consulting with his doctor, we gradually started to reduce his Western medication. He was also put on a Taiyin diet and taught the proper meditation exercises to enhance his awareness and the management of his mental and emotional states.

With the combination of my prescribed treatments and his participation in his own recovery, David found a measure of peace and well-being he had not known before. His mood became more relaxed and his blood pressure dropped to within the normal range after several months of consistent treatment. He reduced his workload and learned to delegate more. In short, he learned how to let go. He was also able curb his excessive need for coffee, reducing his intake to just two cups a day. As a result of his improved physical and mental health, David did not have to fake smiles to his co-workers anymore, because he was in control of his stress and in full charge of his emotions.

Shaoyin

❧ Do not overindulge in either pleasure or joy. Pleasure and joy both cause the body's energy to descend. If a person experiences too much pleasure or joy, then the body's energy will descend too quickly, and in too large an amount. Such a deluge will injure the Shaoyin's weak organ, the Spleen. Through regulation of the emotions, Shaoyins can regulate and balance their internal organs.

☯ Learn to calm down. Shaoyins must try to stabilize their nervous minds, as they are always insecure and anxious. The constant worry afflicting Shaoyins is extremely debilitating and can easily lead to a fastidious personality, such mental problems as phobias, neurasthenia, and obsessive-compulsive behaviors, or even physical problems, like diabetes. When Shaoyins learn how to calm down and relax themselves, their digestive organs will be able to function at an optimal level, ensuring good health.

☯ Practice benevolence and magnanimity. This will naturally balance the minuteness, introversion, and narrow-mindedness that cause nervous system disorders in the Shaoyin constitution. Shaoyins must be especially wary of jealousy and misunderstanding. Shaoyins often are plagued by a constant worry that they are falling behind someone, or being cheated on. They meticulously scrutinize everything they see for evidence to back their worries up. Even if there is nothing to suggest that their fears are true, they often remain caught up in reexamining their world to make certain that things are going their way. Unfortunately, unlike the Shaoyangs, Shaoyins are unable to dispense with their emotions easily. Thus, the only way to avoid the nervous system disorders that result from chronic worry is for Shaoyins to learn to see the big picture and practice being big-hearted. This means setting sights on larger goals and accomplishments and paying less attention to little profits and benefits. They must learn to share things with others, whether material or not, instead of keeping things to themselves.

☯ Be proactive. Shaoyins should practice being more active and optimistic when starting new projects. In this manner, they may learn to rid themselves of their uncertain dispositions. Shaoyins often end up waiting forever for their messiah to arrive, only to hesitate and lose the opportunity in the crucial moment. If they do not learn to take some action, no matter how small, then they will be doomed to remain trapped forever in a world of what might have been.

☯ Be careful of the acquisition of power and authority. Power and authority are easily abused, and easily lost. They thus have the potential to destroy the simple, law-abiding mentality of the balanced Shaoyin. Under the influence of power, Shaoyins quickly forget the rules of respect, growing abusive in their speech, attitudes, behaviors, and actions towards those that deserve deference, like their elders. They must always remember the rules of respect, and their place within the order of things, no matter how much power and authority they may come to attain.

Footsteps on the path

Cathy R. is a 42-year-old consultant in the film industry. She complained of a variety of digestive problems. Cathy stated that she had a fair appetite, but suffered constantly from gas, bloating, and distention in her abdomen after meals. She also suffered from chronic constipation (with occasional loose stools) and left lower abdominal pain. Moreover, she had been suffering from hemorrhoids for about three months by the time she came in to see me.

I first noticed that she had a small face, with gentle, oval eyes, and a well-defined nose and mouth. Her lower body was well developed, with strong legs and wide buttocks and hips, as opposed to her narrow, sloping shoulders. On the whole, she was short in stature, with a small body, and somewhat overweight. Her gait and gestures were gentle and soft. Her voice, too, was very gentle and calm.

As we proceeded with the interview, Cathy revealed that she also had been experiencing an inexplicable drop in energy for about a year and a half. She felt tired throughout the day, but especially after meals. She had not had any viral diseases, and a recent Western medical check-up revealed no abnormalities. Cathy said she occasionally experienced tightness in the neck and shoulders, and pain and weakness in the lower back and knees. Her sleep was not very deep, with some dreaming, and occasionally she woke with palpitations.

Several other symptoms were revealed in the course of the interview: Cathy tended to bruise easily and to breathe in a shallow fashion, sighing several times throughout the day. Her hands and feet were cold all the time and her hands tended to tremble from time to time. She disliked cold weather in general and liked drinking hot water. She experienced blurred vision, occasional dizziness, and a mild headache on the front and sides of her head about twice a month for the past several years.

Cathy then talked about her emotional condition. She said, "I've been suffering from this mild depression for several years, and I always feel this anxiety inside. People say that I look gentle and calm on the outside, but on the inside, I often feel impatient and I always want to get things done quickly." She also revealed that she was emotionally very sensitive.

As far as work was concerned, she expressed a preference for independence and working alone, although she also worked well under the management of others. Although indecisive by nature, she was very precise and meticulous in her work and in home affairs.

Examination of her abdomen revealed tension and bloating over the whole abdomen, but especially in the area of solar plexus, along her rib cage, and in the lower abdomen. There were gurgling noises in several places. The lower abdomen was tense with spasms, but did not have any masses. Although Cathy was somewhat overweight, her abdomen did not interrupt or obscure her hourglass figure.

I looked at her tongue, and noted that it was pale and purple, with tooth marks on the edges, a red tip, and a thin white coating. Her pulse was thready and weak on both sides, with a slightly wiry pulse on the right second position.

Interpretation

Cathy presents a typical example of the Shaoyin constitution in a state of mental and emotional imbalance. As Shaoyin types tend to have introverted tendencies (due to a lack of Yang), they tend to hold things inside. This can easily lead to depression. Also, because Shaoyins have an innate tendency towards nervous minds, they are in a perpetual state of anxiety. In some Shaoyins, this manifests in the need to get things done quickly. Indecisiveness, precision, and meticulousness are hallmarks of the Shaoyin psyche. Cathy's frequent sighing is an example of how Shaoyins want to get rid of emotional congestion in their bodies.

Along with the above mental traits, Cathy also has a clear-cut Shaoyin type body: a strong lower body and a lack of upper body development. The shape of her waist and hips (hourglass) is typical in Shaoyin body types. She also demonstrates many typical Shaoyin physical symptoms.

With Shaoyins, the first and foremost thing that I check to gauge their health is the state of their digestion: this was clearly out of balance in Cathy's case. Her digestive problems were due to Spleen Yang deficiency. As a result of this deficiency, Cathy's energy level was low (especially after meals) and she had cold extremities. Her constipation also resulted from deficient Yang (here, manifesting as weakened peristalsis). The dryness of her stools, meanwhile, was due to a lack of Blood (which in turn resulted from the weakness in the Spleen). Her hemorrhoids and easy bruising were also caused by the lack of Spleen Yang energy because, under normal conditions, the Spleen Yang holds organs in their proper place, and keeps blood running in the vessels.

The tightness in her neck and shoulder arises from Qi stagnation as a result of her stress, and the pain and weakness in her knees and lower back result from lack of Yang energy in her Kidneys.

When there is a lack of Yang energy and a weakness of the digestive system, production of blood in the body will suffer. This lack of blood can be seen from the following symptoms: insomnia with dream-disturbed sleep, palpitations, blurred vision, dizziness, mild headaches, pale tongue, and a thready and weak pulse. The pale purple color of Cathy's tongue indicates that there is stagnation of energy and blood in her body with underlying blood and Qi deficiency. The slightly wiry pulse on the right second position indicates that energy in her Liver has invaded her Spleen. In simple terms, along with the weakness in her Spleen, stress was contributing to her digestive problems.

Treatment and recommendation

Before I gave Cathy her initial acupuncture treatment, I spoke to her about the importance of balancing her mental and emotional dispositions. I explained to her about the four body types and how her body type has an inherent weakness in the digestive system called Spleen. Whenever a Shaoyin is mentally and emotionally affected, mainly due to stress, her digestive system goes off. I said that all of her digestive problems are created by her inherent Spleen weakness, which was worsened by her mental and emotional stress. This is what is known as psychosomatic illness in Western medicine. So, I carefully gave her guidelines in regulating her mind. The first and foremost principle is to relax, and one of the best ways to accomplish this is to breathe properly. Next, I told Cathy to meditate for few minutes each day. I also told her to loosen up a little on her meticulous tendencies and try to be more open and broadminded. Furthermore, I advised her to be more optimistic by seeing the positive side of things. I said, "One reason why you are getting depressed is a lack of energy, so if you can concentrate on building your overall energy, you will become more optimistic and the depression will naturally disappear on its own." I added, "Try to stay calm immediately before, during, and after mealtimes. It is especially important that you do not start working immediately after meals. Try to sit and relax for 15 minutes after meals. You have to be vigilant over this matter in order to improve your digestive system and the whole body."

To further help Cathy's emotional disposition, I put her on an aerobic exercise program for 20 minutes per day. Deep breathing and movements resulting from aerobic exercises are excellent for many Shaoyins, who tend to breathe shallowly and lack energy. Improved breathing and overall circulation, resulting from the performance of aerobic exercises, will do wonders for Shaoyins' passive and oftentimes negative mental tendencies. In addition to the breathing, meditation, and aerobic exercises, I taught her an abdominal massage technique to speed her progress. The goal of the abdominal massage, in addition to strengthening the digestive system, is to help calm the person down.

Cathy was treated with constitutional acupuncture to help strengthen her weak Spleen and normalize her strong Kidneys while calming her mind. In addition to acupuncture, an herbal formula called Shi Quan Da Bu Tang (All-Inclusive Great Tonifying Formula) was prescribed. This formula includes such famous Spleen-energy-building herbs as ginseng and astragalus, as well as cinnamon bark, a very warming herb. Because of Cathy's constipation, I increased the dosage of angelica root (Dang Gui), a superb Shaoyin tonic herb. I also added an herb called cyperus, which regulates the circulation of Qi, to offset her stress and depression.

After the first two weeks of treatment (three office visits per week), Cathy began to notice improvements in her energy level and her digestion, and after three additional months of twice-weekly treatments, the pain in the lower abdomen disappeared completely, and her bowel movements normalized. Cathy stated, "Since my energy level has increased, my depression has gotten much better. I also feel much calmer and have better control over how I feel. Since I am healthier, I have more confidence in myself and am responding to stressful situations a lot better." She has been regular with her daily regimen of exercises and meditation and now comes in once every six months for a check-up or "tune-up" treatment.

Conclusion: Four Virtues and Vices

To attain self-cultivation, you must first realize that everything that you are is interconnected; the state of your physical health is neither separate from your mind, nor separable from the cultivation of your character. Then, you must observe your behaviors, tendencies, preferences, and attitudes until you clearly perceive the Four Beginnings or Four Principles (virtues of benevolence, righteousness, propriety, and wisdom) and Four Desires (vices of rudeness, vanity, greed, and indolence) within yourself. This is the stage of self-understanding.

According to Confucianism, benevolence is the feeling of commiseration (sympathy or compassion). Righteousness is what causes us to feel shame when engaged in activities that are against our conscience, or when we cannot stand up to injustice. Propriety is what allows us to be modest and humble. Finally, wisdom is our inherent ability to distinguish right from wrong, and is the basic common sense guiding us in our daily lives. According to Mencius, these four beginnings or principles are innate within us, and arise spontaneously if our hearts are unobstructed by vice.

In contrast to the four beginnings are the four desires or vices, the evils of our minds. Rudeness occurs as a result of neglecting propriety and doing everything as one pleases. Vanity occurs when a person disregards wisdom and becomes frivolous and superficial in character. Greed occurs in a person who neglects benevolence and thinks only of the fulfillment of selfish desire. Indolence occurs when a person ignores righteousness and remains idle, basking in comfort instead of keeping active. These are the four vices of our minds that we must vigilantly watch for.

Everyone, whether a sage or a commoner, has both virtues and vices. Sages, however, have more of the virtues and less of the vices, while commoners have more vices and fewer virtues. By cultivating the four beginnings or principles, you will strengthen your moral character. At the same time, you will attain a higher state of health. Also, by cultivating the four virtues, you will be helping others to deal with the suffering and imbalance in their lives. Thus, by cultivating yourself, you will benefit others. This is the stage of compassionate action.

Although the cultivation of the four virtues will elevate you physically, mentally, and spiritually, we must keep in mind that we are not becoming better than others. We are merely centering ourselves, so that we may truly become ourselves, and so that others may be allowed to become themselves through us. Notions of better or worse are deceiving in this context. Similarly, we must remember that no one constitution is better or worse than another. Each constitution has its good and bad qualities. Through knowing our strengths and weaknesses, we can make real efforts at correction and balance. If, however, we attempt to deny who we really are, and pretend that we are perfect, we will get nowhere fast. The path to self-realization and self-cultivation lies within ourselves, with all of our imperfections.

Chapter 11

Acupuncture

The basic premise of Sasang Medicine is to treat the root of the problem, rather than just the symptoms. According to Sasang Medicine, this root is found in a person's basic constitutional imbalance. By treating this fundamental imbalance, all pathological manifestations may be addressed. In addition to diet, herbs, and exercise, acupuncture is another healing modality utilized in Sasang Medicine.

The practice of acupuncture is centered around two core themes in Sasang Medicine:

- ☯ To tone, reinforce, and augment depleted Qi in a weak organ.
- ☯ To reduce or sedate excess Qi in a strong organ.

Acupuncture does not transform you from one body type to another. Rather, acupuncture reestablishes the harmony within your given constitution. Remember that you are born with a certain imbalance in the strength of your organs. Emotional, dietary, and daily habits can tilt this imbalance even more, making your strong organs even stronger, and your weak organs even weaker. This can bring about a chaotic, disharmonious state that triggers the disorders particular to your body type. Acupuncture and other Sasang medical modalities return your body to its particular state of balance.

What Is Acupuncture?

The word acupuncture derives from the Latin words "acus," which means "needle," and "punctura," which means "to puncture." Acupuncture is a primary health care modality that has flourished in Asia for the past 5,000 years. According to the World Health Organization, it is currently used by more than one-third of the world's population. A 1997 *Los Angeles Times* report stated that more than one million people received acupuncture treatments in the United States in 1996. Acupuncture has also been officially recognized by the World Health Organization as a valuable and effective treatment modality for various health-related disorders.

Acupuncture is a safe and effective form of therapy when it is administered by a qualified, experienced practitioner. It has few side effects and is both non-addictive and non-toxic. The practice of acupuncture involves the insertion of hair-thin, sterile, stainless steel needles into specific locations on the body called acupuncture points. Unlike hypodermic needles, there is little or no discomfort associated with the insertion of acupuncture needles. They have a very fine diameter, are not hollow, and are not used to inject foreign substances into the body. Furthermore, acupuncture needles do not tear the tissues of the body. Rather, they gently separate body tissues such that when the needles are extracted, the tissues are able to come back together again.

Although we cannot see radio waves with the naked eye, we know that if we tune a radio to the right frequency, we will hear music. The same principle applies to acupuncture. If we place an acupuncture needle in the right spot and tune it to the right frequency, then it will serve as an antenna for receiving healing energy from the universe. The needle can broadcast the energy through the acupuncture point into the body, where it can exert positive changes.

When energy in the body is depleted, the needles can help to restore it, either by tuning in to the energy of the universe, or by redistributing the energy that is already in the body, drawing from regions of the body where there are surpluses. On the other hand, if the body has an excessive amount of energy, then the needles can serve to either drain the surplus out of the body, or redistribute it to regions of the body where the energy is deficient.

In cases of stagnant energy, acupuncture needles can open the circulation so that energy can flow properly throughout the body. All of these techniques are designed to get the energy flowing throughout the body, in the right quantity, speed, and time.

Acupuncture meridians and points

According to Eastern medical theory, an energy called Qi flows throughout the body along certain channels or meridians. There are 12 major channels and a host of collateral or connecting channels. These channels are invisible conduits through which the Qi, blood, and other vital substances circulate. They help to link all tissues, organs, and systems in the body. As both physiological and pathological signals are carried along these channels, any change within the body inevitably manifests externally on the body surface, along the corresponding channel. A practitioner of acupuncture taps into the internal organs and all vital substances through the network formed by these channels.

When Qi is in a state of harmony, it regulates, balances, and promotes physical, mental, and emotional well-being. Conversely, when the Qi is deficient, excessive, or stagnant, its smooth flow is interrupted. Various physical, mental, and emotional problems result. Physical injury, emotional trauma, stress, constitutional imbalance, an improper diet, or unbalanced lifestyles contribute to the blockage of Qi. The goal of acupuncture is to regulate the flow of Qi and re-establish harmony within the body. When this is achieved, the body will be restored to its natural, balanced state, the state most conducive to healing.

In addition to acupuncture, a variety of therapies affect Qi, including moxibustion (the application of heat to acupuncture points using moxa, compressed mugwort), cupping (the application of glass or plastic suction cups over the points), massage, herbal medicine, Tai Chi (moving meditation), and Qi Gong (energy cultivation exercises).

There are more than 2,000 points on and off the various meridians, but in clinical practice only about 150 points are used on a regular basis. If the channels are compared to traffic routes where the Qi flows, then these points may be likened to street intersections where the Qi concentrates. Acupuncture points act as gateways, portals, or valves that can open or close to regulate the flow of energy throughout the body. Many points are located in the crevices and small depressions found between muscles and bones. Some acupuncture points store enormous amounts of energy, thus acting as major vortexes, much like the chakras of Yoga. For these reasons, these points become the focus not only of acupuncture treatments, but of Qi Gong as well.

Acupuncture according to modern science

Scientific studies have verified several benefits of acupuncture. Research has shown that acupuncture influences the central and peripheral nervous systems of the body, thus explaining its effectiveness in the management of pain. It has also been used for anesthesia during major surgeries. But the efficacy of acupuncture has far more uses and benefits beyond the management of pain and anesthesia.

Research has shown that acupuncture affects the levels of sugar, cholesterol, triglycerides, and hormones in the blood. It particularly stimulates the production of endorphins, morphine-like brain chemicals. Acupuncture thus balances the functioning of the gastrointestinal, endocrine, and nervous systems in the body. It can also improve general circulation to reduce inflammation and expedite healing. Furthermore, placing a needle on points such as LI-4 (on the bulge between the thumb and index finger when they are together) helps to produce interferon, a substance that fights infections and cancer cells. Clinical research has also verified that acupuncture reduces cravings and reactions to withdrawal. Thus, it has been used recently for drug, alcohol, caffeine, tobacco, and food addictions.

What to expect during and after treatment

Most people find acupuncture treatments very relaxing, and conducive to a feeling of overall well-being. The minimal pain and the ease involved in the needle insertions, combined with the comfort experienced during the overall treatment, often surprises many people.

During the insertion of the needle, a person may feel a mild pinch or no sensation at all as the needle breaks the skin. This is followed by a dull, achy, heavy sensation alternately described as pressure, a pulsing, or a surge at the location of the needle. This is identified in Eastern medicine as the summoning and realignment of the body's energy. After these initial sensations, people may feel warmth traveling along certain paths. They may also sense energy moving in a region of the body distant from the insertion site. The needle sensations, however, do not necessarily indicate treatment effectiveness.

During the treatment, most people fall into a complete state of relaxation or into a dreamy state. Some people may even fall asleep during a treatment. After the treatment, some people feel animated and invigo-rated with a surge of energy, whereas others want to continue to rest. Pa-tients typically report a general sense of well-being after treatments, in addition to the specific therapeutic benefits. Many patients look forward to receiving acupuncture treatments.

The depth of the needle penetration can range anywhere from a frac-tion of an inch on the fingers or toes to several inches in the abdomen or buttocks. It all depends upon the location of the point, the thickness of the muscle and flesh, body weight, disease condition, age of the patient, and the practitioner's needling technique.

On average, an acupuncture treatment can last anywhere from 15 to 30 minutes, although the duration varies depending on the practitioner and the technique used. Treatment times will also vary with the age, dis-ease condition, and state of health of the patient. With children and the elderly, for example, the needle retention time is significantly reduced, or the needle may be withdrawn shortly after obtaining a needling sensation.

After the treatment, patients may continue to feel a euphoric sensa-tion with diminished pain and discomfort. Some people may find they are tired for several hours after the treatment. On occasion, patients may not find immediate relief; in fact, it may take several sessions before they ob-tain substantial results. A few people may experience what is called a post-treatment "healing crisis" in the form of a temporary aggravation or exac-erbation of symptoms prior to improvement. Even if patients experience immediate results, however, it is recommended that they follow the advice of their practitioners regarding future sessions. This is essential in order to stabilize and firmly establish their newfound state of health.

Footsteps on the path

Cindy P., 53 years old, came to my clinic complaining of chronic lower back pain, which she had been suffering from for the past 20 years. The pain was constant, and radiated down her left side to her buttocks. It was worse when she walked or sat down; lying down provided some measure of relief. In general, the pain started out sharp in the morning, gradually growing duller and duller until she went to sleep. In addition, she noticed that she was beginning to lose sensation on the left side of her back, but-tocks, and legs. She had been taking over-the-counter painkillers for many years to relieve the pain and inflammation. She also said that her lower back felt better with the application of ice.

Cindy was 30 pounds overweight, with a large belly and buttocks, and a weak looking head and neck. Cindy said that she has been overweight all her life. Her facial features were large and dignified, but her eyes had a certain look of fear in them.

Cindy had a tendency to overeat. She basically liked all types of foods at all temperatures (although she had a special preference for cool or cold foods like salads, raw fruits, and cold sandwiches), and often craved cold water. Although she was frequently constipated, it usually did not bother her. Cindy had warm extremities, and although she was comfortable in most climates, she didn't like the hot and damp season (summer or early autumn).

As far as her medical history was concerned, Cindy reported that she had fractured two vertebrae in her back in an automobile accident 30 years ago. Three years prior to seeing me, an MRI revealed her lumbar stenosis, a narrowing of the space around the nerves of the lumbar region. She also developed osteoarthritis in her knees, feet, and neck. In addition, Cindy said that she got bronchitis twice a year, and that she had been wheezing for the past six months.

Cindy worked as a manager at an import and export company. Personal and work-related stress often left her depressed. She also frequently felt anxious, nervous, and tired all the time. Despite her fatigue, she experienced difficulties in both falling and staying asleep.

Cindy's hobbies and interests included reading, gardening, and occasional exercise, like hiking. In general, she liked taking things slowly, allowing enough time to really reflect on her thoughts and actions.

Her tongue was purple in color, with a thin white coat, a red tip, and tooth marks. Her pulse was wiry and choppy and slightly rapid.

Interpretation

I diagnosed Cindy as a Taiyin type, based on her gait, gestures, and body shape. Her lung weakness (an inherent constitutional weakness) helped to confirm this diagnosis.

Her energy level was low because of her weight (remember that more energy is required to maintain the extra weight), and because the congestion and stagnancy to which her constitution was prone (also due to extra weight) impeded circulation, especially when she was under stress. This stagnancy of energy underlies most of the problems in Taiyins, and in Cindy, it was the cause of her lower back pain and arthritic condition.

There is a constitutional tendency in Taiyins to develop heat. When energy and substance stagnates, heat builds up. Her desire for cold foods and drinks, the tendency toward constipation, and warm extremities all pointed towards the accumulation of heat.

This innate tendency toward heat combined with stress creates additional problems. As a result of constant stress, heat began to develop, drying her body. This heat caused many of her emotional problems; its restless energy made her feel anxious and nervous, and the stagnancy of the energy from the heat (largely caused by her stress) caused her to experience frequent bouts of depression.

Like the typical Taiyin, Cindy did not show her emotions easily. Also like most Taiyins, she had a tendency to procrastinate in most of her daily affairs, preferring to ponder decisions slowly, cautiously, and thoroughly. Her hobbies and interests tended to show this preference towards taking things nice and easy.

Cindy's tongue was purple, indicating that her overall circulation was impeded, and that there was a great deal of Qi stagnation in her body. This was further supported by the wiry and choppy pulses, signs that indicated obstruction in energy and blood circulation, along with pain. The buildup of heat in her body made her tongue red at the tip and her pulse beat at a slightly rapid rate.

Treatment and recommendation

After carefully explaining Cindy's condition and her body type to her, I administered a treatment of general and constitutional acupuncture. General acupuncture was used to mitigate pain and help improve circulation of Qi and Blood to the affected region. Constitutional acupuncture, meanwhile, focused on balancing her inherent energetic tilt of strong Liver and weak Lung energies.

I also gave suggestions for therapeutic exercises (both for breathing and for stretching and strengthening the abdomen, lower back, and whole body), together with a prescription of herbal medicine and modifications to her diet.

Cindy started to notice improvements right away. There was a reduction in the pain and stiffness in her back, and the numbness in her left side improved. She also slept better at night, and her energy level began to rise.

After two months of twice-a-week treatments, Cindy felt so much better that she discontinued the use of her over-the-counter painkillers completely. I continued to treat her once every two weeks for six additional months, and as of this writing, eight months later, she has not had to take any painkillers.

Cindy was extremely happy, saying, "I have never felt so much better in my entire life." She added, "I thought that I would have to take the painkillers for the rest of my life. But now, with my daily exercise routine [stretching and walking] and meditation to help my body and mind, I feel confident that I can stay off the drugs for good."

Part III

Love and Work

Chapter 12

Romantic Compatability in Sasang Medicine

But love is blind, and lovers cannot see
The pretty follies that themselves commit.
—Shakespeare, *The Merchant of Venice*

Sasang Medicine body typing arose with the specific goal of detecting patterns in human physiology and psychology, and effecting changes in those patterns to achieve harmony. Although many of the changes suggested by Sasang Medicine involve the individual alone, one of the most powerful applications actually involves being aware of the relationships between oneself and others, particularly with regard to romantically involved couples. If you use Sasang Medicine to understand yourself and your partner, you will be well on your way to finding harmony in your intimate relationships.

Unless you've been living on another planet, you've probably become aware of the premium our culture places upon the ability to communicate effectively in an intimate relationship. Communications during the courtship phase of a relationship may seem effortlessly satisfying, as our initial choices are usually based upon physical attraction rather than psychological understanding. For a few fleeting weeks, we may speak each other's unspoken language fluently. However, as the hormonal surge of courtship begins to wane, so too does our ability to communicate effectively. Why? Because intimate communication—the stuff of which real intimacy is made—cannot be sustained without a deep understanding of ourselves and of our partners. And, in this regard, our hormones leave us high and dry.

Real intimacy requires mutual understanding, which in turn requires work. As with any other work, we can't perform this task without tools. We can try to do the work by listening to and observing ourselves and our partners. But without tools—a way to find meaning—the information we acquire in the process will not provide us with much clarity or guidance. Sasang Medicine body typing not only provides the compass for health but for relationships as well.

Taiyang

In relationships, Taiyangs can pose serious problems. Because of their constitutional predisposition to excess in all things, they are the most difficult to get along with. They are constitutionally predisposed to be in full control and plow forward, with little regard for the feelings or preferences of their partners. Taiyangs do, however, tend to search for the ideal life partner, irrespective of looks or past history, and will endure nearly anything to recapture a lost love.

Two Taiyangs

It goes without saying that a relationship between two Taiyangs is highly combustible. By nature, each has a clear personal agenda, neither intends to yield power, and both have the energetic capacity to cause changes of epic proportions. In a dispute between two Taiyangs, the energy in the room can be enough to peel the paint off the walls. Unless somebody backs down, one person will eventually lose in this contest of wills, with the promise of an ugly aftermath. The only way to avoid this tragic result is for one or both partners to summon the strength to restrain their innate passion, and compromise.

However, even when there is compromise, the Taiyang couple will face many challenges. Their strong Yang energy will draw them both outside the home for fulfillment of their creative potentials. This is particularly true of Taiyang men, who are capable of toiling day and night. Taiyang women, meanwhile, will find little satisfaction in the domestic sphere, due in part to their difficulty conceiving as a result of the constitutional weakness in their reproductive systems. Thus, the Taiyang couple is both physically and psychologically predisposed to seek gratification outside the home and to neglect family life. The problem occurs at the literal and figurative end of the day when they return to a home attended by no one. It is then that they find themselves in a relationship out of balance. In order to restore harmony, one or both partners will have to again override their inherent nature and take time away from their outside goals to cultivate a family life, whether it be to have and nurture children or to simply attend to the comforts of daily living.

In Sasang Medicine, the Liver plays a vital role in sexual activity. Because Taiyangs are defined, in part, by their weak Livers, they have little sexual energy left over once the initial passion of courtship subsides. They are more physiologically predisposed towards goals and ideals than towards procreation or sex. Even in the rare cases where a Taiyang does experience great passion, it usually leads to deep spiritual, intellectual, and emotional awareness rather than sexual prowess. Typically, Taiyangs rarely feel sexual impulses once they have settled into a relationship.

Taiyang-Shaoyang

Taiyangs don't fare well with Shaoyangs. In particular, they will not tolerate the Shaoyang's fickleness. Taiyangs know what they want and have no time for people who don't. Likewise, the extravagant spending habits of the Shaoyang will be enough to send the Taiyang through the roof, as he or she will view this behavior as a sign of weak character. Moreover, the female Shaoyang's affection for a social life will be unbearable to the Taiyang male, who craves subservient obedience from his partner. A social butterfly of a partner is of little use to the selfish Taiyang partner, who seeks to manipulate his partner to advance his own goals. The Taiyang-Shaoyang couple do, however, have one thing in common: curiosity—the Shaoyang for anything and everything, the Taiyang for anything related to his or her own ideological dreams.

Taiyang-Taiyin

At first glance, there would seem to be little hope for the Taiyang-Taiyin combination. Taiyangs will not tolerate the lazy, greedy nature of the Taiyin constitution any better than they will the conservative, status quo attitude of the typical Taiyin. Moreover, Taiyangs are in a hurry. They have a sense of urgency that permeates every aspect of their lives, whether they're on their way to an important meeting or filling up their gas tank. Taiyins, on the other hand, act as if they have all the time in the world and don't like to be rushed. They dislike movement and like to remain still. However, it is the extremely understanding, patient, and magnanimous nature of the Taiyin that makes them the only constitution that can tolerate the extreme behaviors of the Taiyang partner. Taiyins will, in fact, respect and honor the air of authority projected by the Taiyang partner. Thus, it is the Taiyang/Taiyin couple who will realize the greatest degree of harmony without denying their innate constitutional tendencies.

Taiyang-Shaoyin

Taiyangs lack the ability to express passion or affection or praise—feedback the Shaoyin constitution aches for. Shaoyins like someone soft, neat, gentle, well-mannered, sensitive and loving—in short, the antithesis of a Taiyang, whose manner, regardless of sex, is similar to that of an adolescent boy—long on attitude, short on sensitivity. Taiyangs strive for achievement in the workplace and put family second. Shaoyins are family-oriented, a trait which should complement the Taiyang's lack of domesticity but for the fact that Shaoyins aggressively require their partners to share this priority. Taiyangs see the big picture, not the details. Shaoyins are known for their meticulous attention to detail. As such, Shaoyin women are notorious for their nagging, Shaoyin men for their meddling. It is this quality in particular that will serve as a catalyst for discord. The Shaoyin begins meddling or nagging the Taiyang, who, in turn, is innately poised to resist such pressure, particularly in the domestic sphere, and will state this objection in no uncertain terms. The conflict that ensues will be enough to eliminate any possibility that ever existed for them to take advantage of their differences to achieve harmony.

The Taiyang-Shaoyin couple does, however, stand some chance of moderate success if both can restrain their constitutional predispositions and work towards a common goal. However, in this case, it is the Taiyang who benefits at the expense of the Shaoyin. Specifically, the ambitious Taiyang can enjoy great success in using the detail-oriented Shaoyin to do the dirty work, while the Taiyang keeps his or her eye on the big picture.

Shaoyang

A relationship with a Shaoyang can be challenging. On the one hand, they are true romantics, witty, humorous, and eager to please in every way. On the other hand, they are the most fickle of all constitutions and have trouble finishing anything they start.

Two Shaoyangs

A relationship between two people of this constitution has the potential to be like a brilliant fireworks display that burns out all too quickly. This is true both sexually and emotionally. Because both ride an emotional roller coaster and neither remains tied to any set plan, this is a relationship fraught with potential for conflict. When an argument does break out, dishes can fly. It is not uncommon for persons of this constitution to throw things in anger. Still, this anger burns out quickly, and Shaoyangs tend to make up as though nothing ever happened. The only way for the Shaoyang couple to avoid this tumultuous cycle is for one or the other to cultivate patience in his or her daily life.

In addition, someone must impose some restraint on both partners' innate constitutional tendency to act impulsively when it comes to finances. Shaoyangs represent the epitome of the impulsive shopper. This tendency towards extravagant, impulsive buying fits in quite nicely with their innate desire to be the life of the party and to pursue an expensive lifestyle. Without some imposed restraint, the Shaoyang couple will quickly exceed their means.

Finally, when Shaoyangs choose each other, there is no one to tend to domestic matters. Thus, Shaoyangs, like Taiyangs, may find themselves a couple out of balance, unable to find support or solace in their home life. Thus, in a Shaoyang relationship, it is essential for one or both partners to take extra steps to cultivate a home life, and for each of them to nurture their inner selves.

Shaoyang-Taiyin

Because Yang energy dominates the Shaoyang body types (though in a weaker form than in Taiyangs), Shaoyangs complement both Taiyins and Shaoyins, the constitutions in which Yin energy dominates. Unlike Taiyangs, Shaoyangs are more tolerant of differences in others.

Shaoyangs are up and about, unable to remain still; Taiyins dislike movement and prefer stillness. Taiyins place great importance on domesticity and self-indulgence, whereas Shaoyangs focus on outside matters and tend to neglect family and the home. In these ways, a Shaoyang and a Taiyin are well-equipped to handle each other's innate flaws. The obstinate, selfish

Taiyin will not bother the oblivious Shaoyang. Furthermore, the quick decision-making abilities, charm, and cleverness of the Shaoyang will actually balance the dull, conservative tendencies of the Taiyin. Moreover, the fickle, impulsive, and hot-blooded Shaoyang may find solace in the patient, calm, stable, and understanding Taiyin, who will provide encouragement and make amends easily.

This combination can, however, become seriously unbalanced. For example, when Taiyins are consumed in their work, they may become easily irritated by the Shaoyang's curious, intrusive, and fickle nature. Further discord may arise if the Taiyin partner persists in promoting his or her opinion on domestic affairs to the Shaoyang, who would prefer to ignore them. Thus, this couple will also need to cultivate patience, prudence, and understanding in order to take advantage of their innate differences and achieve harmony.

Shaoyang-Shaoyin

The Shaoyang-Shaoyin partnership presents similar potential for either compatibility or discord, as these two constitutions are polar opposites of each other. Shaoyangs have a strong Spleen and weak Kidneys; Shaoyins have strong Kidneys and a weak Spleen. For example, Shaoyins, who are prone to mild depressions, can be cheered back to life by their jovial Shaoyang partners, who know instinctively how to please their mates. Likewise, Shaoyangs, who are in general very sympathetic, will tend to be understanding of the timid and cautious behaviors of the sensitive Shaoyins. On the other hand, however, a Shaoyin will be less tolerant than a Taiyin when it comes to the Shaoyang propensity to neglect family obligations. A Shaoyin wife, in particular, will have little patience for a Shaoyang husband who indulges his innate tendency towards fickleness, impromptu partying, and unpredictable acts of generosity or sentiment. It is not unusual for a Shaoyang man to bring friends home late at night or give money to a friend in need. This unrestrained lifestyle will not suit the ever-calculating, scrupulous, and methodical Shaoyin wife. Her complaints will, in turn, trigger a fiery response from her Shaoyang husband. Thus, like the Shaoyang/Taiyin couple, the Shaoyang and Shaoyin will need to cultivate patience, prudence, and understanding to take advantage of their innate differences and achieve harmony.

The Shaoyang-Shaoyin couple will also irritate each other when it comes to beginning and completing projects. Just as the Shaoyang partner will grow annoyed with the Shaoyin's inability to start anything, the Shaoyin will be irritated by the Shaoyang's inability to follow through. To reconcile this difference, the Shaoyin must learn to trust the judgement of the Shaoyang when it comes to moving forward; and the Shaoyang must take time to reflect before starting a project in order to ensure its completion.

Shaoyang-Taiyang–see Taiyang section

Taiyin

Due to their magnanimous nature, Taiyins are the most tolerant of all constitutions. Their tendency to honor family and to feel at ease with themselves are qualities that often serve them well in relationships. Taiyin women, in particular, usually find great contentment as wives, mothers, and homemakers. Inasmuch as their overly developed lower bodies and strong reproductive organs make them well-equipped to bear children, these are roles as to which they are well-suited. Taiyin men, though also family oriented, tend to focus their efforts on working to support the family. As a result, they may sometimes appear distant from their families, even though they care for them very much.

Two Taiyins

A relationship between two Taiyins has the potential for great longevity simply because they are so similar, and neither is likely to complain when a conflict arises. They tend to view each other as friends and equals. However, because they both dislike moving and lack motivation to begin any new projects, there is the risk that the couple will degenerate into physical and mental laziness. Moreover, their mutual emphasis on domesticity, combined with their tendency towards stillness, can manifest as idleness. The Taiyin couple are prime candidates for turning each other into couch potatoes.

Taiyin women tend to gravitate to traditional homemaker roles and to yield domestic authority to their husbands. Taiyin men likewise tend to hold conservative values and prefer their wives to assume traditional roles as well. Together, Taiyin couples often create a contented and congruent family life. However, with nobody around to initiate activity, the Taiyin couple risks creating a relationship devoid of fun, mirth, or spontaneity. For this relationship to succeed, one partner must override the innate tendency towards idleness and initiate some form of activity. Due to their magnanimous natures, Taiyins are the most tolerant of each other's constitutional behavior; but due to their innate laziness and idleness, overall compatibility between Taiyin couples is merely average.

Taiyin-Shaoyin

The Taiyin-Shaoyin combination is the perfect recipe for either harmony or discord. Taiyins display a deep understanding of life and a magnanimous personality, whereas Shaoyins have a narrow focus and are meticulous and precise. Physically, Taiyins are strong and robust, with a larger frame, and Shaoyins are more fragile and tender, with generally smaller bodies. As such, these two complement each other well.

Taiyin-Shaoyin couples can often lead a very stable family life, as both partners are family-oriented. Because they are both Yin types, each tends to be passive and prefer the status quo over changes—even improvements or progress. Both are content to seek stability in the home. This desire to forge a strong family life generally motivates Taiyin and Shaoyin husbands to work hard to support their families, and Taiyin wives to impose any financial prudence necessary to maintain the household. Taiyins are not concerned with details, unlike Shaoyins, who are meticulous. This Shaoyin feature can compensate for the Taiyin weakness in such matters.

There are, however, a variety of ways in which this combination is not complementary. Laid-back Taiyins may not appreciate their Shaoyin partners' efforts to attend to details left undone, but rather may view this behavior in a negative light and complain about their nagging, meddling partners. Also, the Taiyin's love of domesticity may manifest not as a pride in the home, but rather as a lazy desire to remain housebound. A Taiyin individual may be perfectly content to stay home all day, surrounded by dirty dishes and piles of undone laundry, a situation that would unnerve his or her Shaoyin partner. Shaoyin women can be nit-picky or sulky, complaining that their Taiyin husbands are not sufficiently cheerful in social situations. If a Shaoyin wife gives in to her inclination to complain about every minor household matter as well, she may try the patience of even a Taiyin husband. In order to avoid these pitfalls, both partners must resist their innate tendencies. Shaoyins must exercise restraint over their tendency to be petty and critical, and Taiyins must avoid turning obstinate and lazy, as any one of these behaviors will close the door to communication and intimacy.

Taiyin-Shaoyang—see Shaoyang section

Taiyin-Taiyang—see Taiyang section

Shaoyin

As Yin types, Shaoyins are passive and family oriented and thus well suited to relationships generally.

Two Shaoyins

Two Shaoyins have the compatibility to be a generally loving couple, but they will tend to blow trivial things out of proportion and then hold a grudge. Among couples with the same constitutions, Shaoyins fit each other fairly well. Because both are considerate, tactful, and perceptive of each other's feelings, they largely avoid huge conflicts. In general, they have the potential for domestic harmony. Each seeks a gentle, well-mannered partner, passionate about love. Both are family oriented and neither requires an extravagant lifestyle, unlike Shaoyangs. Moreover, Shaoyins are sexually the strongest constitution of all. They may not explode with initial sexual passion like their Shaoyang counterparts, but they have strong sexual vitality and strong reproductive systems.

Shaoyin women flourish in the role of the attentive and caring housewife or mother. They tend to keep a tidy home and excel in managing household affairs, though they can be stingy with the family funds. However, even though they are of the Yin constitution, Shaoyin women are subject to as much emotional fluctuation as Shaoyang women are. They are prone to jealousy and suspicion, along with stress and anxiety. Unlike Shaoyangs, however, Shaoyin women tend to keep their emotions locked up inside and ponder them until they are absolutely certain about their judgment. Only then do they take action based upon emotion. This restraint does not, however, apply to household affairs, as Shaoyin women are notorious for nagging and interfering when they are the least bit dissatisfied with their husbands or children.

Shaoyin men tend to be kind and considerate towards women. Their ability to know a woman's heart makes them quite sensitive to a woman's needs. Though they attend to their partners' needs with careful consideration, they are said to lack a sense of spontaneity. Like their wives, though, they too tend to meddle in domestic matters, which can drive their partners crazy.

The overactive Shaoyin mind and tendency to obsess over small things can cause a trivial misunderstanding to take on a life of its own and result in serious and long-lasting emotional pain for both. Like Taiyins, Shaoyins disdain physical violence, instead choosing to verbally lash out at each other. They are, however, conscious of those around them and so will argue discreetly, unlike the Shaoyangs, who will engage in thundering combat.

This tendency to blow trivial matters out of proportion will be compounded by the fact that Shaoyins are quite rational, composed, meticulous, and calculating. Thus, in arguments, neither will want to admit a loss. Apologizing or even opening up is distasteful to this easily misunderstood constitution. To make matters worse, both are capable of expressing hatred and contempt in the heat of the moment. Though the conflict may be resolved, these caustic emotions do not readily dissipate, and the negative effects may last for days, weeks, or even months. As such, marital problems are typical for Shaoyin couples. However, as long as the initial flame of affection remains, Shaoyin couples will avoid huge conflicts.

The Shaoyin couple has great potential for domestic bliss. In order to realize this potential, they are best advised to resist their tendency towards pettiness and try to let go of negative emotions. This applies to both their tendency to express caustic emotions to each other, as well as their tendency to hang on to negative feelings long afterwards. Shaoyin women should try to fight their tendency towards jealousy and suspicion and Shaoyin men should do what they can to reassure their partners in this regard. These few measures will go a long way for the Shaoyin couple.

Shaoyins-Others—see previous sections

Chapter 13

Career Choices

The return from your work must be the satisfaction which that work brings you and the world's need of that work. With this, life is heaven, or as near heaven as you can get. Without this...this life is hell.
—W. E. B. DuBois, "To His Newborn Great-Grandson"
(address on his 90th birthday, in 1958)

Job satisfaction is one of the most important factors of a person's well-being. Without it, many aspects of a person's life may deteriorate. One may become physically as well as mentally ill as a result of a stressful job. Consider, for example, the disturbing fact that more people die of heart attacks on Monday morning at 9 a.m. than at any other time of the week.

A job must be more than just a means to make a living. It should be appropriate for an individual's unique disposition, aptitude, and physical makeup. Ideally, it should be the path that actualizes one's highest goals and ideals. Furthermore, it should help one to realize the true goal of life—that of serving and satisfying the needs of others. Ultimately, the practice of benevolence, kindheartedness, and public service should be paramount, no matter what path in life an individual chooses.

Although people of all body types can work at any job, Sasang Medicine holds that constitutional differences can make a person more or less suited to certain types of jobs. This is truer of psychological traits than of physical attributes and capabilities. Sasang Medicine views how psychological traits show up in the different constitutions in the workplace. Sasang Medicine aims to teach how a person of any given constitution can bring out the qualities best suited to the job at hand. Finally, it provides key advice in cases of extreme incompatibility: If a job does not fit your personality and constitution, and does not bring out the best in you, it is best that you keep searching for one that will.

Taiyang

Strengths

The energy and strength of Taiyangs is best represented by the wind element, especially as it manifests in such devastating and destructive phenomena as tornadoes or hurricanes. Such storms inevitably cause dramatic changes; in the same way, Taiyangs alter history by their very existence. Just as the winds of a tornado or a hurricane are uncontrollable, so too is it impossible for Taiyangs to restrain their advancing energy. This lack of restraint is evinced in many ways. First, just as wind, by its very nature, cannot be still, so too are Taiyangs unable to hesitate or wait for things to happen. Fear of others does not hold them back either; like the wind that blows through every corner of the world, untouchable but touching everything, Taiyangs speak and act unreservedly to even perfect strangers, irrespective of position or rank, swaying and blowing them over with their incredible conviction and self-confidence. Fear of the unknown also fails to be an obstacle; it in fact goads them onward, fueling their curiosity like the Zephyr trying to find the end of the horizon. Even questions of sacrifice, method, or morality tend to be irrelevant to the goal-oriented Taiyangs, who continue on their chosen paths like tornadoes or hurricanes, mercilessly tearing up anything in their paths. For all of these reasons, Taiyangs are perfect for corporate operations (preferably at the head of, or outside, the corporate structure), because such work demands their characteristic independence, fearlessness, and ruthlessness. They would be excellent at making initial business connections for developing overseas operations, or as front men leading the company into unknown territories. In any case, it would not be wise for a Taiyang to confine him or herself too much in the "system" of a corporation; like the wind, Taiyangs were meant to have their own space to roam and wreak havoc.

Taiyangs are very creative and original in their work. This is because they are able to transcend the given world around them and hear the Times of Heaven, the source of divine inspiration. In this, they are truly like the wind, which blows according to the will of heaven. Although the other elements (fire, water, and earth) are more or less bound to the ground, the wind is able to traverse freely, no matter what the terrain may be. Thus, Taiyangs are able to exercise the greatest creativity and flexibility of thought with regard to their work. They may find their place as innovators, idea banks, or think tanks. They may become inventors, strategists, or adventurers. They may find their place in the marketing or advertising department, due to their ability to come up with new and brilliantly creative ideas. What's more, their ingenuity may not only be restricted to a single field; many Taiyangs show professional abilities in a variety of fields.

Although Taiyangs can be ambitious and tenacious in achieving success (whether in business, politics, or daily life), they have little interest in monetary rewards. They would rather envision themselves as performing heroic deeds, like a divine wind. Actualizing grandiose, idealistic, and otherworldly visions is more important for Taiyangs than the accumulation of worldly possessions—after all, what wind ever wanted to burden itself with the soil of the earth? As a result, jobs or careers of high social position, fame, or glory are preferable to Taiyangs than those that guarantee the accumulation of wealth.

Weaknesses

Like a hurricane, with winds cycling about an empty center, Taiyangs tend to be self-righteous and self-centered. Oblivious to others, they wipe out anything that happens to stray into their path. Their sole concern is the maintenance of their own spinning fury; the world around them looks only like a calm and placid lake to stir. They fail to see others as sources of advice or wisdom, and in fact will more likely than not actively reject any who employ independent thought in their service. Words like "reconciliation," "harmony," or "camaraderie" have as much meaning for Taiyangs as a town in the path of a hurricane. As a result, Taiyangs tend to evoke animosity and rejection from others, and are frequently estranged and isolated. The only co-workers or subordinates suitable for Taiyangs are "yes men" or "brown-nosers" who allow themselves to be manipulated by their

G-force winds. As such weak and collapsible scarecrows usually have neither backbones nor brains, Taiyangs often find it impossible to find good help in the form of an effective, diverse staff.

When things go wrong, it is impossible for Taiyangs to introspect and see any fault within themselves. In this, they resemble the wind, which never pauses to examine itself (partly because it is invisible). Instead, Taiyangs can only find fault with others, criticizing people even when they themselves are at fault. It is no surprise, then, that when danger or misfortune hits, not many people are willing to jump in and help a struggling Taiyang out. When there is no hope of redemption in a situation, Taiyangs will not only remain on the sinking ship; they will make sure that everyone else remains as well. They live by a simple, albeit twisted, motto: "All for one, and that one is me."

For these reasons, Taiyangs often fail in businesses requiring personal relationship skills, or in politics, where they must govern others through persuasion. Although they have many leadership qualities, the inability to coax others or to give in and compromise leaves them high and dry, like a boat without a sail.

Although Taiyangs are typically unsuccessful at business or politics, on those rare occasions when they do manage to hold a position of power, they are likely to abuse it in various ways. They have an inborn tendency to become dictators or autocrats (though always in a charismatic way).

Taiyangs live by the philosophy that the ends justify the means. If they are unable to overcome barriers in ordinary, moral ways, then they will not hesitate to take the low road. Like the wind, they will find a way to flow, whether it be over the mountain, or through the valley. This "freedom at all costs" spirit is also related to the Taiyang's tendency to overlook details. If situations are too complex (morally or practically), then Taiyangs will merely gloss over them, like a broad stroke of wind through a tangled forest.

Conclusion

Although Taiyangs are natural born leaders, it is best for them to find positions with some degree of space, solitude, and independence, as they tend to rub people the wrong way. Typically, Taiyangs are well suited for careers of independent mental exploration; they make excellent strategists, inventors, scientists, musicians, and scholars. Also, Taiyangs are great groundbreakers and trailblazers; they were the revolutionaries, conquerors, pioneers, and adventurers of the old days, and in the modern world, they often serve as the spearhead or front man in new business territory, whether this be a foreign market, or a potential client. Because pioneering careers are rarely found in today's shrinking world, the competitive edge is no longer found in the Taiyang's gung-ho attitude, but rather in a sense of politics and the ability to establish and maintain smooth relations. Taiyangs should therefore learn how to swim with the new school in order to survive—or, at the very least, they should hire politically-minded individuals to help them interact with others.

Shaoyang

Strengths

Shaoyangs are best represented by the fire element. Fire has many qualities: it is bright, passionate, hot, quick, and full of energy and excitement. Because fire provides light, it creates the clarity necessary to distinguish right from wrong, whether it be in matters of justice, or in matters of taste. Because fire provides warmth, it is the opportunity for social gatherings, like the campfire that binds people together against the cold and darkness of isolation and the wilderness.

Fire's clarity is seen in the Shaoyang's straightforward nature. Shaoyangs are well suited for jobs requiring a great deal of honesty; they are excellent at carrying out inspection duties, like auditing, for example. Their uncompromising attitude towards injustice, coupled with their fiery bravery and burning spirit of self-sacrifice make them ideal for careers in public service (such as social work) and public defense (such as the police or the military). As the Shaoyang fire can also distinguish matters of taste, Shaoyangs are perfect for creative ventures in the fashion industry. They are skilled at running small businesses, such as those involved with garments, interior design, and trendy gifts.

Fire's warmth is manifested in Shaoyangs' excellent social skills. They possess a bright, cheerful, agreeable personality, and a wit as sharp and humorous as a dancing, flirtatious flame. For these reasons, it is easy for Shaoyangs to make a lot of friends. The Shaoyangs' dynamism and natural inclination for meeting and dealing with people make them well suited for jobs requiring a great deal of social interaction. They would do well in the corporate operations department, the public relations department, the dispatch or field service departments, or in departments that select materials or gather information. Such positions are better suited for Shaoyangs than the mundane day-to-day tasks of clerical work.

The Shaoyang fire not only sets alight the spark of humanity in others; it also makes those around them burn with the desire to help, not just with advice, but with money as well. Whether Shaoyangs need contributions for a political office, capital for a startup business, or rescue funds for a failing enterprise, their friends are always there to help.

Although Shaoyangs tend to take defeat hard, their flame is rarely extinguished. Their competitive spirit and their constant desire for change allows them to ignite themselves after any damper, with hardly a regret. One of the reasons Shaoyangs recover so easily is that they tend to burn their bridges behind them instead of rekindling old flames. Like an advancing blaze, they quickly spread to new goals or projects. Thus the consequences of pain, sorrow, or setback have less of an impact for Shaoyangs than for the other constitutions. This tendency to distraction is actually a strength of sorts, for, as any firefighter will tell you, it is hard to put out a fire that refuses to be contained.

Weaknesses

It is the nature of fire to burn swiftly and spread. This being the case, Shaoyangs tend to lack patience. It is hard for them to sit still and concentrate. Thus, Shaoyangs should avoid any detail-oriented, repetitive work that involves sitting for extended periods of time.

As fire ignites and spreads randomly, so too do Shaoyangs tend to open up new businesses without much planning. As a result, it is easy for them to fail miserably. Of course, when they fail, they simply begin something new, usually with as little planning and foresight as in their original venture. Thus when the going gets tough, Shaoyangs will get going—to greener (unburned) pastures. It is actually better for Shaoyangs to stay at a job that has stability; a fire in a furnace, for example, is guaranteed its fuel for the day. Unfortunately, coming back to the same business day in and day out is not easy for the easily bored Shaoyang.

Occasionally, a fire strikes upon a field of dry, dead brush, and is able to blaze bright and hot for a few glorious hours. In the same way, Shaoyangs sometimes experience quick success in their unpremeditated business ventures. But, just as the brushfire swiftly burns itself out, so too do Shaoyangs experience equally swift descents into failure. With success, the Shaoyangs' extravagant and opulent tendencies emerge, and they overspend or improperly manage funds, like a brushfire exhausting its fuel. But this isn't the only reason; the other half of this financial one-two punch is that Shaoyangs put less effort into their work once they think they've attained success. Shaoyangs also tend to fail because they try to expand their businesses unnecessarily, like a brushfire that thins itself out. Also, just as a fire burns quickly and restlessly, so too are Shaoyangs rash in their business dealings, and they lack tenacity or willpower with projects that are difficult to ignite.

When they fail or lose in their ventures, Shaoyangs experience a tremendous shock. This is clearly evident on their faces, which resemble a wavering flame on the verge of being put out. In this state, Shaoyangs may easily become lost and without direction. Nevertheless, as mentioned earlier, their moment of despair is truly momentary, and they soon arise, oblivious and innocent, like a phoenix.

When a campfire is not properly restrained, it can transform from a center of social gathering to a destructive, all-consuming force. In the same way, when Shaoyangs become unbalanced, and their fire nature is unrestrained, their impulsive, vain, and self-centered qualities take over, and they become overly rough and aggressive when solving problems or dealing with others. They may over-exaggerate and follow their reckless sentiments.

Nevertheless, Shaoyangs are for the most part less greedy than the other types, and do not set grand financial goals. Rather, they act out of simple and pure motives, especially when helping others. At times, this can be a disadvantage, especially in practical settings. In business and politics, for example, qualities such as prudence, cold-heartedness, and firmness, as well as the ability to formulate strategies on the basis of gain and loss, are basic requirements. The simple, honest, straightforward, frivolous Shaoyangs, who are unconcerned with and unaware of the financial bottom line, will not be as successful as members of the more savvy and practically-minded constitutions.

Conclusion

Shaoyangs will excel in fields requiring a great deal of guileless sociability. For example, they make great talk-show hosts, radio disc jockeys, tour guides, comedians, and news reporters. In a business, they would do well in any position requiring heavy social interaction. For example, they would do well in personnel or public relations departments, and would make excellent field men. They would not be able to sit the long hours required of most clerical or office positions, however. As Shaoyangs have a naturally compassionate, self-sacrificing bent, and are inherently brave, they would feel comfortable with all forms of public service, such as counseling, social work, police work, and the armed forces. Shaoyangs also have a natural sense of style, and a fiery creativity; thus, careers in interior design, art, modeling, and fashion would suit them. Finally, as Shaoyangs possess a free and easy wit, they are the most amicable of the constitutions. Therefore, they can serve in positions intended to ease friction and soften hard edges. For example, they make excellent traders, diplomats, ambassadors, and mediators.

Taiyin

Strengths

Taiyins can be likened to mountains, great accumulations of earth. Like mountains, Taiyins are physically massive; in fact, they are the most massive of the four constitutions. This mass serves as surplus energy for the Taiyins; it is their reserve gas tank, or the extra oil in their lamp. This surplus allows them to outlast others in work, and prevents them from quitting a job until it is complete. Furthermore, it gives them the capacity to take on jobs that most would consider boring, simple, repetitious, or tedious. Like mountains sitting immobile through the changing storms of time, Taiyins have the capacity to weather setbacks and distractions. The one thing that Taiyins find intolerable is work involving a great deal of detail; like mountains, they were meant for grandiosity, not minutiae.

Like mountains weighing heavily into the earth, Taiyins bring their full weight to bear upon their chosen tasks. In this, they are similar to Taiyangs. Yet, whereas Taiyangs attack problems with the swiftness and ferocity of the wind, Taiyins tend to attack them with the persistence and patience of mountains. They move slowly, like mountains evolving over eons, pacing themselves whenever they work. They will skip meals and go overtime, double-overtime, or even all night if necessary, to get the job done. Furthermore, they take their work home and focus on it late into the night, and even work on weekends and holidays. They constantly think about their work, often sacrificing their personal or domestic lives to their professional careers. Even their social lives are not purely social. They will frequently go out to dinners, drinking engagements, parties, games of golf, and so on just to meet with business associates and potential clients. In these dealings, they get help from their constitutionally strong physique, which can tolerate large amounts of food and drink.

When faced with serious obstacles or hostile environments, Taiyins will remain as steadfast and unperturbed as a mountain. They will not give up when things go counter to plan. Even if they fail on several occasions, they will come back and continue trying until they succeed. Huge financial losses or a smeared reputation will not stop them. Also, unlike Shaoyangs or Shaoyins, they will not show loss, discouragement, or despair on their faces when confronted with failure. They will remain as calm as the face of a white-capped mountain.

Taiyins show good leadership qualities, and often find success at the top of the business or political ladder. They actually look like leaders, possessing the natural dignity of great mountains. Furthermore, like the wide foundations of solid mountains, Taiyins have the broad-mindedness required of true leaders. This is evident both in their professional disposition (the drive to learn all they can about their work), as well as their strong interpersonal and social skills, through which they build and maintain support.

Weaknesses

If mountains are steadfast and eternal, then they are also inertial, or even immobile. Taiyins, like mountains, may suffer from being too lazy or slow, with an innate tendency towards procrastination and fixation. Sometimes this laziness shows itself in the Taiyin's lackluster efforts to earn a living. This inertial quality makes any job requiring outgoing or adventurous endeavors unsuitable for Taiyins. Also, jobs that require quick and timely responses, dependent upon up-to-the-minute information or communication, are probably unsuitable for the lumbering, slumbering Taiyins.

Mountains are of the earth, which helps to explain the Taiyin's often excessive love of material (earthly) wealth. Taiyins ultimately desire that which is tangible, and of practical or profitable value. In fact, for Taiyins, all things are ultimately measured by these criteria. In a Taiyin's eyes, things are important only if they can be linked to some sort of profit. What's more, to hold their attention, the profit must be big, whether it is money, fame, power, or position. Just as mountains will not concern themselves over molehills, so too will Taiyins ignore ventures resulting in meager benefits.

By their very nature, mountains accumulate mass and earth into themselves. If they did not, and they dispersed the mass that they contained, then they would flatten out, and no longer be mountains. In the same manner, Taiyins have a greedy, accumulative tendency. They tend to concern themselves only with gathering money, power, and profit for themselves, and will rarely sacrifice time, energy, or effort for the benefit of others.

Taiyins tend to overrate themselves, like mountains, each silently claiming to be the top of the world. From this vantage point, they believe that they can accurately see the entire expanse of the universe, thus they feel their opinions represent the absolute truth. This being the case, Taiyins will refuse to compromise or budge an inch once they make up their minds. The struggles of others to persuade Taiyins otherwise after they have resolved themselves can resemble the struggles of ants trying to push a mountain out of the way.

Although Taiyins usually have the most broadminded perspective of the four constitutions, when they are unbalanced, they can be obstinate and biased. It is in these instances that their mountain-like stubbornness is particularly damaging.

Conclusion

Although Taiyins are excellent workers, with the persistence and patience to handle most tasks that come their way, they enjoy neither minute, detailed tasks involving a great deal of thinking, nor tasks requiring a great deal of adaptability and flexibility. Furthermore, Taiyins tend to have a grandiose vision of their lives and their possibilities. Thus, they will only commit themselves to those tasks that eventually allow them to realize success on a grand scale. Taiyins will work persistently in almost any field, but only if it furthers their ambition to get to the top positions, where they seem to belong. They often aspire to be politicians, corporate leaders, or high-ranking officers in the armed forces. As Taiyins have a grand vision of the world, they also succeed in careers requiring the capacity to see the big picture. They make excellent authors, historians, and philosophers. They are better at syncretistic thought. In other words, they are better at thinking in terms of breadth rather than depth. This is not to say that Taiyins are incapable of profound thought or penetrating insight; however, it is to say that such depth is not primary, and is usually the result of seeing the big picture and putting things in perspective. Taiyins would enjoy careers requiring a worldly sense of culture; they could serve as critics, for example, whether it be of society, or films, or food. Again, though, it is their breadth of experience, rather than their discriminating taste, that supports them in such endeavors.

Shaoyin

Strengths

Shaoyins are best represented by water. It is water's nature to flow, descend, percolate, and pool together. Although it would be wrong to call water's path predictable, it is nevertheless true that water's course is the one of least resistance. Moreover, water always tends to gather and collect, whether in deep wells, or in the vastness of the sea. The path of water demonstrates simple wisdom, and the gathering, reuniting tendency of water demonstrates composure. These two qualities, wisdom and composure, aptly characterize a Shaoyin in the workplace. Shaoyins' wisdom manifests in the way that they plan well ahead of time before beginning any business undertaking, thus ensuring a smooth and easy course of action (the path of least resistance); they carefully investigate all possible contingencies, leaving nothing to chance. They are good at drafting or drawing up plans for a project, gathering the necessary materials, or scrutinizing complicated matters related to a project. No other constitution can match a Shaoyin in this regard. The composure of Shaoyins, meanwhile, is evident in their ability to get down to business without any personal feelings or sentiments. They do not allow themselves to be scattered by unnecessary emotions.

Water's gathering, reuniting tendency shows up in another way. Shaoyins are good at gathering people for social organizations, school organizations, or even recreational groups. Unlike Taiyangs, they are able to clearly discern the strengths and weaknesses of people, as well as their compatibility with others. Thus, they have a talent for gathering the right people for the right jobs. For all of these reasons, Shaoyins are well suited to working in the planning, accounting, or personnel departments when in a corporate structure.

Water is tasteless, and dilutes all things. Because of this, paradoxically, water affords the possibility for true taste. A food critic will drink a glass of water to clear his palate, for example. In the same way, Shaoyins have a well-developed sense of taste. This, combined with their neat, tidy, meticulous nature allows Shaoyins to excel in the food industry.

Water is resilient and flexible. Like water, Shaoyins possess excellent dexterity. This, combined with their natural sense of aesthetics and their penchant for detail, makes them well suited for jobs in tailoring, interior design, hairstyling, cosmetics, and the like. No matter what the undertaking may be, a Shaoyin will be meticulous, calculating, systematic, and sharp.

Weaknesses

Because Shaoyins lack fire or Yang energy, they do not have the adventurous spirit of Taiyangs or Shaoyangs; Shaoyins shy away from risky ventures, and are thus apt to miss out on many golden opportunities. They will not venture into unknown territory when they already have a stable business (just as water will not venture out of its well-established waterways); they tend to work best within an established framework, where there is stability and support from other workers.

Also, Shaoyins tend to lack the basic aggressiveness required to spark action. Thus, although they may draw up detailed plans to get a project underway, their passive nature may prevent them from finalizing decisions on those plans, and in particular, will keep them from bringing them to life. They will need someone with more dynamic energy, like a Taiyang or Shaoyang, to jumpstart and spark their plans into action.

Shaoyins are excellent planners because they are terrible worriers. Water has no backbone. This being the case, it is easily disturbed by others. When water meets with earth, for example, it gets absorbed, or its flow becomes impeded. When it meets cold air, it freezes into ice. When the wind blows, it becomes turbulent. So, although water can nurture and help other things to grow, its identity tends to be fragile and blurry, constantly threatened by the presence of others. The worry that others will take advantage of them often acts as a self-fulfilling prophecy for Shaoyins, because it gives others the opportunity to cheat them. Because of this, Shaoyins do not feel at ease with strangers and people that they do not know well. They become cautious and apprehensive in situations where they must interact with strangers. They prefer to be around familiar people and surroundings. Thus, work that involves meeting a lot of new people, such as sales, fieldwork, or customer relations, may not be appropriate for them. Also, Shaoyins are less suitable for leadership positions, because of their social discomfort and their inability to initiate and inspire action. Again, it must be stated that, although water flows well in deep channels, the loss of boundaries leads to an immediate loss of direction.

Shaoyins, like Shaoyangs, get shocked when they experience failure in business. When Shaoyins experience failure, they lose their composure, meticulousness, brightness, and correct judgment and become confused, like rippled, turbulent water. They begin to manifest uncharacteristic and irrational behaviors, like a quick temper, irritation, and nervousness, and will often slander and defame others. Lacking a backbone of substance, as well as the fire of aggression, Shaoyins will quickly lose all desire to come back and struggle again, and will tend to give up the fight completely. Even minor setbacks can plunge Shaoyins into despair. Thus, whenever there is misfortune, Shaoyins are usually ill equipped emotionally to handle it. They will torture themselves, and sometimes begrudge or even hate others as well. Like water carrying the ripples of even the smallest disturbances long after they are gone, Shaoyins become attached to even the most frivolous trifles of the past. This is the very reason that Shaoyins take so much trouble to plan their course of action.

Conclusion

Shaoyins are comfortable in jobs that are stable, perhaps even boring and repetitive. Shaoyins commonly work as salaried employees, slowly climbing their way up the ladder, rather than as entrepreneurs or tradespeople who gamble their careers on risky ventures. Jobs requiring a meticulous bent and a quiet personality are suitable for Shaoyins. They can make great librarians, teachers, scholars, translators, bank tellers, secretaries, clerical workers, statisticians, or accountants. Shaoyins are also great for many jobs in the technical fields, excelling as engineers, mechanics, plumbers, carpenters, architects, or doctors. Shaoyins have good taste and pay attention to detail, so they may also excel as sculptors or cooks. Shaoyins can also run their own businesses quite adequately due to their skills in planning, personnel discernment, and composure.

Making Work Work

As we have seen from the previous descriptions, individuals with differing body types display differing tendencies in their work life. It is important to understand and work with these tendencies, instead of attempting to force oneself to fit the requirements of one's job. A common attitude nowadays is that work is merely something that we *have* to do, not something that we *want* to do. Therefore, "work" has "play" as its antonym, and "business" is often the opposite of "pleasure." The word "labor," meanwhile, connotes difficulty, as in "labored breathing." It is small wonder, then, that most people perceive work as something that *must* be unpleasant and endured. If a person changes his or her work in order to make things easier or more pleasant, then that person is seen as shirking duty or lacking backbone.

Although it is true that there is an element of discipline involved in work, it is also true that people function best in the correct contexts. A hammer, for example, finds its true nature when it is hitting nails. It would not make sense for a hammer to be used to cut material. This would damage the hammer, and botch the job at hand as well. We, like hammers, would do best to find out what our strengths and weaknesses are, not only for our sake, but for the sake of efficiency and productivity as well. When work is seen in this light, then it becomes a vital part of who we are and not just a necessary burden. Work becomes both an expression of our individuality and a way for us to express our gratitude to the universe. Work becomes an ennobling act, the highest achievement in the universe, in fact, and the worker, an agent of sincerity, truth, and service.

Part IV

Application

Chapter 14

Famous People and Their Sasang Body Types

To help you to gain a deeper understanding of the individual constitutions, this chapter analyzes eight historical figures in the context of Sasang Medicine. These people were chosen from diverse fields such as politics, science, arts, and the movie industry.

Although careful examination of pictures, portraits, and biographies has been used to determine the constitution best matching these figures, these analyses are not to be taken as absolutes. First, all of these analyses are based upon my personal impressions of these historical figures, which are further based upon the general impressions that these figures have made upon history. Thus, they may not reflect these individuals as they truly were. Also, although an individual's constitution never changes throughout his or her life, the manner in which a constitution manifests may vary widely. Nevertheless, for the purposes of edification and education, these analyses should prove helpful.

Taiyang

Ludwig van Beethoven

Ludwig van Beethoven was not a handsome man. Like many Taiyangs, he was somewhat short (5'4"), with a disproportionately large head. Also like many Taiyangs, Ludwig was not an easy person to get along with. From a very young age, he displayed a rebellious, misanthropic nature. As a child, he never played with his peers, due in part to the fact that his father imposed strict musical training upon him from a very young age. As an adult, he could neither keep a servant because of disagreements, nor please his neighbors because of his piano playing late into the night. It was this quality of rebellious individuality that set him apart from the rest, both socially, and more importantly, musically.

Taiyangs are revolutionaries by nature, and Beethoven was no exception. His music shattered several classical conventions, often with deliberate purpose. In one notebook, for example, he worked out one exercise 17 times, just to prove that a rule of harmony was wrong. And, in what was to be a turning point for himself and for music as a whole, he composed the *Eroica*, the longest and most challenging symphony written up to that point in time.

Beethoven's life outside of his music was somewhat dull. It was true that he was able to move within aristocratic circles despite his social failings. However, like many Taiyangs, he seemed to lack a sense of social position, and often approached others as a cresting wave would approach the receding shoreline, with an expectation of homage, respect, and subservience. Once, Beethoven walked with the highly respected German writer, Goethe, through the city. People passing by repeatedly bowed down to them out of respect, and in response, Goethe repeatedly removed his hat in acknowledgement. When Goethe complained of the inconvenience of this ritual, Beethoven replied quite matter-of-factly that the passers-by had all the while been bowing to *him*. What is most laughable and revealing about this little vignette is that Beethoven was absolutely convinced of the truth of his statement; he was not just saying it to compete for honor against Goethe. Taiyangs do not belittle themselves by competing. Their command of respect is so implicit that they look upon the world as a conquered realm, and themselves as sole sovereign.

Goethe both respected and admonished the wildly individualistic Beethoven. On the one hand, he said, "I have never met an artist who is so concentrated, so energetic and so profound." Yet, on the other hand, he felt that Beethoven was, "a completely unrestrained personality who is surely not wrong to detest the world, but in this way he does not make things more pleasant, either for himself or for others." Unfortunately, what Goethe liked and disliked about his contemporary could not be divorced. The concentration, energy, and profundity that made Beethoven such a revolutionary composer were the very qualities that forced him to detest the world around him. An unbalanced Taiyang, he had little choice but to hate the real world in favor of that perfect other world that he occasionally managed to hear and capture in his compositions.

Although it was rumored that Beethoven fell in love now and then, it seems that he always set his sights upon unattainable women. There is little evidence that he ever allowed his feelings to be crowned by physical conquest. Thus, his passions occupied the same idealized other world that his music came from. Such is the nature of unbalanced Taiyangs—their truest passions can only be invested in other, more perfect worlds of their own imagining. They can be stuck in a state of suspended animation, caught between the despised real world and the sacred worlds that they fashion within themselves.

Much of the time, Beethoven lived alone amidst the squalor of his home. His most debilitating affliction came at age 30, when his hearing began to deteriorate. Beethoven's hearing affliction appears to contradict Sasang Medicine theory, because Taiyangs are supposed to have the most well developed ears of all constitutions, that they may hear the Times of Heaven. However, Sasang Medicine explains Beethoven's hearing loss through the saying, "When Yin reaches its extreme, it converts into Yang; when Yang reaches its extreme, it converts into Yin." In other words, Beethoven's hearing, like a needle, grew excessively fine, until it shattered and dulled. Surprisingly, Beethoven composed the *Eroica* during this period. In fact, many of Beethoven's most significant pieces were composed in the muffled silence of his affliction. Deafness may have paralyzed lesser composers, but Beethoven was, and always had been, different. He was a true individual and a true Taiyang, familiar with deep silences, and the strength required to work beneath them. As he once wrote to a friend, "Strength is the morality of the man who stands out from the rest, and it is mine." Beethoven's strength endures within his music, able to reach us across the silence of time.

Napoleon Bonaparte

Physically, Napoleon had clear Taiyang characteristics. He had the broad chest and shoulders and large lung capacity typical of Taiyangs. His head was noticeably large, and beneath it was a very stiff looking neck; both of these are distinctive physical features of Taiyangs. Although a healthy, energetic man, Napoleon occasionally suffered from dysuria, a condition involving painful or difficult urination. This is an important indicator of imbalance in Taiyangs. He died of stomach cancer, a disease that Taiyangs are susceptible to.

Napoleon made an indelible mark on history both as a military leader and as a statesman. In both cases, he displayed Taiyang characteristics. It is interesting to note how the same constitution can provide the fundamental qualities necessary for success in both war and peace. For instance, Napoleon's immense willpower led the way for his daunting military campaigns, as well as for his struggles to establish his form of government. Napoleon himself was aware that his successes were due to his will; he once wrote, "I have succeeded in whatever I have undertaken, because I have willed it. I have never hesitated, which has given me an advantage over the rest of mankind."

Related to this, but perhaps more relevant on the battlefield, was Napoleon's emphasis on discipline. Napoleon felt that discipline was the most important quality in the army. He himself lived a strict, disciplined routine in his daily life, and he expected no less from his men. He treated those that were undisciplined severely, and provided incentives for anyone demonstrating bravery during a battle.

Another Taiyang quality particularly advantageous to Napoleon on the battlefield was his speed and lack of hesitation. If we take even a quick look at the major events in Napoleon's life, we can see the velocity with which he hurtled towards his destiny. He became a brigadier general at age 24, commander of the army of the interior at 26, first consul at 30, and emperor at 35. He desired to do everything at high speed, whether it be getting married, making love, fighting enemies in a battle, taking over a new government, or implementing changes. This quality, of course, was vital on the battlefields, where quick decisions were a basic requirement.

But Napoleon, like most Taiyangs, possessed not only speed, but also tremendous drive and determination. During battles, he was able to keep going for 18 to 24 hours for days at a time. In daily life, too, he generally worked long hours with short breaks, often waking up in the middle of the night to dictate to his assistant. The constancy of Napoleon's Taiyang energy is made clear in Vincent Cronin's description of Napoleon's daily activities in his book, *Napoleon*. He writes that Napoleon was, "nearly always standing or walking, rarely seated, and [did] an unusual amount of talking." It is significant to note that Napoleon, like most Taiyangs, preferred to stand and move about; unlike Shaoyins or Taiyins, he was not suited to long hours of sitting still. Such is the nature of Taiyang energy—restless, active, pacing the world as though seeking to conquer it with anxious footsteps.

Despite the fact that Napoleon often overstepped himself in his attempts to realize his ambitions, he never regretted his actions. Like most Taiyangs, he looked upon each setback as another opportunity to recollect himself in preparation for the next attempt. Even after the disaster of his Russian campaign, he was able to demonstrate extraordinary optimism, remaining productive. Similarly, after he had been abdicated and sent to live on the island of Elba, he was able to return in 11 months, fresh and ready for his last battle at Waterloo.

Under fire, Napoleon manifested another Taiyang trait—unshakable courage. No matter how disturbing his circumstances were, he refused to falter. In fact, his motto was, "Fear last." He was even able to sleep amidst thundering bombs and guns.

This bravery played no small part in Napoleon's successes on the battlefield. However, a more significant role was perhaps played by his Taiyang revolutionary zeal. Napoleon was the first to utilize artillery cannons to their full potential. This, combined with other unorthodox tactics that he invented, made him a nearly unstoppable force on the battlefields.

Napoleon was also possessed of the Taiyang ability to speak well. Like all Taiyangs, he was able to speak to anyone whether above or beneath him, in a direct and straightforward manner. Furthermore, he had the Taiyang charm and charisma, allowing him to influence large crowds and instill confidence in his soldiers on the battlefields.

Of course, Napoleon had his fair share of negative qualities. He possessed the short temper typical of Taiyangs, a natural consequence of his swift Taiyang energy. Napoleon also tended to be insensitive toward others, another negative trait of Taiyangs. Thus, Henri Clarke, a French government spy, reported that Napoleon "does not spare his men sufficiently.... Sometimes he is hard, impatient, abrupt, or imperious. Often he demands difficult things in too hasty a manner." It is said that when he lost his temper on the battlefield, he would slap his generals in the face. Napoleon was also cursed with the overconfidence of a Taiyang, as manifested in the crucial and decisive Battle of Waterloo.

Shaoyang

Bruce Lee

Most people know of Bruce Lee through his martial arts films. With his lightning swift kicks, high jumps, and unbelievably fast hand techniques, he introduced the world to the finesse and power of martial arts. He played roles in which he personified anger and fury, yet exemplified justice and righteousness, all with energetic presence and perfect skill. He was an undeniable superstar from the start, whose instant popularity helped to break down the racial barriers stifling Hollywood. Still, Bruce Lee was far more than just an actor. He was, first and foremost, a martial artist who created his own system of martial arts, Jeet Kune Do, or the Way of the Intercepting Fist. He was also a philosopher and a teacher, and a loving husband and parent.

Bruce demonstrated the warrior aspect of Shaoyangs. Although he was only 5'7" and weighed 135 pounds, he was extremely well-built and had clear muscular definition, with the characteristic Shaoyang wide shoulders tapering down to a narrow waist and hips. He also had the sharp, bright eyes of the Shaoyang, capable of withering any opponent with their intensity and ferocity.

Like many Shaoyangs, Bruce felt that he was driven by a spiritual force within himself propelling him to accomplish many things in a short span of time. A natural consequence of this force and urgency was another Shaoyang trait, the propensity to be extremely direct and straightforward. His wife, Linda Lee, wrote that "Throughout his life, Bruce had never feared to state openly and frankly how he felt about people or problems." Although Bruce, like most Shaoyangs, had a temper, it was merely a manifestation of this straightforwardness. This is the quality that gave vitality and force to his creative and artistic temperament.

There are many more Shaoyang traits that Bruce demonstrated. One was the fact that he was often described as being a comedian. He was always amusing everyone with his jokes and was fun to be around. Second was his charm, wit, and self-assurance, with which Bruce always became a life of the party and a center of attention. He was also a show off (a primary trait of Shaoyangs) who enjoyed demonstrating his strength. He would do push-ups on his thumbs or on the index finger and thumb of one hand, or perform his famous one-inch punch.

Bruce was also a deep philosophical thinker. He had an extensive library, consisting of 2,500 books with extensive marginalia. His handwritten notes, meanwhile, amounted to about 6,000 pages. Furthermore, his teachings in martial arts were not flat, technical instructions. Bruce Lee's statements were infused with his beliefs about the very nature of life:

"To live is to express and to express you have to create.Creation is never merely repetition. Remember well my friend that all styles are man-made and man is always more important than any style. Style concludes. Man grow."

Bruce displayed several other Shaoyang traits and qualities. He had an irrepressible, positive nature. He had acute powers of observation, combined with instinctive good judgment. He had an indomitable will, which allowed him to overcome racial prejudice and several career disappointments.

Elvis Presley

Elvis Presley represents the glories and consequences of ultimate masculinity. He was dubbed the King of Rock and Roll, with his unique, charged mix of country, pop, blues, and gospel. But to the world, and especially to Americans, he was much more than this. He founded a culture of his own, complete with its own fashion and attitude. It was so influential that no description of American culture could be considered complete without it. Elvis's legacy continues to endure to this day, so well, in fact, that tabloids resurrect him daily with alleged Elvis sightings.

Elvis was obviously a Shaoyang. Only a Shaoyang could combine enormous sex appeal and charisma, a creative and innovative sensibility in fashion and music, a need for extravagance, and a rebellious, but chivalrous, temperament. Moreover, he always had a broad-shouldered Shaoyang physique, distinct even after he gained a great deal of weight in his later years.

During his teenage years, Elvis was considered to be shy and eccentric. Yet, this was merely the deceptive appearance of a seed before sprouting. What was called eccentricity, meanwhile, was merely young Elvis's experiments in expressions of rebellious fashion in clothing and hairstyle. In truth, Elvis had a powerful need to "show 'em." In fact, more than anything else, he did not want to be ignored. Therefore, he set out to be recognized through sports, dancing, singing, and his clothes. Shaoyangs, more than any other constitution, have a deep need for the attentions of others.

When Elvis broke into show business, one of his early managers, Bob Neal, said of him, "He had ambition to be nothing in the ordinary, but to go all the way." One manifestation of this ambition was his onstage usage of gestures and manners that were unruly, arrogant, surly, and vulgar, as well as fresh, lively, and powerful. He eventually became known as "Elvis the Pelvis" for his uninhibited hip swivels and gyrations. In later acts, he incorporated a mix of martial arts to his repertoire to add a bit of flash. Another consequence of his drive for recognition was his outrageous, flamboyant fashion, which included his distinctive hairstyle, clothing, and sunglasses, as well as his Cadillacs, mansions, and gigantic rings.

Elvis's success was not due solely to his showy behaviors, however. He was first and foremost an innovative musical pioneer, combining the varied elements of his background to form the unique sound representative of early rock and roll. He set forth a new style of American music. His influence was even felt by those other giants of rock and roll, the Beatles. John Lennon once said, "Before Elvis, there was nothing." This artistic judgment is particular to Shaoyangs.

Elvis clearly displayed several of the psychological traits of Shaoyangs. He was extremely masculine, extroverted, and rebellious, and yet, partially due to his Southern upbringing, extremely polite, chivalrous, and generous. He bought Cadillacs for friends, and once even gave one to a teller at a local bank.

In his later years, the consequences of his lifestyle began to catch up with him, and he began to manifest several of the negative behaviors of Shaoyangs. According to Red West, his former bodyguard, "Elvis became arrogant and abusive to those around him." Once he attained fame, money, and power, he became lonely, bored, and friendless. He lost himself in drugs, food, and women. Like many Shaoyang superstars, he followed the pattern of the short, oil-soaked wick: phenomenal success at an early age, followed by a swift death at the age of 42. No exact reason was given for his death. Yet his health had been failing rapidly, in no small part due to the fact that he had been overworking himself with an endless schedule of touring. The massive doses of prescription drugs that he took either to pep him up before a performance or calm him down at night only worsened his condition. Repeatedly sabotaging his own foundation of health, his tower of glory could do little else but fall short of heaven, and collapse into the dust.

Taiyin

Martin Luther King Jr.

Balanced Taiyins have a well-rounded personality, encircling a strong, centered sense of self. With such a structure serving as a foundation, Taiyins are able to accomplish deeds requiring extraordinary courage and forti-tude. Such is the case of Dr. Martin Luther King Jr., the figure who most clearly represents the civil rights movement of the 1960s.Like many Taiyins, Dr. King's personality was balanced, having both a hard side and a soft side. The hard side allowed him to accomplish great things, and the soft side allowed him to remain human. On the hard side, it must be said that Dr. King possessed extraordinary courage. He never shied away from a fight, despite the fact that his enemy, prejudice, was deeply entrenched. He remained at the forefront of the struggle for equal rights, whether it led him through a Chicago riot in the midst of flying bullets, into white mobs, or into jail. He remained steadfast, despite the beatings, bombs, and death threats, taking disparaging remarks, insults, cruelty, bitterness, and pain as matters of course.

On his Mississippi campaign, reports that he would be assassinated daunted his associates, who begged him to cancel. But Dr. King refused. "I have a job to do," he said. "If I were constantly worried about death, I couldn't function." He felt that his cause was "so right, so moral, that if I should lose my life, in some way it would aid the cause." This is the cour-age of the Taiyins—solid, sure, and relentless.

Dr. King was also a great leader. Although there were some complaints about his weaknesses as an administrator, it was his guidance and his skills as a preacher that united the civil rights movement, and propelled it into the public eye. He felt as though his co-workers were his family, and that he was the father of that family. Thus, he was able to harmonize well with his co-workers, while instilling a sense of reverence in them. Taiyins commonly inspire such fatherly reverence in those around them.

Dr. King had a great deal of commitment. This he demonstrated through his persistence, perseverance, and complete dedication—hallmark Taiyin traits. When writing a book, he would work 12 to 14 hours a day to meet his deadline. When campaigning in Chicago to improve living condi-tions, he actually lived in the slums with his family so that he could identify completely with those he was fighting for.

Although Taiyins are usually taciturn and silent, Dr. King demonstrated the fact that Taiyins may become excellent orators when given the proper cause or opportunity. His rich, resonant voice, his majestic physical pres-ence, his uncanny oratory skills, and his soul-stirring speeches all combined perfectly when he took the podium. Perhaps one reason that his words were so convincing was that they were reinforced by his own life. As staff member Hosea Williams once said, "He not only talked the talk; he walked the walk."

Behind the public hard side, Dr. King maintained a soft side. This softness was not a liability; in fact, it allowed him to become a better leader. As balanced Taiyins are broad-minded, they have a great capacity for tolerance and compassion. Dr. King exemplified this quality. His dream was all-inclusive; he wanted every man and woman, whether white, black, Chicano, Jew, or Catholic, to join hands and live a life of equality, justice, and freedom. Related to this was his extremely forgiving nature, which is also a strong trait of the balanced Taiyin individual. Once, while giving an address at the Southern Christian Leadership Conference (SCLC) in Birmingham, he was punched in the mouth and knocked down by a young, white, 200 pound self-styled Nazi, but he did not try to defend himself. When the police and several SCLC delegates restrained the man, Dr. King only made him sit back down, refusing to press any charges. Afterwards, he said, "This system that we live under creates people such as this youth. I'm not interested in pressing charges. I'm interested in changing the kind of system that produces this kind of man."

Dr. King was extremely humble despite the fact that he maintained a very public life. Attention from the media sometimes even embarrassed him. He continually emphasized that it was his movement that deserved attention, not himself. Like many Taiyins, Dr. King also had a humorous side, which he maintained despite the serious and often life-threatening situations he faced while following his calling. Dr. King loved to tease and didn't miss an opportunity to laugh at himself. Once on his way to a meeting, dressed in a suit and tie, he was mistaken for the elevator operator by a white woman. Amused, he kept quiet and pressed the floor she needed, but as soon as she stepped off, he broke into laughter with his friends and laughed the hardest amongst them.

Dr. King was also a very scholarly, intelligent individual. By age 15, he had finished high school without graduating, having passed the college entrance exams of Morehouse College. By age 17, he chose to become a Baptist minister like his father. By the spring of 1948, at 19 years of age, he graduated from Morehouse with a degree in sociology, and elected to study for his bachelor's degree in divinity at Crozer Seminary. He received his Ph.D. at the age of 26. He was *Time* magazine's "Man of the Year" in 1963 and won the Nobel Peace Prize in 1964.

Dr. King was assassinated in the prime of his life in Memphis while trying to organize a poor man's march to Washington, D.C. Yet, the heavy boulder that he started rolling only gained momentum after his passing. Today, the principles and ideals he fought so hard for have been established in the nation's conscience. Perhaps we have not fully realized the dream of universal brotherhood and peace that Dr. King set into motion, but we are definitely closer to it because he was a dreamer who dared.

Thomas Edison

Thomas Alva Edison, the father of modern electronics, is a clear example of the Taiyin's resemblance to a sphere. His face was large and fleshy, as was his body, carrying a fair amount of mass in the center. In the same way that a sphere diminishes near its top, Edison's lungs were relatively weak. He suffered frequent respiratory infections as a child, as well as some hearing loss. (The ears are related to the Lung system according to Sasang Medicine.)

Although Edison was a genius, he was neither sublime nor otherworldly, like Taiyangs, nor clever and stylish, like Shaoyangs. Instead, his genius was more well-rounded. Like all geniuses, he would become suddenly inspired. However, these inspirations resulted primarily from a combination of several related Taiyin traits. Edison had great perseverance and could focus and concentrate on one thing for a long time. From an early age, he demonstrated this propensity to work throughout the day on laboratory experiments. Sometimes, he concentrated so hard and long upon one thing that he became oblivious to those around him. His ability to remain in a rut was truly astounding. When pondering a certain subject, he was able to read a pile of books 5' high day and night, eating at his desk and sleeping on a chair for six weeks. This persistence was also reflected in his strong work ethic: he expected his workers to put in at least 11 hours a day, and he worked 18 hours a day himself, taking catnaps and eating very little. In fact, he basically worked continuously from his teens until his death, only stopping when he was injured by an experiment or when he was seriously debilitated by an illness at an advanced age. His persistence may best be summed up in his own words: "Genius is 1 percent inspiration and 99 percent perspiration."

Arising from this persistence was an ability to remain flexible. Edison's flexibility was neither weak-willed nor escapist. Rather, it was like a rolling sphere, always moving, not to escape from problems, but to return to them from other angles. He kept the ball rolling in his daily operations by rapidly switching his focus from one project to another, asking questions, giving instructions, or making decisions in a laboratory running several unrelated experiments simultaneously. When confronted with a difficulty, he did not give up, but instead cheerfully considered alternative possibilities. As he tried to keep his mind active and in touch with every possible aspect of his field, he had an inexhaustible store of perspectives from which to choose. He was in a unique position to turn limiting problems into liberating solutions. As Edison demonstrates, Taiyin geniuses are not precisely revolutionary in their thinking, but are instead persistent and able to bring a well-rounded breadth of knowledge to bear upon their problems.

Another Taiyin characteristic exemplified in Edison was his focus upon the practical. Although he had a great capacity for experimentation, Edison was not a theorist. For him, it was more important to make something work than to understand how or why it worked. Another aspect of Edison's practicality was his business-mindedness. He did not undertake a new invention unless he felt there was a market demand for it. He said of himself, "The point in which I am different is that I have, beside the inventor's usual makeup, a bump of practicality...the sense of the business-money value of an invention." This emphasis on money was not, however, an end in itself. He only needed it because it allowed him to invest more in future inventions. "As fast as profits were realized... he would plough the money earned into research and development work in new fields, for his curiosity about the facts of science remained undiminished to the end," writes Matthew Josephson in his 1992 biography of Edison. Both his inventions and the money that resulted from them were merely the grease that kept the Taiyin Edison rolling along the track of his scientific curiosity.

Edison, like most Taiyins, was both stoic and solitary at heart. Yet, like a sphere, he was able to maintain a smooth appearance that allowed him to operate effectively and efficiently with others. Although he was fundamentally taciturn and reserved, he became lively when he spoke about his novel schemes and inventions. Although he was shy and timid in front of women and crowds when young, he proved to be an excellent boss to his workers. He knew how to bring out the best in his associates and workers because, according to Josephson, he, "had an intuitive knowledge of human psychology." Although he was always a serious, aggressive businessman, there was a lighter side to him. For one thing, he was never indifferent to his wife and children. For example, he took his family to the beach or played with his kids on Sundays. He loved and esteemed his wife, and, writes Josephson, "was capable of very genuine and strong affection." Like many balanced Taiyins, he occasionally played practical jokes with his inventions, and was known for his sense of humor.

Edison was a well-rounded individual. Although he had the typical Taiyin dedication to his work, he never allowed it to force him to adopt a one-sided or myopic view of life. Like a true Taiyin, he had expansive vision, which enabled him to create new inventions; his practical sense insured that they would be well received by the world. At the same time, he maintained a good family life. He was a powerful inventor and businessman, and a sound and stable individual, as all Taiyins have the potential to be.

Shaoyin

Marilyn Monroe

Shaoyins have a tendency to become victims. They are gentle, timid, and indecisive by nature, and are often forced or duped into playing roles that are not to their liking. This is true especially when Shaoyins find themselves in the spotlight. A heightened awareness of oneself and the way one influences others can force issues of identity, power, and control that most other Shaoyins in stable, secure roles are able to avoid.

Marilyn Monroe represents the victimized Shaoyin. Her life demonstrated how a normal girl could swiftly rise up from the obscurity and hidden tragedies of domestic life to find herself a star—and how, just as quickly, that star could lose herself in the vast darkness of the heavens, cold and alone.

Marilyn Monroe was born Norma Jeane Mortenson on June 1, 1926. Her father abandoned her and her mother when she was very young. The stress of raising young Norma Jeane alone proved to be too much for her mother, and she was institutionalized. Norma Jeane was forced to live first at a children's home, and then with friends of her mother's. Norma Jeane married Jim Dougherty when she was only 16 years old. She proved to be an immaculate housekeeper. She was also excellent with children, who seemed to trust her instinctively.

Jim was in the merchant marines and soon went off to war. Norma Jeane, meanwhile, took part in the war effort by working in a defense plant called Radio Plane. There, she worked as an assembly line chute packer and a glue sprayer, winning several awards for her excellent work. By this point in her life, Norma seemed to be a secure individual. She was a good wife and a capable worker. In other words, she was a typical Shaoyin, taking satisfaction in the comfortable roles and routines that life offered her. Like most Shaoyins, she was good at managing the domestic sphere; also like most Shaoyins, she got along well with children, because of her gentle nature. In the working world, she proved herself by relying upon the Shaoyin propensity for detailed, monotonous work.

This idyllic state changed one day when a photographer came to the plant to do a layout on women helping with the war effort. He singled Norma Jeane out as a natural model, and decided to use her in the layout. From that day forward, Norma Jeane was to awaken to the power of her beauty. Gradually, modeling and acting took up larger and larger portions of her life. She divorced Jim, changed her name to Marilyn Monroe, and dyed her hair blonde. She starred in two 20th Century Fox movies, *Niagra* and *Gentlemen Prefer Blondes.* She then married Joe Dimaggio. Their brief marriage ended after the famous photo of Marilyn standing over a subway grill, her skirt blown up by the hot air.

Marilyn slowly became aware of herself and how she wished to portray herself. She began to fight with the studios over her roles. She wanted to do dramatic parts, and not just the musicals and comedies that she had been restricted to. This period was largely one of self-exploration; one result of it was her May-December marriage to the playwright Arthur Miller. She starred in *Some Like It Hot* and *Let's Make Love.* Then, during the filming of *The Misfit,* she divorced Arthur Miller.

Marilyn had come a long way from her life as a dutiful housewife. She had become aware of her beauty and its influence. This had given her a sense of power that she had not known before. Yet, even as she grew famous through film roles, she remained somewhat indecisive as to who she was, and how she was to present herself, and left the decision making to others. This is a typical Shaoyin reaction to most important decisions, even those that concern identity and personal power. Late in her career, she began to find her voice, but by then, it was too late. She had already become a pawn to too many people—the Strasbergs, Frank Sinatra, and President Kennedy—and felt as though she were being used by all of them. At this point, she succumbed to a great despair, for she felt that she had nowhere left to go.

Her last picture, ironically titled, *Something's Got to Give,* was left unfinished, because Marilyn claimed she was too sick to work. The studios denied this excuse, and said that they would sue her for millions of dollars. This, combined with an increasing sense of loneliness and isolation, led her to commit suicide on August 5, 1962. In a sense, she had predicted her own death very early in her career, for she had once written about herself that she, "was the kind of girl they found dead in a hall bedroom with an empty bottle of sleeping pills in her hand."

Marilyn also exhibited the Shaoyin perfectionism towards work. Her half sister wrote of her, "Marilyn was not a dumb blond. She was thoughtful and determined and a workaholic. She insisted on perfection from herself in her scenes. Her insistence frustrated several of her directors who were happy with the first take and had to suffer through dozens more at her request."

Marilyn was a true Shaoyin. She had the archetypal Shaoyin body, well proportioned, with well-rounded hips. Her face was soft, with gentle eyes that always looked sleepy and half-closed, and full lips. Psychologically, she dealt with several key Shaoyin issues throughout her life. She always wrestled with her lack of self-confidence, and her inability to make decisions. The mild manifestation of this insecurity was a certain shyness she possessed. Another manifestation was her vulnerability. She had an emotional baseline of constant worry, depression, and hypersensitivity.

Mother Teresa

Mother Teresa was an extraordinary woman. Her compassionate deeds stagger the mind and challenge the soul, both in their breadth and in their depth. During her later years, she was even considered to be arguably the most powerful woman on the planet, for she had easy access to presidents, kings, prime ministers, princes, princesses, generals, and dictators, all of whom were influenced by her presence and her words. And yet, those close to her continually described her as being ordinary, simple, and humble, which are all typical Shaoyin traits. What few words she had for herself always referred to the glory of God, of whom, she said, she was nothing but an instrument. Such extreme self-abnegation and compassion is only found among the most balanced Shaoyins.

Mother Teresa was born Mary Teresa Bojaxhiu on August 26, 1910 in Skopje, Yugoslavia. Her family had always been very religious, especially after the death of her father when she was only seven. Young Mary was especially so, deciding that she wanted to become a nun when she was only 12 years old. At that time, her mother refused her, because she was yet a child, but when she repeated her wish six years later, her mother acquiesced. On March 24, 1931, Mary took the vows of poverty, chastity, and obedience as a sister of Loreto, and became Sister Teresa. After completing her novitiate, Mother Teresa spent 17 years at St. Mary's school in Calcutta, first as a teacher, and then as a principal.

Mother Teresa received a Call from God while riding the train to Darjeeling on September 10, 1946. God commanded Mother Teresa to leave the convent and serve only the poorest of the poor. Although she had been happy at St. Mary's, she could not refuse such an important calling. There were two ways that Mother Teresa could have achieved her mission. She could have either gotten an "indent of secularization," that would have meant that she would serve as a lay person, and not as a nun, or an "indent of exclaustration," which would have allowed her to keep her status as a nun. Although the latter alternative took longer to approve, Teresa decided that it was important to remain a part of the church. This demonstrates the Shaoyin characteristic of obedience, which was particularly strong in Mother Teresa. She was both obedient to God in following her calling, and obedient to the church. She could, after all, have simply left the church to follow her calling alone.

Mother Teresa then founded the Missionaries of Charity, an order that vowed to give, "wholehearted and free service to the poorest of the poor." To this end, her order taught and cared for poor and unwanted children, served leprosy patients, and gave peace and comfort to the terminally ill. Her love was all encompassing, and transcended the boundaries of race, creed, nationality, and especially religion. She once said that she wished to inspire religiosity—but not necessarily her religion—in others.

If Mother Teresa's vision was all encompassing, her actions were decidedly small. In fact, she encouraged those of her order to never stray from humble works. "Nothing is ever too small," she said, "not the writing of a letter for a blind person, nor the helping of an elderly neighbor to clean her house or to wash her clothes. Let the big things be done by other people.... Acts of neighborly kindness are as important." This focus on humble dedication also explains her reluctance to get involved in politics. She once said that war was the fruit of politics or business. In this sense, she was definitely representative of the Shaoyin, for Shaoyins concentrate on the small, meticulous tasks, even when their overall visions may be grandiose.

Physically, Mother Teresa had a small body that appeared frail, soft, and gentle, consistent with Shaoyin body types. She projected a pure, quiet, serene, and settling energy, a Shaoyin energy, which had a tranquilizing effect on those in her company.

Although Shaoyins are often considered to be the "least" of the constitutions, Mother Teresa demonstrated how, "The meek shall inherit the Earth," or, to use an Eastern philosophical perspective, how extreme Yin may become extreme Yang. In many ways, she was like that most humble and potentially powerful element, water, which by nature sinks to the lowest point, nourishing and nurturing wherever it goes. Mother Teresa, a woman who claimed to be nothing, literally changed everything in the world, simply by flowing down and out, with outstretched hands and downcast eyes.

Chapter 15

Heroes and Villains

The appeal of fiction lies in the fact that it is larger than life. It can take the most minute characteristic of an individual and project it onto the big screen, transforming it into a heroic or grotesque caricature. While watching or reading about how these grandiose beings weave their stratagems or gamble out their destinies, we temporarily forget the complications of our own relatively small lives. Yet, the possibility of our entertainment in fiction lies in the fact that, somehow, we recognize those larger-than-life characters. Somehow we know that they are reflections of ourselves or of people that we know. Furthermore, the relationships that they have with each other reflect relationship patterns that we implicitly know and understand. If we examine fictional characters closely, we begin to see that, far from being strangers from other realities, they are the essence of our own reality.

This being so, it is particularly interesting and edifying (not to mention simple and fun) to look at famous fictional characters and try to identify their Sasang body types. As fiction reflects life, so too can an examination of fictional characters teach us something about people in general, the people we know and love, and most importantly, ourselves.

Taiyang

Taiyangs in fiction often play the roles of true heroes or true villains. Whether they wear the white hat or the black hat, however, they are always extremely serious and driven. They typically have vague, ill-defined, or even absent personalities. What little is revealed of their inner self usually hints at some tragic or traumatic event, one that consumed their personality, and drove them to follow their present path. For example, heroes, such as Superman, Batman, Ripley from the movie *Alien,* or Captain Ahab from *Moby Dick,* all present an opaque, impenetrable face to the world. Behind this facade exists little more than the memory of some traumatic event. In Superman's case, this was the destruction of his home planet, Krypton; for Batman, it was the murder of his parents; the entire crew of Ripley's ship was slaughtered by a single alien; Captain Ahab's leg was bitten off by the elusive white whale.

These tragic events traumatized these individuals, driving them to adopt heavy responsibilities. Superman claimed Earth as his new home planet, swearing to protect it at all costs; Batman donned a disguise of fear and darkness to combat crime; Ripley was driven to destroy the aliens whenever she came in contact with them; Captain Ahab was obsessed with pursuing and killing Moby Dick, the white whale.

Traumatic events are not only reserved for protagonists. Some of the darkest Taiyang villains also suffered from tragic events. These events effectively broke their spirits or their sanity, driving them to the dark side or off the edge. In *Star Wars,* Darth Vader, who was once Anakin Skywalker, was defeated by the Emperor. As a result, he turned to the dark side of the force. The Joker, though originally a criminal, only became the manic nemesis of the somber Batman when he fell into a vat of acid. Some Taiyang villains, like the Terminator, did not suffer from a traumatic event, but were made to play their part. The Terminator was a cyborg, programmed to kill.

Although Taiyang villains, and Taiyangs in general, are ultra-serious, the Joker seems to be an exception to this rule. He seems to take nothing seriously, making a joke out of everything. Because he takes this flippancy to an extreme, he is a Taiyang villain of the highest degree.

Driven by their lives' missions, Taiyangs seldom have the time or the capacity to form relationships. An apparent exception to this is *Star Trek's* Captain James T. Kirk; he romances practically every woman in the galaxy. However, the next episode always finds him alone in the captain's seat. Ultimately, his only true love remains his ship, the vehicle that carries him on his endless, or, at least five-year, mission. Symbolically, this represents the fact that he is married to his mission, as all Taiyangs are. Other Taiyangs have sidekicks. Batman is accompanied by Robin, Don Quixote has Sancho Panza, the Lone Ranger has Tonto, Sherlock Holmes has Watson, and Xena has Gabrielle. Superman, meanwhile, has an unrequited love in Lois Lane. Of these partners, Sancho Panza is a Taiyin, Tonto and Watson are Shaoyins, and Robin, Gabrielle, and Lois Lane are Shaoyangs.

Taiyangs are paired with characters of other body types in order to soften or humanize them. If they were presented alone, as they sometimes are, then their stories would be too far removed from human realities. Sometimes this is the desired effect, as in epics that seek to wrestle with universal, abstract themes. This is the case in *Moby Dick*, in which Herman Melville attempts to represent man's universal pursuit of the elusive mystery of life and death in Captain Ahab's hunt for the white whale. In other stories, however, the Taiyang's powerful character must be balanced.

Don Quixote is representative of the Taiyang fool—he has created an idealized world within his head where he lives almost exclusively. In order to balance this dreaminess and near complete misperception of reality, Quixote is paired with Sancho Panza, a Taiyin. Sancho Panza has a slower, more pedantic style (he rides a mule), and a relatively pragmatic view of the world.

Sherlock Holmes, like Quixote, is also heady, but in a different sense; he is extremely intellectual and rational. Sherlock Holmes has his rough edges, and is reminiscent of Beethoven in many respects. He is relatively antisocial, and is addicted to cocaine. He is paired with Watson, not to ground him, but to soften him and tone him down. For the same reason, the Lone Ranger is paired with the soft-spoken Native American, Tonto. Shaoyins are excellent at softening and toning down, as they have gentle, timid personalities. They also have an eye for detail, although Watson doesn't usually see things until Holmes points them out.

Shaoyangs like Robin, Gabrielle, and Lois Lane are paired with Taiyangs to add an element of play and mischief to the story. The spirit of play is usually absent in Taiyangs. Quite often, they have had to grow up too quickly. Batman lost his childhood when his parents were murdered, and Superman lost his when his home planet was destroyed. Robin, the "Boy Wonder," thus serves to soften up Batman's incredibly dark destiny, acting as the child that Bruce Wayne could never be. Gabrielle accomplishes the same thing for the warrior Xena, introducing her to the less savage aspects of life.

Lois Lane is a special case. Superman wishes to win the love of the vivacious, independent Lois Lane, but not as an alien with super powers. He wishes to win her love as an Earth man, a normal, everyday Joe: Clark Kent. In other words, he wants to relate to her not as a superior being, but as a humble man who has managed to win her affections. This is why Lois Lane must be a Shaoyang. Aside from Taiyangs, who tend to be too independent, Shaoyangs are the most free-willed. Superman, a man for whom most tasks are ridiculously easy, must experience a challenge when it comes to love. He must win over the free-spirited Shaoyang Lois Lane, not as the powerful superhero, but as the average mortal.

Shaoyang

Shaoyangs are more playful and mischievous than Taiyangs. Although they too sometimes play the main protagonist or hero, there is something fallible about them. Though brave, they also tend to be reckless, making several mistakes in the course of their travels. They also often have an element of curiosity that enables them to see the way out of dangerous situations. Yet, more often than not, it is this very curiosity that gets them into the cannibal's pot in the first place. For example, in *The Odyssey,* Ulysses allowed his curiosity to get the better of him on several occasions. Most notably, he unleashed the Zephyrs from the Alveolus after being warned not to open it until after he had returned home. As a result, Ulysses' ship strays further off course, making an already long journey home an almost interminable odyssey. Another Shaoyang cursed with curiosity is the archaeologist Indiana Jones in *Raiders of the Lost Ark,* whose quest for ancient treasures leads him to cross paths with everyone from Nazis to vengeful angels. He, like Hans Solo from *Star Wars*, has a certain playful quality that does not allow us to take him seriously, no matter how great his deeds may be.

James Bond is another Shaoyang hero. Although he may seem anything but fallible, he can only be a Shaoyang because of his one ever-present quality: style. James Bond uses the cleverest gadgets, drives the hottest cars, and beds the most beautiful women. Whether he defeats a super-villain or two in the process seems almost irrelevant. In this, he differs sharply from a Taiyang. A Taiyang would be obsessed with completing his mission; Bond, meanwhile, stylishly remains shaken, but not stirred. Similar to Bond is the Fonz from TV's *Happy Days.* The epitome of masculinity, he is always very resolute and straightforward. Although he is secretly aware of his insecurities and weaknesses, he uses bravado and macho to conceal them and maintain his cool.

The damsel in distress, especially in Disney movies, has traditionally been Shaoyin—demure, passive, and dependent. Yet, perhaps because of growing social awareness, these roles have gradually been shifting. Many of the recent Disney movies, for example, have come to depict women in Shaoyang roles. These women demonstrate more independence and spirit than their precursors, challenging the status quo by their actions, but more importantly, by their personalities. These women have, as a result, become more active and vital elements in the story. No longer are they simply the static pivot around which the story turns; rather, they determine their own destinies and the entire story line. Ariel from *The Little Mermaid,* Belle from *Beauty and the Beast,* Jasmine from *Aladdin,* Pocahontas, and Mulan are examples of this growing evolution from Shaoyin to Shaoyang.

Oftentimes, Shaoyangs play roles in which they are the source of mischief. Witness Bart Simpson, Dennis the Menace, Bugs Bunny, or the Mask, characters whose entire purpose in life seems to be to get into trouble and then try to get back out again. Shaoyangs also serve as excellent sidekicks to Taiyangs, providing comic relief. Such characters as Robin and Gabrielle add a somewhat human element and charm to the dark, somber Taiyangs.

Shaoyangs also have a certain ageless quality about them, one reminiscent of the endless playtime of summer. Peter Pan, the boy who never grows old, is perhaps the best representative of this aspect of Shaoyang energy. Another is Snoopy, the spirited beagle from the Peanuts comic strip. He is always involved in some sort of dramatic escapade, like saving the world from the dreaded Red Baron, or stealing a kiss from Lucy. Sometimes he is depicted doing a frivolous skipping dance, expressing the zest for life that Shaoyangs often feel. It is interesting to note that both his keeper, Charlie Brown, and his little bird companion, Woodstock, are Shaoyins. Shaoyangs may complement the gentle Shaoyins well, sometimes as the disturbance that forces Shaoyins out of their shells, or as the protector that comforts and soothes Shaoyins' vulnerabilities.

As villains, Shaoyangs can be clever and maniacal, but they, like their heroic counterparts, cannot be taken very seriously. The Riddler in the movie *Batman Forever* provided more entertainment with his exaggerated behaviors than with his pure villainy. His scheme to collect brain waves, and thus have god-like intelligence, would seem to make him more of a Taiyang. But his neurotic personality, and his obsession with turning everything into a riddle can only qualify him as a Shaoyang. Unlike the Joker, there is no all-consuming darkness behind the light facade of his riddles; the Riddler is mischievous, and little more.

Taiyin

As energy accumulates and settles, it becomes mass. Large accumulations of mass have a great deal of inertia. In other words, they are hard to start moving, and they are hard to stop moving once they are in motion. Think, for example, of George of the Jungle. Although he has the physique of a Shaoyang, in spirit and in motion, he was a Taiyin. Clumsy, stupid, tactless, gullible, and honest, he swung through the trees like a typical Taiyin swings through life. Despite their inevitable collisions with trees, it is in Taiyins' nature to remain true to their course, breaking either it or themselves in the process.

Taiyins, the most massive of the body types, make excellent paperweights. As fictional characters, they often serve to stabilize the story. They are often the father figures in domestic comedies or dramas, because their weight, both physically and socially, holds the home together. Think of Fred Flintstone, Homer Simpson, Heathcliff Huxtable from *The Cosby Show,* and Howard Cunningham from *Happy Days.* Even Al from *Happy Days*, or Mr. French from *Family Affair,* though not literal fathers, serve the same purpose. Their mass holds the home or hangout together.

This role is not restricted to males, of course. In a sense, the traditional matriarchal figure has always been a Taiyin. Think of Shirley Partridge from *The Partridge Family.* Alice, the housekeeper from *The Brady Bunch,* is also a Taiyin. Although she is not the literal mother of the family, it is she who holds this unconventional household together.

Roseanne, though not someone most would consider a traditional mother figure, accomplishes the same function despite, or perhaps through, her ever-present sarcasm.

The accumulated mass of the Taiyin can also be reinterpreted as accumulated wealth. This wealth can be used in good or evil ways. When it is used in good ways, as the source of generosity, then you find characters like the Buddha and, in particular, Bodhisattvas like Jizo or Santa Claus. When it is used in evil ways, as the foundation for wicked or greedy activities, then you find villains like Goldfinger, James Bond's nemesis, the Penguin, one of Batman's enemies, or Jabba the Hutt from the *Star Wars* series. The Penguin is a particularly interesting character as a villain. He is generally considered a freak or an oddity and not much more. Yet his rotund figure hides a most insidiously vicious mind. Taiyins can disguise incredibly wicked propensities beneath their magnanimous appearances.

Bluto, from the *Popeye* cartoon, and King Kong are also Taiyin villians, obsessed with acquisition. In their cases, they seek to woo the girl, Olive Oyl and Fay Wray, regardless of her wishes. Scrooge from Charles Dickens's classic, *A Christmas Carol,* begins the story as a typical Taiyin villain concerned only with the acquisition of money. His transformation into the generous saint at the end of the story demonstrates the latent possibility of all Taiyins to become truly compassionate and giving people.

Shaoyin

Shaoyins are gentle, quiet, and mild-mannered. They are rarely cast as villains, because they appear too soft, and seem unable to pose a threat to anyone. Instead, they play the role of the innocent victim of the story. Many Shaoyins are damsels in distress who need a knight in shining armor to save them. Cinderella, Snow White, and Olive Oyl are Shaoyins.

When Shaoyins are cast as protagonists, they are usually innocent bystanders who get picked on or abused by villains. They usually suffer more than other protagonists, taking their blows patiently, until finally, they have no choice but to take action, which can sometimes be violent. Cain from the *Kung Fu* television series is a prime example. An innocent drifter, he somehow always manages to get into the center of trouble, and although he does not willingly commit violence against others, he always convinces the evil-doers in the end. Edward Scissorhands is also an example of a Shaoyin protagonist. Although he has blades for fingers, he always uses them for peaceful, minute, delicate tasks, like hedge trimming, haircutting, or ice sculpting. Shaoyins are great at detailed tasks. It was only when he was pushed too far that he used them once to kill. Charlie Brown also exemplifies the abused and disrespected Shaoyin, who, despite his problems, endures life with a sigh, a warning sign of ill health for Shaoyins!

Many Shaoyins play the role of the nice guy. Richie Cunningham from *Happy Days* and Casper the Friendly Ghost are examples. Their role in stories is to show how nice guys can get into trouble, and, more importantly, how nice guys can get out of trouble responsibly, maintaining their integrity. Shaoyins also serve as alter-egos for characters of other constitutions. The mild-mannered Clark Kent is a Shaoyin who is abused and overlooked by Lois Lane. Bruce Banner is the compassionate scientist who transforms into the raging Incredible Hulk whenever he gets angry. On the darker side, Norman Bates is the timid man who wouldn't hurt a fly, yet becomes the psycho with the knife when the occasion is right. The Shaoyin's nice, polite behavior, after all, can mask inexpressible feelings that, more often than not, are directed inwards, failing to see the light of day.

Afterword

Now that you have come to the end of this book, and the end of our journey together, it is important to look at the nature of the path we have taken. As I indicated early on, the path to health is not a linear one, taking us from point A (disease) to point B (health). Rather, it is a circular one. There are many significant ideas encompassed by this circle. First of all, a circular path never ends; its starting point and its ending point merge and disappear. Thus, the end of this book is actually the beginning of your journey to health, a journey that never ends.

Another idea contained within the circle is the fact that it articulates a boundary, determining an inside and an outside. This boundary is significant, because it helps us to be clear about who we are (the inside of the circle), as opposed to who we are not (the outside of the circle). By staying within our circle, through appropriate awareness of our limitations, we can maintain a healthy, balanced life.

This was actually one of the bases for Dr. Lee's creation of Sasang Medicine. He wished to spread the practicality of Confucianism through the core principle of Joong Yong, or the Middle Path. Joong means "center": the state of impartiality and absence of bias, neither excessive nor lacking, leaning toward neither right nor left, front nor back, up nor down. Yong means "application," "usage" or "perpetual Tao." Dr. Lee believed that the practice of Joong Yong could lead people to the very center, otherwise known as enlightenment.

Through Joong Yong, one would realize that too much or too little of anything results in disharmony of the mind and the body. Although constant joy and happiness might seem to be good, when experienced too much or too strongly, they damage the mind and the body. Thus, Dr. Lee felt that it was necessary to cultivate an inner centeredness that could not be overwhelmed by joy, anger, sadness, or pleasure. In other words, he felt that we had to know the boundaries of our circle, and stay within it.

A third idea contained within the circle is its representation of the whole, the universe, or the Tao. If we combine these three ideas together, we can approximate a statement such as this one: "Through the endless path of circling our boundaries and discovering who we are through knowing our limits, we realize our wholeness, the potential of who we are; and, when we realize who we are, we simultaneously realize the wholeness and potential of the universe around us."

Dr. Lee was not content with discovering the path to enlightenment for himself alone, however. He did not circumscribe himself in his own circle, and leave things at that. In fact, perhaps his most distinguishing characteristic, and the measure of his compassion, was his struggle to find a path to health for all people. It was through this struggle that he discovered the profound truth of Sasang Medicine that we are born as one of four different constitutions. As a result of this discovery, he approached the realization of his dream: an accessible form of medicine and self-cultivation that could be understood and practiced by all. He once wrote:

> There will be a lack of vases, if only one person makes vases in a town of 10,000 households; there will be a lack of medical treatments if there is only one doctor in a town of 100 families. Only after we develop the medicine widely so that each household understands it and individuals know the process of disease can we expect longevity, and preserve the life of humankind.

In the spirit of this great man, I have endeavored to translate his profound teachings to the Western world, that all may practice self-cultivation and realize their highest potentials. It is my hope that Sasang Medicine will be studied and practiced by all, that we may "preserve the life of humankind."

It is a common saying that the true path of the Tao is one of returning. Sasang Medicine is all about returning. By paying attention to the Compass of Health articulated by Sasang Medicine, we are reminded of our basic biases, and the means to adjust ourselves to return to our true alignments. We are called on to return to the four beginnings (benevolence, righteousness, propriety, and wisdom) that are innate within us. In writing this book, I have tried to follow the path of the Tao and sought to return to the ideas of the esteemed master, Dr. Lee.

As you end this book, I strongly urge you to always return to yourself and your journey, in whatever you do. If you just return to your true self, you will make progress on the circular path that leads to the realization of the true Tao.

Remember the saying by Lao Tzu: The journey of a thousand miles begins with a single step. Best wishes on your journey.

Select Bibliography

Books in English

Beinfield, Harriet, and Efrem Korngold. *Between Heaven and Earth*. New York: Ballantine Books, 1991.

Carnegie, Dale. *How to Develop Self Confidence Through Public Speaking*. New York: Pocket Books, 1956.

Chawla, Navin. *Mother Teresa: The Authorized Biography*. Boston: Element Books, 1996.

Cho, Hun Young. *Oriental Medicine: A Modern Interpretation*. Translated and revised by Kihyon Kim. Compton, Calif.: Yuin University Press, 1996.

Chopra, Deepak. *Perfect Health*. New York: Harmony Books, 1991.

Cohen, Misha Ruth. *The Chinese Way to Healing: Many Paths to Wholeness*. New York: Berkley Publishing Group, 1996.

Cronin, Vincent. *Napoleon*. London: HarperCollins, 1994.

Fung, Yu-Lan. *A Short History of Chinese Philosophy*. New York: Free Press, 1966.

Gray, Michael, and R. Osborne. *Elvis Atlas: A Journey Through Elvis Presley's America*. New York: Henry Holt, 1996.

Hall, Calvin S., and Gardner Lindzey. *Theories of Personality*. New York: John Wiley and Sons, 1978.

Josephson, Matthew. *Edison: A Biography*. New York: John Wiley and Sons, 1992.

Kaptchuk, Ted. *The Web That Has No Weaver*. New York: Congdon and Weed, 1983.

Koolbergen, Jeroen. *Beethoven*. New York: Smithmark Publishers, 1996.

Lad, Vasant. *Ayurveda: The Science of Self-Healing*. Santa Fe: Lotus Press, 1984.

Le, Kim. *The Simple Path to Health: A Guide to Oriental Nutrition and Well-Being*. Portland, Oreg.: Rudra Press, 1996.

Lee, Jae Ma. *Longevity and Life Preservation in Oriental Medicine*. Translated by Seung Hoon Choi. Seoul: Kyung Hee University Press, 1996.

Lee, Linda. *The Bruce Lee Story*. Santa Clarita, Calif.: Ohara Publications, 1989.

Legge, James. *The Works of Mencius*. New York: Dover Publications, 1970.

Little, John. *Bruce Lee: Jeet Kune Do*. Boston: Tuttle Publishing, 1997.

Marsh, David. *Elvis*. New York: Thunder's Mouth Press, 1996.

Miracle, Bernice Baker, and M. R. Miracle. *My Sister Marilyn: A Memoir of Marilyn Monroe*. New York: Boulevard Books, 1995.

Monte, Tom. *World Medicine*. New York: G. P. Putnam's sons, 1993.

Ni, Mao Shing. *The Yellow Emperor's Classic of Medicine*. Boston: Shambhala Publications, 1993.

Oates, Stephen B. *Let the Trumpet Sound: A Life of Martin Luther King, Jr.* New York: HarperCollins, 1994.

Pitchford, Paul. *Healing With Whole Foods*. Berkeley, Calif.: North Atlantic Books, 1993.

Remnick, David. "Vladimir Ilyich Lenin." *Time*, 13 April 1998, 82-85.

Sachs, Robert. *Health for Life: Secrets of Tibetan Ayurveda*. Santa Fe: Clear Light Publishers, 1995.

Schonberg, Harold. *The Lives of the Great Composers*. New York: W. W. Norton and Company, 1997.

Sunu, Ki, *The Canon of Acupuncture*. Compton, Calif.: Yuin University Press, 1985.

Tierra, Michael. *The Way of Herbs*. New York: Pocket Books, 1998.

Books in Korean

Chang, Moon Sun, et al. *Sasang Constitutional Medicine*. Seoul: Yuh Kang Press, 1991.

Forty-Second Graduating Class of Kyung Hee University. *Constitutional Medical Theory of Korea*. Seoul: Dae Sung Cultural Press, 1994.

Han, Dong Suk. *Annotations on the Longevity and Life Preservation in Oriental Medicine*. Seoul: Sung Lee Hye Press, 1967.

Han, Hee Suk. *Western Examination—Eastern Treatment According to Sasang Constitutional Medicine*. Seoul: Suh Won Dang Press, 1991.

Hong, Soon Yong. *Life Preservation Treatments in Sasang Constitutional Medicine*. Seoul: Suh Won Dang Press, 1991.

Hong, Soon Yong, and Eul Ho Lee. *The Principle of Sasang Constitutional Medicine*. Seoul: Haeng Lim Press, 1973.

Hong, Won Sik. *Interpretation of the Yellow Emperor's Inner Classic*. Seoul: Ko Mun Press, 1971.

Kim, Dal Rae. *224 Foods That Become Medicine According to Constitutional Types*. Seoul: Kyung Hyang Press, 1996.

———. *Who Should Eat Ginseng*. Seoul: Kong Kan Media Press, 1996.

Kyu, Yong Chi, and Suk Ahn Kyu. "An Inquiry Into the Physiology and Pathology of Four Emotions in the Discourse on the Four Principles." *Journal of Constitutional Medicine* 5 (1993): 53-59.

Lee, Chol Ho. *Let's Live According to the Body Types*. Seoul: Ki Lin Won Press, 1988.

———. *Marital Harmony of the Body Types and Creating Happiness*. Seoul: Ki Lin Won Press, 1995.

Lee, Eui Won. *People, Society, and Constitutional Medicine*. Seoul: Sam Hua Press, 1996.

Lee, Jae Ma. *Longevity and Life Preservation in Oriental Medicine*. Seoul: Yuh Kang Press, 1992.

Lee, Tae Ho. *Canon of Sasang Constitutional Medical Treatment*. Seoul: Haeng Lim Press, 1978.

Oh, Soo Ill. *Oriental Medicine in Daily Life: Qi Therapy*. Seoul: Sports Cho Sun Press, 1994.

Park, In Sang. *A Story of Sasang Constitutional Medicine*. Seoul: Dong Il Oriental Medicine Clinic, 1995.

———. *Essential Principles of Sasang Constitutional Medicine*. Seoul: So Na Mu Press, 1997.

Park, Suk On. *Canon of Sasang Constitutional Medicine*. Seoul: Eui Do Han Kuk Press, 1977.

Park, Won Jong. *Marital Harmony and Body Types in Daily Life*. Seoul: Ha Na Media Press, 1995.

Shin, Jae Yong. *Constitution and Physiognomy*. Seoul: Dong Hua Cultural Press, 1989.

Song, Il Byung. *Sasang Constitutional Medicine Made Easy*. Seoul: Sasang Press, 1993.

Song, Il Byung, et al. *Sasang Constitutional Medicine*. Seoul: Jip Moon Dang Press, 1997.

Yim, Jin Seok. *Visualization in Oriental Medicine: New Understanding of Sasang Medicine*. Seoul: Gaseowon Press, 1997.

Yon, Sang Won. *Body Types and the Yin-Yang and Five Element Theory*. Seoul: Da Na Press, 1996.

———. *What Is Disease and What Is Medicine?* Seoul: Da Na Press, 1997.

You, Sung Hoon. *Understanding People Through Their Body Types*. Seoul: Ko Rye Won Media Press, 1996.

Yun, Kil Young. *Theory of Sasang Constitutional Medicine*. Seoul: Myung Bo Press, 1973.

Index

T

Y

About the Author

As a third generation practitioner of Eastern medicine, Dr. Joseph K. Kim, O.M.D., Ph.D., specializes in Sasang "Constitutional" Medicine. He has served as Chairman of the Department of Oriental Medicine at Emperor's College of Traditional Oriental Medicine in Los Angeles, and is currently an acupuncture researcher at University of California at Irvine, studying the effects of acupuncture on brain patterns as translated by a functional MRI.

Dr. Kim received advanced clinical training in China and Korea and has translated and revised Hun Young Cho's *Oriental Medicine: A Modern Interpretation*, published by Yuin University Press in 1996.

Dr. Kim also possesses more than 20 years of martial arts training, including Qi Gong and Tai Chi. He served as team doctor for the United States Tae Kwon Do team of 1988. He maintains a private practice in Encino, California.

For more information on Dr. Kim's seminars, workshops, books, adn other resources, contact him at:

Toll-free: 888-600-5155
E-mail: sasangmedicine@prodigy.net
Internet: www.ichingmedicine.com